I077924T

The Medici Quest

3

Jeff Raymond

Come now, you who would indulge a better curiosity, if you would apply it to the business of your salvation, run over to the apostolic churches, in which the very thrones of the apostles are still pre-eminent in their places, in which their own authentic writings are read, uttering the voice and representing the face of each of them severally.

Tertullian
Christian Theologian
180 AD

Prologue

Florence, Italy 1458

Alone figure moved through the streets under a canopy of stars. The twinkling orbs stood guard over a moon that appeared large enough in the night sky to be within a person's reach. The man wore a simple, but stylish cloak, indicating a person of means, but not of nobility. He walked with a slight limp and carried a worn leather satchel in one hand. A tuft of grey hair was visible above a long forehead, sunken eyes, and a narrow nose. Evidence of a cool, winter evening was apparent with each breath coming from his mouth.

Poggio Bracciolini felt every one of his seventy-seven years as he walked through the darkened streets of Florence toward his destination. He requested this late evening meeting to ensure some privacy, but his aching back tempted him to rebel against those plans. Once he reached the Palazzo Medici, he managed to shuffle through a torch-lit entryway and move forward to the columns surrounding the interior courtyard. The cool marble of the columns provided a place to lean for a few moments of rest.

Bracciolini traveled many miles during his lifetime, though the steps he took now to see Cosimo Medici felt like the longest and loneliest journey of all. The news he must reveal weighed him down, making his progress more labored than usual.

He pushed away from the column and ascended a stone set of stairs to the second level of the palazzo. The need to wipe sweat from his brow forced him to stop several times during the climb despite the coolness of the evening. Bracciolini whispered prayers for strength until he reached the top of the stairway. There, he gently knocked on the door blocking his path. He heard no reply, so gradually opened the carved wooden door and took a tentative step inside.

Though he had been to the Palazzo Medici several times since the completion of the large residence, Bracciolini had never been to this room. Only a few candles lit the chamber he entered, but the illumination flickered throughout the space to reveal an intricate and ornate chapel; a chapel designed solely for the use of the Medici family.

Cosimo knelt at the altar in the small apse, eyes lifted to a painting of the Christ child. A floor laid in an elaborate marble mosaic surrounded the leader of the Medici clan. A fresco painting covered the majority of the walls. The fresh, vibrant colors of the painting seemed to jump off the walls, despite the lack of light. Rumors had reached Bracciolini that many of the characters depicted in the painting had faces resembling members of the Medici family and other dignitaries of Florence.

Thankful for the respite to catch his breath, Bracciolini enjoyed his surroundings and waited alone with his thoughts while Cosimo spent a few more minutes in prayer.

Despite working for several Popes and meeting many wealthy and influential people during his lifetime, Bracciolini remained in awe of the man who soon rose to greet him. Cosimo inherited the Medici Bank from his father but expanded the family business with branches throughout Italy and as far away as London. Those ventures produced great wealth for the Medici family.

Cosimo was the unofficial ruler of Florence, worked diligently to promote peace in northern Italy, and was an avid supporter of the arts. He collected books and manuscripts from throughout Europe and the East and taught himself to read several languages. He even provided the funding to build multiple libraries throughout Tuscany.

Bracciolini's relationship with Cosimo started many years prior when the Medici family financed the young scholar on various travels to search for rare books.

"Poggio, my good friend. I thank you for meeting me at this late hour," said Cosimo. "You appear tired. Come sit with me and tell me your news."

Cosimo was not a handsome man. His hazel eyes were too close together, his nose was too long, and his ears seemed to be too big for his head. Nevertheless, he carried himself with an assurance that accompanied men of wealth and power.

The pair moved to recline on wooden benches so intricately carved that they appeared to be pieces of art.

"It is I who am honored. When I requested to meet, I did not plan to be invited to your family chapel. It, indeed, is astonishing in its craftsmanship." Bracciolini looked down at the satchel in his hands while he spoke. "The news I bring is also astonishing; though it will not bring you pleasure."

"Tell me," was the only reply from Cosimo.

Bracciolini took a deep breath before beginning.

"As you are aware, I recently sent an envoy to the Ottoman Empire to meet with Sultan Mehmed in our continued search for rare books and manuscripts. The Sultan conquered the city of Constantinople four years ago. It is said that the ancient library in Constantinople once held thousands of ancient writings, and some may have survived both fires and invaders over the centuries. Despite his viciousness in war, Mehmed is recognized as a learned man with a sincere interest in literature and art."

"I have heard this about the Sultan," said Cosimo. "I also know my friends in the Vatican are worried about his continual thirst to expand his empire. The Pope has discussed a crusade to retake parts of the territory captured by Mehmed."

Bracciolini continued. "It seems that Mehmed was well aware of my envoy's relationship with your family, and of your families' influence with the Pope. He sent back a letter with my representative and enclosed a single page from a manuscript. The Sultan claims the manuscript was miraculously saved from the destruction of the Library of Constantinople."

"Why the secrecy of this late-night meeting, Poggio? It sounds as if we now have a portion of a very rare manuscript to add to our libraries. Is that what you are holding in the satchel?"

Bracciolini again stared at the satchel that now sat in his lap, wishing it held better news.

"Yes, it is, my friend. But there is more to the story." Bracciolini cleared his throat, which was dry as the desert, and continued. "Mehmed made two demands to my envoy. First, the letter was not to be read until received here in Florence. Second, he wants Pope Pius himself to read it and to see the page of the manuscript as soon as we can get it to Rome."

"I assume you have read the letter and seen the manuscript?" asked Cosimo.

"Yes. Reading them has both filled my soul with wonder and caused me great distress. I am confident it will do the same to you and the Pope."

"What kind of written word can cause the anguish that I see in your face?"

Bracciolini opened the flap of the satchel and handed it to Cosimo. "I think you should read the documents for yourself and then we can talk further."

He watched as Cosimo found the letter from Mehmed rolled like a scroll and tied with a single blood-red ribbon. The elder Medici unrolled the letter and began to read, an audible gasp emerging from his mouth after only a few moments. Once finished, Cosimo carefully removed the fragile manuscript from the bottom of the satchel.

Bracciolini saw a tear become visible on Cosimo's cheek as the elder Medici read the words on the parchment. Cosimo then used his right hand to make the sign of the cross against his chest.

"My dear Poggio, I think you can leave me now to examine this letter and the manuscript on my own," Cosimo said without looking up. "Do not speak of this to anyone. I will send for you in the coming days once I decide how to proceed."

Bracciolini nodded, stood on shaky legs, and retraced his steps out of the chapel, down the gloomy stairway. He became absorbed into the darkness as he left the palazzo.

The moon and stars that shined so bright earlier in the evening now hid behind a thick cover of clouds.

———•●•———

Cosimo, still in the chapel, continued to read the manuscript, squinting in the glimmer of candlelight. The breaths labored in his lungs and his heart pounded against his chest as the full realization of the contents became clear.

Mehmed knew exactly what he was doing when he sent this manuscript, thought Cosimo. *Mehmed knew that if Pope Pius II believed there was more to this manuscript and possibly others like it, the Vatican would never encourage an attack on the Ottomans. Mehmed would feel safe, simply by threatening to destroy the manuscripts.*

After reading the letter and manuscript multiple times, Cosimo returned the documents to the leather satchel with great care. He then moved with deliberate steps back to the apse and knelt in prayer once again, beseeching the Lord with a passion he had not felt in many years.

Chapter 1

Present Day

*G*o. Go. Go!"
The jumpmaster shouted his command over the roar of the C-130 engines. Hand signals accompanied the words, making it clear that it was time to jump out of a perfectly good airplane.

Ethan Montgomery and other members of the 173rd Airborne Brigade shuffled forward toward the open door and stepped one by one into the open expanse of wind and clouds. The landscape fifteen thousand feet below appeared as faint outlines of fields, forests, and roads as the paratroopers descended in free fall.

Within a few seconds, parachute canopies began popping open like mushrooms magically materializing in the sky. A dozen parachutes opened. Then eight more. Ethan pulled his ripcord.

The cool air continued to rush by like being in the midst of a wind tunnel. Something wasn't right. His descent should have been slowed by now. Looking around through his fogged-up goggles, Ethan watched as other parachutes floated with their passengers toward the ground. With his body spinning and falling at a perilous speed, a voice calling for help broke through the howling wind. Ethan locked eyes with another ill-fated soldier speeding downward. He strained to steady his body and reached out a hand. He grabbed a wrist. Maybe they could both be saved.

Ethan grasped the emergency pull cord and ripped it away. The auxiliary chute broke free and began to fill with air, rapidly slowing his descent. But he was now alone; the tenuous grip broken; his friend falling away.

Strangely, as the other man continued to plummet downward, the patch on the doomed soldier's shoulder seemed to glow. It was his brigade's unit insignia, creatively combining a parachute, a sword for strength, and a lightning bolt for speed.

"Godspeed," Ethan said.

Then he screamed into the void of the heavens as he glided down to the grassy terrain.

With perspiration across his forehead and his heartbeat visibly moving his chest cavity in rapid succession, Ethan sprang up from his bed. His hands were shaking. The dream again—or maybe it was a nightmare. It didn't come to him often, but it was always the same.

Though he never shared the dream with anyone, Ethan assumed a psychologist would have a heyday deciphering all its meaning, picking through the fears and phobias that roamed around his subconscious.

Deep down Ethan understood what the dream was about, but resisted admitting it, even to himself. Parachuting out of airplanes during his time in the Army certainly elevated his heart rate, but never made him panic. He never had a narrow escape during a jump. However, he did lose a close friend from his unit and blamed himself for not being there to help.

The late-morning sun warmed the air to the edge of being uncomfortable by the time Ethan left his apartment, located just minutes from the historical center of Florence, Italy. The days of wearing a light jacket in the mornings began to disappear as the calendar changed from May to June.

Over the next couple of months, the temperatures and the number of tourists would continue to rise. Florence transformed into a different city at the height of the tourist season; the restaurants, hotels, and markets burst with daily activity to accommodate thousands of visitors from around the world. The permanent residents endured this onslaught, very aware that much of the city survived off the dollars, euros, pounds, rubles, and yen that flowed from the pockets of guests.

The central district of Florence boasted history at almost every turn; from a variety of palazzos and piazzas to museums and historic churches, the birthplace of the Renaissance offered visitors the maximum value for history per square mile. Indeed, the ease of walking to the primary destinations caused many streets to be nearly unpassable in a car as tourists felt it was their inalienable right to walk down the center of the narrow roads. Some locals resorted to bikes or mopeds to get around the city, often fantasizing about running over a picture taker or a kissing couple blocking their path. Fortunately, these fantasies rarely played out in reality.

After spending most of his morning working on his Master's thesis, Ethan had enough time to cross the street and grab a takeout pizza from Fuocco Matto—or Crazy Fire for those who didn't know Italian—and make it to a lecture at the University of Florence. Now a graduate student in Renaissance History, he was in the final days of his study semester in Italy.

"Farò andare la pizza Margherita," said Ethan in passable Italian, asking for a cheese pizza to go. This wasn't the pre-made pizza that Americans ate by the slice. The fresh mozzarella and tomatoes, along with several oils and spices added to the crust, produced a taste that far exceeded the ingredient-packed *supreme* pizzas that Ethan devoured growing up in Indiana. He read over some class notes as he waited and fifteen minutes later stepped back onto the Via Ventisette for a short walk to the University. He would savor each bite of the pizza on the way.

Before reaching his destination, Ethan's phone rang. He managed to chew and swallow his last morsel of pizza and sat down on a bench on the south side of the Piazza San Marco.

"Pronto," he said, using the Italian way of answering the phone, though Ethan saw by the incoming number that it was his roommate, Dale Carlson

"Hey, Monty, it's Dale." Ethan never liked the nickname Monty, even though his last name seemed to provoke the moniker throughout his life.

"Make this quick Dale. I have to be in class in a few minutes."

"No problem. Just wanted to let you know that

a very attractive young lady is looking for you." Dale said this with all the subtleness and intonation of a teenager.

Knowing that Dale, a semi-serious architecture student from upstate New York, spent more time studying the signorinas in Florence than anything else, Ethan assumed this was some kind of joke. Dale regularly attempted to set Ethan up with a local Italian girl. Ethan countered with constant reminders that finishing graduate classes and heading back to the States were his top priorities.

"Dale, I'm not in the mood for your matchmaking," said Ethan in a firm voice. "I'll talk to you tonight."

Ethan hung up, but his phone rang back within seconds. Dale again.

"What?" Ethan answered, now getting upset.

"Don't hang up," Dale responded. "There really was a girl here looking for you. She just missed you when you left."

Ethan took a deep breath, still not sure Dale wasn't playing games.

"Okay. Who was it and what did she want?

"Said her name was Chloe Conrad and that you knew her father. She was hoping to talk with you about something important."

Conrad. Could she be the daughter of Kenneth Conrad? thought Ethan, remembering his former military commander. *If this woman was Colonel Conrad's daughter, how did she know I was in Florence and what could she want?*

"What did you tell her?" Ethan responded to Dale.

"I told her you were in class at the University, and I gave her your phone number. I hope you don't mind."

"I'll deal with it if she calls, but please don't give out my number to anyone else without my approval."

"Yah, yah. Sorry," mumbled Dale. "But she was a very good-looking signo...."

Ethan hung up before Dale finished the sentence.

————•●•————

Ethan spent six years of his life in the U.S. Army, the last five as a member of the 173rd Airborne Brigade stationed in Vicenza, Italy. Nicknamed the Sky Soldiers, the 173rd provides a rapid response force in Europe, Africa, and the Middle East. Despite his relative youth, Ethan proved mentally and physically ready for the challenges of the unit. He impressed both his squad members and superiors with his tactical and leadership abilities.

Almost five years into his deployment, Ethan received two phone calls in a matter of days that precipitated a change in his life's direction. The first was an early-morning call from his mother. She revealed that Ethan's father had been diagnosed with colon cancer and would be having surgery within days. The cancer appeared to be in the early stages and the overall prognosis was good, but it still presented many unknowns and possible complications.

The second was an urgent call from Colonel Conrad's office with orders to report immediately. After arriving at the Colonel's office, the commander informed Ethan that a member of his unit—and one of his closest friends—suffered a fall and died in a hiking accident. Cam Williams fell down a steep ravine while trekking a difficult, mountainous trail on one of his few days off from duty. Ethan planned to go on the hiking trip with Cam but backed out at the last minute. It was a decision that continued to haunt Ethan—and invaded his dreams—even several years later.

The double-barrel blast of bad news forced Ethan into several weeks of deep thought and doubts. The shield of invincibility he felt for most of his life shattered and disappeared. He came out on the other side with a shaken confidence and a new plan. With his six-year Army enlistment nearing completion, he informed his superiors that he would not be re-enlisting. Colonel Conrad, among others, attempted to convince Ethan to remain on active duty.

After returning from his tour in Italy, Ethan completed an undergraduate degree in history and immediately began pursuit of a Master's degree. A six-month program in Florence allowed Ethan to study history up close and do in-depth research for his master's thesis on the Medici Family, often considered the Godfathers of the Renaissance.

No more battles; no more danger; no more losing friends. It was the safe route.

———•●•———

A light breeze flowed down the narrow streets as Ethan left his afternoon class. He glanced straight down the Via Ricasoli and saw the dome of the Santa Maria del Fiore, better known as the Duomo or the Florence Cathedral. The sight of the dome never failed to make Ethan think of the incredible construction project that took place in the early 1400s, creating what was still the tallest structure in Florence.

Thoughts of architecture, history, and the nagging pressure to complete his thesis filled Ethan's mind as he walked toward his apartment. He stepped out to cross the Via Cavour and an ambulance blazing toward the center of the city came within inches of running him over. Normally hyper-aware of his surroundings, Ethan somehow missed the high-pitched shrill of the ambulance as it approached. He jumped back onto the curb just as the white emergency vehicle with a bright orange stripe rushed by.

One deep breath slowed his heart rate. He then looked both ways before entering the crosswalk.

Just as Ethan reached the other side of the street, his phone vibrated. He didn't recognize the number.

"Pronto."

"Is this Ethan Montgomery?" The voice was female, with no discernable accent. Most likely American.

"Yes. Who's this?"

"This is Chloe Conrad. Colonel Kenneth Conrad is my father."

Ethan had almost forgotten the call from his roommate earlier in the day.

"My roommate said you came to our apartment earlier. What can I do for you?"

"I'm sorry to bother you, but I didn't know who else to contact. My father mentioned one of his former soldiers was studying in Florence, and I needed to talk to someone I can trust."

Ethan was unaware that his former commander knew of his academic pursuits. He always had a deep respect for the Colonel and felt that the respect was mutual. Still, he didn't know whether to be flattered or worried that Colonel Conrad kept track of him even four years after leaving the service.

"I'm not sure what you need, but I'll certainly help if I can." There was no way Ethan could brush off the daughter of Colonel Conrad.

"Can we meet soon?"

"I suppose I can find some…."

"Can we meet now?" she broke in, sounding impatient.

Ethan hesitated. Something about a woman he didn't know suddenly desperate to meet him set off mild alarm bells.

"I think I've made a discovery that involves the Medici family," Chloe continued, not waiting for Ethan's response. "I need some advice and some help following the leads I've found. You're an expert on the Medicis, aren't you? That's what you're doing in Florence, isn't it?"

"Well, I don't know that I'm an expert, but I'm doing a thesis on the Medici family. What is it you've discovered?" Ethan found himself at least curious now.

"Not over the phone. I need to see you in person,

and it's important that we meet soon. I think someone is following me so I'm a bit freaked out." Chloe's voice sounded more distressed as the conversation continued.

"What do you mean, someone's following you?" Ethan sensed his attitude changing from curiosity to concern. "I don't understand."

He heard Chloe take a deep breath and noticed a hitch in her breathing as if she was choking back tears. "Look. I'm going to be standing by the statue of Giovanni Medici near the Basilica of San Lorenzo for the next thirty minutes. If you can meet me, I'm wearing a blue top with white Capri pants. If not, good luck with your thesis."

Chloe disconnected the call. Ethan found himself standing on the sidewalk with the phone still to his ear, wondering what just happened.

Chloe did sound sincere and genuinely in distress, and he could walk to her proposed meeting place in ten minutes. Ethan looked down the street that would take him back to his apartment, but turned and walked toward the center of Florence.

Do I want to get involved with this? Ethan thought. *I used to jump out of airplanes, so going to meet a girl who I don't know should be a piece of cake. Plus, how bad can the daughter of Colonel Conrad be?*

Ethan took off at a brisk pace, following the Via Cavour in a southwest direction for several blocks. The decorative flags on the buildings billowed and flapped. The puffy clouds sailed across the blue sky in the afternoon breeze.

He took a right turn on the Via de'Gori and then

attempted to blend in with tourists and shoppers buzzing around a souvenir shop. He wanted to get a look at Chloe before she spotted him.

A waist-high fence surrounded the statue of Giovanni Medici—the first of the Medici bankers and Cosimo's father. The fence looked more like a place to hold up bicycles than a barrier to keep out unwanted visitors. Most tourists passed right by the statue and went straight to get in line to enter the Basilica of San Lorenzo and the attached Laurentian Library, which stood across the piazza.

Chloe appeared as she rounded the statue, the blue blouse and white Capri pants blowing a bit in the gentle wind. Her shoulder-length brown hair hung freely, and dark sunglasses covered her eyes. She carried a canvas bag with long straps draped over her left shoulder.

Ethan started to make his approach but stopped in his tracks when a commotion started to his left. The crowd near the Basilica spread apart as the din of voices and human movement caused a stir in the natural flow of tourist activity. With his focus being on Chloe, he hadn't noticed an ambulance parked close to the Basilica's doors.

He saw Chloe also become aware of the quick movement of the crowd—drawn in by the commotion—and start walking toward the ambulance. Medical attendants pushed a gurney out of the Basilica. They moved in sync while they worked feverishly on the patient. Chloe arrived just as the gurney slid into the waiting ambulance, which gave her a clear view of the patient. She also saw a circle of red showing through the white sheet covering most of the body.

Chloe's hand moved to cover her mouth. Her body shook with a slight tremor.

Ethan observed from a distance before he approached, aware that Chloe's actions indicated that she knew the person being put into the ambulance. He watched her attempt to talk to one of the medical personnel just before the ambulance turned on its lights and siren and dodged pedestrians as it pulled into traffic.

Ethan wondered if it was the same ambulance that had almost run him over a few minutes earlier.

The two ran into each other as the crowd of tourists scattered to make room for the ambulance. Many still kept an eye—and some cell phone cameras—on the commotion. To the visitors who paid good money to travel to Florence, a little tragedy at the Basilica would only add to the adventure and look better on their social media posts.

"Excuse me. Sorry," Ethan said as he bumped into Chloe from behind.

She turned and looked up at him, pulling off her sunglasses to reveal eyes that were already wet with tears.

"It's okay," she said. "I just need to get out of this mess."

Chloe started to push her way out of the crowd, moving away from Ethan.

"I'm Ethan Montgomery," he said to her back. "You're Chloe Conrad, aren't you?"

She stopped but didn't turn around right away, taking a moment to wipe her eyes with the back of her hand and replace her sunglasses. Once she did turn to look at Ethan, she didn't say a word, but grabbed his arm and pulled him away from the tourist.

"I'm really glad you came to meet me," she said once they were away from the crowd. "But this thing has gone way too far, and I need to get out of here."

"I think I also said this on the phone, but I don't understand," stated Ethan. "What thing has gone too far?"

Chloe now had a death grip on the straps of her satchel and shifted her weight back and forth on each foot, looking like a nervous job applicant waiting for an interview.

"That man being put into the ambulance was Pietro Vesuchi, the director of the Manuscripts Office for the Laurentian Library. He's the one who helped me with the information I found on the Medici family."

"I'm still not sure I'm following what exactly is going on," said Ethan.

Chloe yanked off her sunglasses again, the tears running down her cheeks now overshadowed by the intensity in her eyes.

"Pietro guided me through my research and was there when I made a discovery that might lead to something priceless; something he warned me that others would do about anything to possess. I just talked with Pietro yesterday and now he's on the way to the hospital with what the ambulance driver told me was a gunshot wound. A wound that could very well be fatal."

Chapter 2

Ethan and Chloe hurried down a side street filled with vendors selling every kind of leather bag, belt, and wallet that any tourist might want. They took a right turn on Via San Antonino and found themselves amidst more vendors under white pop-up tents.

Navigating the crowd, the pair worked their way through the tents and found an entrance to the Mercado Centrale. Built in 1870, the large indoor structure served for more than a century as the primary marketplace for Florentines. The building's designer modeled it after Milan's famous shopping arcade, complete with soaring glass windows, oversized arched entryways, and a wrought iron ceiling.

Ethan visited the Mercado Centrale several times during his time in Florence. It featured a variety of stalls offering anything from gourmet Italian specialties to simple takeout meals. He always saw it as an upgraded version of a food court in an American mall but assumed the locals wouldn't appreciate that comparison.

Chloe grabbed Ethan's hand and pulled him toward a table in the far corner of the expansive seating area. The busyness of the Mercado made it much easier to blend in and hide in plain sight. The aromas of various meats, kinds of pasta, and sauces could cause real or imagined hunger pangs as they rose in a culinary blend and settled over the crowd.

Once they found an open table, Chloe placed her satchel on the ground between her feet while Ethan situated his six-foot-three frame on a stylish but uncomfortable chair. He looked at her with attentive blue eyes, which highlighted a rugged face of high cheekbones, a chiseled nose, and a two-day growth of stubble. His short-cropped sandy-blond hair confirmed he remained comfortable with the Army grooming style.

Chloe spoke first. "I'm sorry for dragging you here. You have no reason to listen to anything I say, but I'm glad you found me in that crowd at the Basilica. After seeing Pietro taken away in an ambulance, I would have completely fallen apart if you weren't there."

"I'm glad I could help. Although I'm not sure that I did anything."

With her sunglasses off, Ethan now noticed Chloe's jade green eyes framed by her tanned face.

The words of his roommate from earlier in the day came back to him and made Ethan smile. He had to agree that Chloe was an attractive Signorina.

"You're probably wondering how I found you," Chloe inquired. She saw Ethan nod and continued. "I called my father, who is retired and living back in the States, and told him a few details of the discovery I made and that I might need some help. He keeps track of many of his former soldiers and told me about you."

The comment surprised Ethan, but he tried not to show it.

Chloe continued. "He knew about your studies in history and that you were spending a semester abroad. I did a Google search and brought up a posting you put in the University of Florence student newspaper a few months ago looking for a roommate. The posting gave the address of your apartment, plus an email contact. I figured the email wouldn't reach you as soon, so I went straight to the apartment this morning."

"That's quite the piece of detective work. But I still don't know anything about you other than that you are Colonel Conrad's daughter."

Chloe spent a few minutes telling Ethan her story. She grew up moving frequently with her parents as her father's career took him to various posts around the world. She went to a boarding school in Switzerland during Ethan's time in Italy and then headed back to the U.S. to attend college and study art history. During her sophomore year, her mother passed away after a long fight with breast cancer and her father came back home for good. That was two years ago.

Chloe recently graduated and wanted to spend time in Florence before returning to the States and looking for a real job. Renaissance art was one of her favorite periods, so Florence was the obvious place to be.

"First, sorry about your mom," Ethan said when she finished. "My dad has had cancer. He is doing well right now, but it's always something that's on my mind. Right now, though, I hope there is some way I can help you. Other than the fact that you've found something about the Medici family and that it might lead to an important discovery, I still don't have a good grasp of what this is all about."

"This is where I could lose you," Chloe said. "What I'm going to suggest will sound farfetched and you'll most likely just get up and walk away."

"I promise I won't walk away. Besides, the smells in here are starting to make me hungry, so I might stay for dinner," Ethan quipped, trying to lighten the mood.

Chloe showed a slight smile.

"I'll just hit you with the big reveal up front and see if you decide to bolt." She looked around to make sure no one else could hear. "I think I've found some clues to a manuscript that the Medici either possessed or knew how to find. And I believe that manuscript is an original copy of an epistle written by the hand of the Apostle Paul."

Ethan stared at Chloe, trying not to show the activity going on behind his eyes. He didn't know what to say.

"Aren't you going to say anything," Chloe said after a few moments. "Maybe call me crazy or even just laugh."

"You're talking about the Apostle Paul from the Bible?"

"Yes."

"An original manuscript of an epistle he wrote in the first century?"

"Yes."

A long pause.

"I want to call you crazy," admitted Ethan. "But nothing I have seen of you so far would support that hypothesis."

"I guess that's a vote of support," said Chloe.

"Tell me how you came to your conclusions."

Chloe talked for almost an hour while Ethan listened intently, asking occasional questions.

Then he paid for dinner.

———•●•———

Giancomo Morelli leaned back in his plush leather chair, resting his polished designer shoes on the edge of the mahogany desk. His fingers intertwined themselves behind his bald head while his dark brown eyes stared at the ceiling. The window behind Morelli's desk provided a panoramic view of the Capitoline Hill area of Rome and the Piazza del Campidoglio. He never wanted to be stuck in some high-rise office complex in the modern section of the city. His fourth-floor office was part of an otherwise nondescript building on the Via Montanara, only minutes away from many of the historic sites in the Eternal City. The office included a small reception area, a conference room, and his own well-appointed space where he planned his business ventures and displayed some of his most prized possessions.

His business—the acquisition and sale of antiquities with an often suspect provenance—was booming. Those who thought badly of Morelli would describe his ventures as shameful and illegal; perhaps say he played a major role in the so-called black market of historic artifacts.

Morelli himself would boast that he is a supplier of rare pieces of history to those who are willing to pay an appropriate price. It was a simple matter of supply and demand. He also had to support his family: a beautiful younger wife who had grown accustomed to the nicer things in life, and two young children who would soon enter pricey private schools.

As he leaned back in his chair, Morelli dreamt of a potential life-changing payday. The news he received from Florence only days ago set his competitive juices flowing. It prompted visions of buying a secluded tropical island, complete with servants and tutors to take care of all the mundane tasks.

The few minutes of daydreaming came to an abrupt end when Morelli's cell phone buzzed on his desktop. The device was one of several burner phones he kept in supply. He only gave out his numbers on a need-to-know basis and only to those he trusted to be discreet. Any of his past associates who failed to use discretion either were no longer among the living or too frightened to fail Morelli again.

"Pronto." Morelli assumed it was Adolfo Caputo, his contact in Florence.

"Signore Morelli. I have news from Florence." Caputo was obviously out of breath.

"Yes, Adolfo. What has happened?"

"I talked to the man in the Laurentian Library like you asked." Caputo took a couple of quick breaths. "He did not jump at the bribe you authorized, and he put up more resistance than I expected."

Negative thoughts began to enter Morelli's head, just minutes after being filled with sweet dreams of riches and tropical islands.

"Please tell me you were able to acquire the information I needed. Please tell me you were successful, Adolfo."

There was no immediate reply. Morelli's face began to flush, and he saw that his grip on the phone was turning his fingers red with effort. He forced himself to inhale deeply and let the breath out slowly. He set the phone on the desk and tapped the speaker icon.

"Adolfo?"

"I must report that Signore Vesuchi died only minutes ago. I just ran out of the hospital to call and give you the news. I must also report that I did not get all the information you requested." Another long pause. "I'm sorry."

Morelli struggled to control his anger, speaking in as calm a voice as he could manage.

"Please tell me what happened, Adolfo. Don't leave out any details."

"I went by to speak with Signore Vesuchi in his office during the lunch hour as you suggested. I made him aware that I wanted information on the research by the American girl Chloe Conrad. I made sure he realized that he would be paid very well for the information, but he continued to insist that he didn't know an American girl by that name."

"What did you do then?"

"I pulled out my gun and screwed on a silencer,

hoping to frighten Vesuchi into talking. He surprised me by lunging for the gun. We struggled in his office, and the gun went off hitting Vesuchi in the chest. I left quickly and don't believe I was seen. It was over an hour before anyone discovered Vesuchi and called for an ambulance. I went to the hospital and hung around the emergency room until I heard a doctor say the patient died."

If he were able, Morelli would reach through the phone and choke the life out of Adolfo.

"You said earlier you didn't acquire *all* the information I wanted. Did you find out anything?"

"Yes, Signore Morelli, I believe I did. After our struggle, many papers became scattered throughout the room. I hurried to leave but saw Chloe Conrad's name handwritten on a note partially hidden under other items on the floor. Several letters and numbers were written below her name. The figures don't mean anything to me, but I thought you would want to see it."

"Well, that might be something, Adolfo. Take a picture of the note and text it to this number. Then I want you to stay in Florence and continue to follow this Conrad woman. If you see a chance to get your hands on any of her research or computer, take it. Then make sure she will no longer be any trouble."

Chapter 3

Careggi, Italy 1464

No air moved through the bedroom where Cosimo lay for the third consecutive day. The sweltering August days proved oppressive, even in the hills overlooking Florence where a cooling breeze was common throughout the year.

Wool tapestries covered two of the stone walls in the bedroom. A pair of paintings hung on the wall above the large bed; early works from Brunelleschi and Donatello. The final wall contained a series of shelves, holding little except for a clean towel, a pitcher of water, and seven leather-covered books lined up in a neat row.

Cosimo ate very little food and drank only small portions of water in the days since his family brought him to their villa in Careggi. The swollen joints in his legs continued to throb with pain, leaving him no hope of walking across the room on his own. The distinctive facial features that made the seventy-four-year-old the most identifiable person in Florence now seemed to be melting away, leaving a washed-out and unrecognizable shell.

"My dear Contessina," Cosimo whispered to his wife of nearly fifty years. "I believe my days on earth are coming to an end."

"Don't talk that way, Cosimo. You know you always return to health after these bouts of illness. How will the city of Florence survive without you?"

"You have been a loyal wife, even though I haven't always been the best companion."

A grimace filled his face as the pain continued to contort his body. He managed to continue. "Making money took up most of my life, but I lay here now with a broken body and a soul hoping for release."

"You know I would do anything to take away your pain."

"Will you use my wealth to bring back our dear son Giovonni or my beloved brother? Are you able to use our gold coins to buy me a few days of comfort? Can you take my riches and keep away the specter of death which hovers over me?"

Contessina didn't reply, accustomed to Cosimo's rants in recent days. She understood that, in a way, he was paying earthly penitence for his failures, hoping to assure his entrance into heaven.

Cosimo rested for several minutes, eyes closed and body unmoving.

"Please send for Piero," Cosimo suddenly stated, startling Contessina, who had fallen asleep in her chair.

"He is at the Palazzo in Florence, but I will summon him immediately," she replied.

"Also, tell him to bring our grandson Lorenzo

without delay. I want to speak with them before the end of the day."

A bit of coolness finally came to the villa after the sun dropped below the horizon on the other side of the Arno River. A breeze returned, finding its way through the open windows and making the flames of the candles that lit the residence dance in unison.

A few hours later Piero hobbled into the bedroom, looking almost as bad as his ailing father. The second son of Cosimo had been thrust into a leadership role after his older brother died unexpectedly only a year earlier. Cursed with some of the same maladies that were about to take his father, Piero spent much of his time secluded in the Palazzo Medici, orchestrating the family business from his bedroom.

While Cosimo had a great love for Piero and appreciated the efforts he made in overseeing the banking business, it was Piero's son Lorenzo who would be the future of the Medici family. At only fifteen years of age, Lorenzo already showed a magnificent intellect, work ethic, and ingenuity. His grandfather knew that he would one day guide the Medici clan.

A servant girl leaned over Cosimo, trying in vain to spoon a warm broth past his cracked lips. Upon seeing his son and grandson enter the room, Cosimo sent the girl away and asked the pair to come closer.

Piero bent to kiss his father's cheeks and then grimaced as he sat in a nearby chair, his knees aching mightily. Lorenzo hopped onto the bed with an energy that the other two men in the room could scarcely remember having in their youth. Cosimo marveled at the boyish exuberance of his grandson, despite the responsibilities of manhood that Lorenzo would soon be required to accept.

"The time has come for me to pass on a secret that I have kept for several years," the elder Medici began. "Only one other knew of the secret, but that man passed on from this earth. I will soon join him."

Cosimo paused to take a few labored breaths, trying to gain strength for what he understood would be a long—and perhaps his final—conversation.

He began his story with the visit of Poggio Bracciolini to the Medici Chapel on a cool evening six years earlier. Cosimo spoke of the letter from Sultan Mehmed and of the single page of the manuscript that served as confirmation of Mehmed's claims. He admitted that he never showed the documents to Pope Pius II, choosing to keep the news to himself until a solution was found.

"I counseled Pius throughout his reign to avoid a confrontation with the Sultan, but never revealed the true motivation for my advice. Though the Pope often talked about a campaign to retake lands conquered by Mehmed, he was unable to follow through because of his failing health.

"I often prayed for Mehmed to fall in one of his many crusades," Cosimo admitted. "Or that I would find an artifact that would entice him to exchange the holy manuscripts. To my great disappointment, neither opportunity came about. The Sultan dismissed even my attempts to pay a large sum for the sacred writings.

"I still hold out hope and will beseech the Lord

until my dying breath that the manuscripts can someday be saved and returned to Christendom. Tonight, I am passing on that hope and challenge to you."

Piero and Lorenzo had not spoken throughout Cosimo's discourse. They remained silent as the great man gathered his fleeting strength for a final revelation.

"I have hidden the documents I received from Mehmed and devised a code to direct others to their location in future years. The seven books you see on my shelf are the start. Once I tell you the secret, you will be able to find the documents, if needed. You will also know the process to add more clues in the future if additional information is revealed."

"What is the code, grandfather?" Lorenzo asked, without hesitation.

Cosimo described his unique method for recording the secret information and the process of decoding the clues. Then he looked straight at his grandson.

"I trust you Lorenzo to pursue the manuscripts in the Sultan's possession with a fervor sparked by the power of the Lord. If you do not find success, pass on the secret to the most trustworthy member of the Medici line before your final days."

Cosimo turned to look at his son. "And to you Piero, support young Lorenzo in all possible ways as he continues the quest that I was unable to fulfill. Will you do that?"

Piero nodded in agreement.

Contessina reappeared to check on her husband.

"He is tired and needs to rest," she said to Piero

and Lorenzo. "Dinner has been prepared for you and is waiting in the dining hall."

The two younger men kissed Cosimo on the forehead, eliciting a weak smile.

"I am finally ready to rest," he whispered as his family left the room.

Only days later a huge crowd accompanied the body of Cosimo Medici through the city of Florence to its burial spot in the Basilica of San Lorenzo.

Chapter 4

Present Day

The dream interrupted Ethan's sleep for the second straight night, something that was uncommon. He awoke with an elevated heart rate and a profound sadness. The years had not dimmed the memories of Cam Williams nor the burden of guilt that still weighed Ethan down.

Before Ethan calmed himself, another memory invaded his morning thoughts. Right after the hiking accident that claimed Cam's life, a military situation put Ethan's unit into harm's way. His 1st Battalion, 503rd Infantry Regiment dropped into Afghanistan to protect a U.S. compound after U.S. Special Forces took out a vicious Iranian general. The Iranians pledged revenge and urged their allies in the Middle East to do the same. The battalion spent a very tense month on the ground, including a stretch of forty-eight hours without sleep. Several members of the regiment were wounded as they dodged and hunted the enemy snipers.

Despite winning praise—and a medal—for his efforts in the capture of two of the snipers, Ethan felt shaken. His most prominent memory of the event was coming back to his barracks on many nights, shivering uncontrollably as the fear and adrenaline coursed through his body. A month later his time in the Army ended.

Finally reaching a state of calm, Ethan dressed and then checked the breakfast selections in his apartment. A couple of eggs to scramble and the last few drips from a jar of honey to spread on toast were his best options. And, of course, coffee.

Two cups of his morning jolt might be needed after a late night and a restless morning due to the recurring dream. The discussion with Chloe lasted well into the evening, which forced him to start his nightly thesis work later than usual. He didn't call it quits until after 1 a.m. when his eyes—not to mention his brain—were no longer able to focus.

Getting the late-night work done did allow Ethan some time to meet Chloe today. He agreed to help with her research and help discern if she truly was in any danger. Perhaps she imagined someone following her and the shooting of the man at the Laurentian Library was unrelated. The more Ethan heard, though, the more he started to believe Chloe might be justified in her fears.

Research Assistant and Body Guard. Quite the job description, thought Ethan, bringing a smile to his face.

"What are you smiling about?" asked Dale, walking into the small kitchen still wearing his sleeping attire of boxers and a worn-out Buffalo Bills t-shirt.

"Uh, nothing. Just getting ready to head out," said Ethan, setting his dirty dishes in the sink.

"I didn't think you had class today. Thought

maybe we could hang out and grab lunch," said Dale. "I heard of this little place just over the Ponte Vecchio that serves a great American cheeseburger."

"I don't have class, but I am meeting Chloe to help with some research." As soon as Ethan said Chloe's name, he realized his mistake.

A childish grin spread across Dale's face. "Chloe! Isn't that the name of the girl who was looking for you yesterday? The one with pretty green eyes who told me how much she needed to find you?"

Ethan just stared at his roommate, not willing to reply.

The silent admission was all Dale needed. "Way to go Monty. Have fun with your *research*," he chided.

Ethan shook his head and walked out.

Chloe met him at the Giovanni Medici statue a few minutes past 10 a.m. The tourist rush had not picked up yet, as visitors slept off their heavy pasta dinners and large quantities of Italian wine from the previous evening. She wore comfortable khaki pants and a bright green tank top covered with a white blouse. Her hair was loosely arranged in a ponytail, with sunglasses resting on top of her head. Just like the previous day, a satchel hung over her shoulder.

Her red-rimmed eyes gave away the fact she had been crying.

"Are you alright?" Ethan asked as he drew close.

She seemed embarrassed by her emotions and reached to pull the sunglasses over her eyes.

"I just found out Pietro Vesuchi died yesterday.

I held out hope last night that he would make it, but found a report in the newspaper this morning about his death. It makes me scared, and I just don't know what…"

A sob escaped Chloe's mouth. She cleared her throat and took a deep breath to steady herself. Then she stood up straighter and pulled her shoulders back, trying to look in control. Ethan wanted to comfort her but was unsure if his gesture would be appropriate after their less-than-twenty-four-hour relationship. He put his arms out and she hesitantly stepped forward for a brief, awkward hug.

Anybody watching would have determined it was a hug between friends and not anything remotely romantic.

Ethan moved back a step, no words coming to mind. Chloe did the same.

"Are you sure you're up for this?" Ethan finally found some words.

"I don't have the luxury of waiting," she answered, still wiping away tears. "The pass I have to examine manuscripts in the Laurentian Library expires in two days. We need to hope that Pietro has an assistant who will help us out."

Chloe turned and walked toward the library entrance with a determined look; what some would call a *game face.*

—•●•—

Across the street, Adolfo Caputo watched as the two stepped away from their hug and walked together toward the door leading to the cloister of the

Basilica of San Lorenzo. From the cloister, there was easy access to the Laurentian Library wing.

Who's the guy and what's he doing with the Conrad women? thought Adolfo. *Why are they going back to the library? Don't they know that Vesuchi is dead?*

Adolfo decided to wait until the two came out and then attempt to follow; maybe find out who the guy might be. He made a call to his contact inside the library and told him to keep an on eye the pair and report back. The contact—a former childhood friend of Adolfo's who had gambling problems unknown to his superiors—already supplied the original tip on Chloe Conrad's research, angling for some type of reward. Once Pietro Vesuchi died, Adolfo knew his contact would be scared and greedy enough to do anything asked of him.

Adolfo purchased a copy of the La Nazione newspaper and found a small café in sight of the Basilica. He ordered a croissant and some strong coffee, then settled in for a long wait.

———•●•———

Ethan and Chloe entered the office where those wishing access to the library manuscripts or rare books must check in. Each person requesting access had to submit an application with a reason for their research and written confirmation from their organization or university. Since she already finished her degree and was jobless, Chloe had her former college advisor email a letter of support to Pietro Vesuchi. A few days later Chloe received notification of the approval of her research pass for a two-week duration. That approval ended in two days.

A bulky desk made of dark wood and looking almost as old as the Basilica greeted them when they entered the office. The office itself was empty and yellow tape blocked the hallway leading to Pietro's office, which confirmed it was still a crime scene. Ethan and Chloe wondered if using her pass would be possible today. Maybe the entire library would be unavailable.

Just as they turned to leave, a small side door opened on their left and an older woman emerged, blowing her nose and looking haggard. She looked up and recognized Chloe.

"Buongiorno, Signora Chloe," greeted the woman in a weary voice. "I did not expect to see you today. I'm afraid I have some very bad news about Signor Vesuchi."

The woman appeared to be having a difficult time holding in her emotions.

"I heard," Chloe said as she walked toward the woman and the two embraced. Once they parted, both made efforts at composure.

"This is Adelina," Chloe pointed out while wiping her eyes for the second time in only a few minutes. "She is the secretary for the Manuscripts Office. Adelina, this is my friend Ethan."

"Buongiorno Adelina. E molto bello conoscerti. Mi Dispiace per la perdita del Signor Vesuchi." Ethan impressed with his Italian, saying it was nice to meet Adelina and that he was sorry for the loss of Mr. Vesuchi.

"I can't believe he is gone," said Adelina in

Italian, forgetting that Chloe was not fluent. "I left for my lunch break yesterday and came back an hour later and found him in his office. Who would do such a thing? He was such a good man."

Adelina dabbed at her eyes with a well-used tissue, then looked at Chloe and continued in her heavily accented but adequate English. "I came by only to do some necessary tasks and then have been allowed to take a few days away. My husband is taking me to Lucca to see my grandchildren.

"Before I leave, is there something I can do for you?"

"I know this is not a good time, but I need to look at a few more of the books from the Medici collection," Chloe explained. "Is there someone here today who can help?"

"Yes. Mario Ranallo has been Signor Vesuchi's assistant for the past two years. He should able to find the books or manuscripts you request."

Adelina left to find Ranallo and returned with the assistant in tow. He was a small man, who looked to be in his late twenties, with a receding hairline and mouse-like facial features. Ranallo's eyebrows raised noticeably when he entered the office and saw who requested his help. He introduced himself to Ethan and Chloe, confirmed Chloe's pass, and vowed to help in any way possible. He reminded them of the rules: only one manuscript or book could be examined at a time and only ten total requests per day.

Well aware of the rules, Chloe pulled a prepared list from her satchel and handed it to Ranallo.

"These are the ten books we would like to see

today," said Chloe. "I believe we will need about thirty minutes with each book—plus a short break for lunch—so we will be here until late afternoon. Will that work for you?"

"Yes, yes," Ranallo said a little too eagerly. "You and your friend go down the hall to the conference room on your right and I will bring in the first book."

"Have you met that guy before?" asked Ethan as he followed Chloe to the conference room.

"I've seen him during previous visits, but have never been introduced to him. Why do you ask?"

"It's just that he seemed to recognize you when he first came into the office. Also, he didn't even look at the list you handed him before agreeing to help. It's like he already knew what type of books you would request. Maybe I'm imagining things, but the guy gave off a strange vibe."

Chloe shrugged. "Maybe Pietro told him about me. I don't care as long as he brings us the books I requested." The *game face* was back.

They settled into a conference room featuring wood-paneled walls, a high ceiling, and terracotta floors. It was a scaled-back representation of the historic Reading Room of the Laurentian Library, designed by Michelangelo and located in another portion of the building. The original room featured a series of wooden benches, called plutei, down each side of the elongated space. The benches functioned as both lecterns and bookshelves. A wooden panel on the side of each bench listed the titles available at that particular plutei. Many of the original books acquired by the Medici family were leather bound and stamped with not only the Medici crest but also a number corresponding to the appropriate plutei. The sixty-three oldest volumes—collected by Cosimo Medici—originally sat in the first plutei.

"So how did you get started looking at the old Medici books?" asked Ethan once they sat down. "This seems a long way from your interest in art history."

"I was looking at all the places in Florence where the Medici family crest is displayed," explained Chloe. "You probably recognize the crest of five red balls and one blue ball on a golden shield. It shows up on buildings all over the city and in some minor artwork as well. After I saw a picture of the crest stamped into the leather cover of a centuries-old book, I thought I would take a look at the real thing. Once I got access, I noted the coded text along the bottom of some pages in a few of the books. That piqued my interest."

Chloe pulled out a laptop computer from her satchel and brought up her notes.

"I have all the information I've collected so far on this laptop. That's why I carry it with me all the time. It's also backed up automatically on the cloud when there's sufficient Wi-Fi available. Plus, I save the info each night on a USB drive that I keep hidden in my room."

"That sounds smart," said Ethan. "Would you let me take a look at the material and see if anything new jumps out at me?"

"I can do that." She turned the laptop toward Ethan. "Here are the first few pages I put together. You can read through them until Mario brings us the first book I requested."

Ethan read for several minutes, asking a few clarifying questions.

"Where is Mario, anyway? It usually doesn't take this long to bring me the books."

———•●•———

Mario Ranallo sat in his office with a cell phone to his ear.

"It's just as I told you. She introduced the man as a friend. She said his name was Ethan something. I don't remember his last name." Ranallo listened for a few seconds. "Yes, I will try to find out his full name, and yes, I'm sure the list of books I gave you is all she requested."

Another pause to listen.

"There is a way to look at the books online. We are testing a new digital library that has not been made known to the public yet. Every page of every book has been photographed and can be enlarged on a computer screen for closer examination."

Ranallo stated the web address of the digital library. He went over it three times to make sure the man on the phone wrote it down correctly.

"Now Adolfo, I've given you the information you wanted. How much is it worth?"

Satisfied with the response, Ranallo ended the call. He then headed to the underground repository where climate-controlled vaults held many of the historic books and manuscripts.

Several hours later, Ethan and Chloe exhausted their limit of examining ten books in a day. Mario Ranallo served them well, delivering each book requested and hovering around the conference room throughout the afternoon. Ethan sensed Chloe's discouragement because their efforts hadn't produced any new information. Both felt they were missing something, but were unable to come up with any fresh leads. Only one more day remained on Chloe's research pass.

"I know you're disappointed, but let me buy you dinner," said Ethan as they exited the library complex. "You must be starving since we didn't take time for lunch."

"You paid for dinner last night. Let me treat you tonight," said Chloe. "I know a nice little place on the other side of the Santa Maria Novella called Tirabaralla. It's still early enough that it shouldn't be too busy."

"I'll take you up on that. I'm hungry enough to eat about anything."

The pair walked along the Via de Panzini in a constant flow of pedestrian traffic. They turned to take a shortcut through one of the alleyways that wound through many of the older buildings in Florence. Late afternoon shadows darkened the empty ally.

"Chloe Conrad," someone behind them said.

Surprised, they turned to see a young man pointing a gun at them. Chloe gasped and Ethan didn't hesitate to step in front of her. "What do you want? We don't have much money, but you can have it." Ethan was willing to sacrifice a few Euros to defuse the situation.

The man walked forward with a confident look on his face. He wore ripped black jeans and a light jacket over an old T-shirt. Disheveled hair and a scraggly black beard covering much of his boyish face gave him the appearance of a street person trying to shake down some tourists.

Chloe realized that this was not a normal robbery. "How did you know my name?" she asked over Ethan's shoulder.

"I know much about you Signora Conrad and your research at the Laurentian Library," the man said in stilted, accented English. "I even know your friend is named Ethan."

Chloe's claim that she had been followed over the last several days now looked accurate.

"Now, you give me that bag over your shoulder. Then you two can go."

Ethan sensed Chloe's hand on his arm and could feel her grip tighten. He knew by looking at the gun the man carried that they were in a serious situation. The pistol was a newer Beretta 92 that took fifteen 9mm rounds when fully loaded. The silencer on the front made the situation more concerning. Not many street crooks carried silenced Berettas.

"What should I do?" Chloe spoke quietly, just loud enough for Ethan to hear.

"Hand me the bag," he said. Chloe slipped the satchel off her shoulder and handed it to Ethan.

"Here it is," Ethan said. "We don't want any trouble, so just come and get it." He hoped the man wouldn't ask him to set it on the ground and move backward. The assailant rewarded his hopes, confidently closing the gap with the gun pointed at Ethan's chest.

Ethan extended his arm holding the satchel and the man reached to grab it. Just as the man's fingers closed around a strap, Ethan jerked back, pulling the man off-balance. Ethan took advantage with a kick to the man's gun hand—sending the Beretta scooting across the brick pavement. He followed with a punch to the head. The man somehow kept hold of the satchel as he dropped to his knees. Ethan was ready to throw another punch, but the man bolted toward the gun.

"Ethan, let's go," shouted Chloe.

He grabbed her hand and the two sprinted to the opposite end of the alleyway, guessing the man wouldn't follow them toward a crowd of people. They soon burst back into the sunlight and found themselves on a piazza across from the Santa Maria Novella and amid a throng of tourists. Ethan glanced back, but the man wasn't in sight.

They stood against a wall catching their breath and kept their eyes peeled for the young man with a bushy beard. After more than fifteen minutes, they were confident that their assailant grabbed the computer and disappeared.

"Are you alright?" asked Ethan.

"Just scared," said Chloe.

"Let's go report this to the police," he said, then started walking before Chloe had a chance to notice his trembling hands.

Chapter 5

Adolfo wound through the darkening streets of Florence, crossed the Ponte alla Carraia Bridge, and trekked to his small, one-room apartment, located up two flights of stairs above a pharmacy. His beard helped hide his swollen left cheek, which was already turning purple from absorbing a punch. His jaw ached and a finger might be broken. Overall, though, he felt satisfied that he had possession of the computer from the Conrad women and that he could continue to build a relationship with Giancomo Morelli. Working behind the scenes for the shady antique dealer could be very profitable. It was also much safer than other options available to a person like him—namely, working for the mafia.

He wrapped a few cubes of ice in a towel and held it to his face with his injured hand. Using the other hand, he tapped in Morelli's number and activated the speaker function while his phone sat on the cracked tile counter of his kitchenette. Morelli answered the call after two rings.

"Yes, Adolfo. What news do you have for me?"

"Good news, Signor Morelli. I have the laptop from Chloe Conrad." Adolfo smiled to himself in satisfaction, even though it hurt his bruised face.

"That is good news, my young friend," stated Morelli.

"My contact in the library also gave me a new way for a person to research the old books. It's a website that is not yet available to the public so very few people know about it."

"Very good. That information should also prove to be helpful. What about the woman? Is she going to cause us any further trouble?"

"She had a man with her when I confronted them. Unfortunately, they both got away." Adolfo left out the part about taking a few punches.

Morelli was not happy that the woman had developed into a loose end. Now, an unknown man was also involved. Morelli didn't like loose ends. He knew that too many loose ends sometimes found a way to tighten and cause problems; like a noose around your neck.

"This is what I want you to do," said Morelli after some thought. "You should be able to catch the final train this evening from Florence to the Termini Station in Rome. Bring the computer and I will meet you there. You can return to Florence in the morning and then I want you to focus on permanently wrapping up these two loose ends. Can you do that, Adolfo?"

"Yes, Signor Morelli."

"This is extremely important to me and to your future. Do you understand?"

Morelli ended the call before Adolfo responded.

Adolfo knew very well what Morelli was talking about when he alluded to the future. Failure meant that Adolfo's future could come to an abrupt end.

Maybe this isn't safer than the mafia, he thought.

———•●•———

Ethan kept his shaking hands in his pockets as he led Chloe up the stairs to his apartment. After an hour spent giving statements and descriptions to the Polizia di Stato—the State Police—they thought Ethan's place would be safer, not knowing if their assailant knew where she lived. The police promised to contact them if they found any leads or retrieved the computer, but made no promises. The influx of tourists in a place like Florence also brought out the element of society hoping to relieve the tourists of their cash and valuables.

Once they entered the apartment, Ethan introduced Chloe to Dale and made it clear that they needed some privacy. Dale smirked but said he was going out for some food and left the apartment.

"I've never experienced anything like that in the alley," Chloe said after sipping from a glass of water provided by Ethan.

"That's a first for me as a civilian," said Ethan. "Even in the army, most of our confrontations were long-distance. I've never had a gun pointed at me from such close range."

"You didn't seem scared. How do you do that?"

Ethan shrugged his shoulders, unwilling to admit his panic manifested itself in body tremors—and one particular reoccurring nightmare—after a fear-inducing situation. "Believe me, I do get scared.

I guess I've just learned to deal with it," he said, not being entirely truthful.

"So, what now?"

"You can stay here for a while until we know it's safe. I should go check out your apartment and try to get the backup drive."

"What if that guy's there looking around? I don't want to put you in any more danger," said Chloe. "I can still retrieve the information from the cloud."

"I can handle myself and I'll be very careful. Will you give me your key?" asked Ethan. "We shouldn't leave that backup drive for anyone to find."

Chloe dug the key out of her pocket and gave him the address of her apartment. It was fifteen minutes away on foot. Ethan said he should be able to be back in less than an hour if everything went well.

"The USB drive is hidden under a loose floorboard in my bedroom, directly beneath the only window. You'll hear a hollow sound if you knock on the correct board. The board will pop up if you push on the edge. My passport is also in there, so you better grab that, too." Chloe handed him the key.

"Don't leave the apartment and call me right away if you need anything," said Ethan. "If Dale comes back, just ignore him. He can be a pain at times, but he's fairly harmless."

Ethan used the walk to Chloe's apartment to help reduce the bottled-up tension he felt but tried not to show. For now, the overwhelming dread and doubt that accosted him after a traumatic encounter showed outwardly only on the back end—never in the heat of the moment. His greatest fear was that someday that blanket of indecision would fall on him when he needed to react, when he most needed to protect someone. That fear weighed heavily on his decision to leave the Army and dive into the supposedly safe world of academia.

— • ● • —

Ethan found Chloe asleep on the couch when he returned an hour later. He attempted to be quiet, but she soon stirred and sat up, still groggy from her impromptu nap.

"You're back. How did it go?" she asked.

"No problems. I didn't see anyone lurking around your apartment and found the loose floorboard right away."

Ethan handed her a small shopping bag.

"The USB drive and your passport are in there. I also picked up a change of clothes. I don't have much fashion sense, so hope they're okay."

Chloe pulled out the drive and the passport, then checked through the clothes and gave Ethan a thumbs up. "These will work. Thanks."

"I also picked up some dinner." He walked into the kitchen and brought out a pizza box. "I got this across the street at my favorite pizza place. I'm starving."

The two combined to devour the pizza in a few minutes and washed it down with a couple of sodas from in the fridge.

Afterward, Ethan pulled out his laptop and let Chloe type the password to her cloud account, allowing him to download her research files. Her laptop and a few supplies were lost, but the two of them and Chloe's research were safe.

Unfortunately, someone else now had Chloe's laptop and access to her research. If there was something to find, it just became a race to find it first.

"Can you explain to me again how you deciphered the code in the Medici books?" asked Ethan as he scrolled through some of Chloe's notes.

"It all started with a research paper I wrote in college," Chloe began. "Many artists hid secret messages in their paintings or sculptures, especially artists in the Renaissance period. Most of the messages were harmless and held very little meaning, just artists giving themselves a kind of self-adulation. Writing that paper made me aware of the use of ciphers to transmit information in the fifteenth century and of a Florentine named Leon Battista Alberti, who became known for devising secret codes.

"With that knowledge in the back of my mind, a series of random letters written on the pages of some of the Medici books caught my attention. The letters only appeared in a few books and the writing looked different from the original text. Pietro Vesuchi suggested that it might be some type of Renaissance shorthand, but no one had ever come up with a complete explanation.

"I found four instances of the random letters, all in the earliest books collected by Cosimo Medici," said Chloe. "I played around with some possible ciphers and all of a sudden the random letters in those books started to spell out recognizable Latin words.

Each short passage revealed seems to be part of a longer message, but it still feels like some of the parts are missing."

"So the code you figured out has something to do with shifting letters?" asked Ethan.

"Yes, it's a type of substitution code, putting one letter down that represents another letter. This method is rumored to have started as far back as Julius Caesar, but the Alberti guy I mentioned took it a step further. Instead of just moving each letter of the alphabet a set number of spaces, Alberti suggested changing the number of spaces throughout a message. So, as an alternative to jumping one space for an entire message—B represents A; C represents B; and so on—the Alberti method might jump one letter for the first word, but then jump two letters for the next, and keep increasing the spacing for each word. The jumps in letters could also be random, so the recipient would have to know the right sequence to figure out the message. To anyone else, the jumbled letters would never make any sense.

"The code in the Medici books is ingenious," Chloe continued. "The original message I decoded started with the first word being just one letter off and then added another jump for each word. The second message I found began with the first word being three letters off—like A equals D and B equals E—and then progressed from there. The other two started with jumps of five and seven letters. I was fortunate to catch onto the pattern as I fooled around with potential solutions."

"I see you have a chart here in your notes with the alphabet repeated in staggered rows and columns," said Ethan, looking at the computer screen. "But why are there not twenty-six letters?"

"I thought you would know that," Chloe chided. "The Classic Latin alphabet developed from an original twenty-three letters. Other forms of Latin varied slightly, but with trial and error, I found the messages in the Medici book didn't use the letters J, K, and W. So, I made my chart with only the appropriate letters. I still had to download a translation app to read the Latin message once I got it decoded."

"Let's look again at the messages you have decoded so far and see what we've got." Ethan looked through each of the short messages as they appeared in Chloe's notes, both the Latin and English translations.

1. Ego, Rossi Medici, fuisse beati portionem de epistola beati Pauli Apostoli ad Ephesios, scriptum in sua manu.

I, Cosimo Medici, have been blessed to see a portion of a letter from the Apostle Paul to the Ephesians, written in his own hand.

2. Ego diu acquirere plena literis et revelabo illis mundus, sed Soldano non mitigavisset.

I long to acquire the full letters and reveal them to the world, but the Sultan will not relent.

3. Oro, ut solutionem inveni in conspectu meo tempore in terra completa est. Si ego, ut transeat ex hoc mundo, argumentum mea dicta sunt occulta, quia unum dignus, ut semper hoc quest.

I pray that a solution will be found before my time on earth is complete. If I should pass from this world, proof of my claims is hidden for one worthy to continue this quest.

4. *Iuvenes Lorenzo equitat super abscondita est locus. Faxit Deus tibi successus.* Young Lorenzo rides over the concealed location. May God grant you success.

Ethan and Chloe discussed the passages for an hour, trying to find meaning in each word as they hashed out various scenarios. They both agreed that too much information was missing, and they needed another day in the library.

Chloe remained pessimistic.

"Each of the books I've found with the secret code came from Cosimo Medici's personal collection. The collection includes sixty-three volumes and some of those volumes are split up into smaller texts. That totals over a hundred books to look through. With the limit of ten books a day, there are still close to thirty to examine and tomorrow is the last day my research pass is valid."

"Maybe Mario will let us go over the limit or give you an extra day or two on your pass," suggested Ethan. "He seemed anxious to help out when we were at the library earlier today."

"I hope you're right."

Ethan showed Chloe a couch that pulled out into a small bed and brought her some sheets and a pillow.

"I know you're tired, so try to get some sleep," he said. "I'll make sure Dale realizes you're staying here, but be forewarned, he still might wander out in his boxer shorts in the morning."

"Thanks for the warning."

Chapter 6

Sasha Stasevich served as Giancomo Morelli's go-to guy for anything computer-related, and Morelli wasted little time in getting the stolen laptop into Stasevich's hands. The computer wiz could drain every bit of information from a computer's drives and memory, and do it without asking too many questions. A native of Russia, Stasevich spent several years living and working out of Rome. Whether it was a hacking job, sending malicious malware, or getting past a login password, many on the dark side of Italian commerce knew Stasevich and helped keep him awash in cash and vodka.

Placed in the conference room at Morelli's office, the computer surrendered its secrets in only minutes under Stasevich's talented hands. He got around the password and checked for any failsafe processes built into the machine. Feeling confident that all the available information was safe, he turned the laptop over to Morelli and quietly left the room. The fee for the computer guru's efforts would be wired into his account by the end of the day.

Morelli spent an hour searching through the files with keywords like Medici, library, or manuscripts.

He easily found the notes that the Conrad women had made and saw that the details in the computer files—plutei and volume numbers—matched up with the scribbled note Adolfo found in Caputo's office. Morelli's excitement level rose, but he soon realized that there was no X marking the spot where the original epistles of Paul could be found.

There is still work to be done, he thought. *That's the bad news. But the good news is that Chloe Conrad didn't have all the answers either. If Adolfo does his job, she won't be able to continue the search much longer.*

———•●•———

Ethan and Chloe walked back to Laurentian Library the next morning, sticking to well-populated streets and making a constant check of their surroundings. After yesterday's incident, there was no doubt that Chloe and her research were the targets. Caution remained a requirement if they chose to keep working on the codes.

Once entering the library, Mario Ranallo soon had the first book from the Medici collection delivered for them to examine. Mario seemed just as eager to help them as he had the previous day. The book, marked with a P and a 1, along with the number 46, indicated placement in the first plutei of the library and the forty-sixth position. The title was Expositio in Ionam in Latin—Exposition on Jonah—and included fifty-six pages of script and a few blank pages. They slowly examined each page, looking for a random grouping of letters that might appear to be out of place.

"The system to place books in the library came about after Cosimo Medici's death. So, the order that the books appear in each plutei would have no relationship to the actual order in which Cosimo entered the code," explained Chloe. "We are now on book forty-six of sixty-three, but we don't know if we're looking for an early part of the coded message or the final part."

"Once we find something, we will see where it fits," said Ethan. "At this point, we just have to keep working."

Moments later, after carefully turning a page in the fragile book, Chloe's eyes locked onto the unique script written horizontally below the final paragraph.

"Look!" she pointed. "This is the same handwriting as the others I've found, although I think it's the shortest string of letters so far."

Only twenty-two letters appeared along the bottom of the page. Both Ethan and Chloe scribbled them down on a notepad.

QAMY THPRA TICOC CPNBPDEV

"The other portions of the coded message that I found started with letter offsets of one, three, five, and seven," said Chloe. "So, if this is part of a logical sequence, it should either start with offsets of two, four, or six. I also could keep going up in odd-numbered intervals and start with nine or eleven. Does that make sense?"

"Yes, I think I've got it," Ethan said as Chloe put a copy of her Latin alphabet grid on the table between them. "Why don't I start with an offset of two and you start with nine."

They started counting on the grid and writing down letters, hoping that some sequence would make sense.

"Remember that each word should increase the offset by another letter; two for the first word, three for the second, and so on," she said.

Ten minutes later, neither made progress in finding a combination that worked.

"I've got one more to try," said Ethan. "I'll start with an offset of six, meaning that counting back from the letter Q would be an I, and counting back from A would be a T." He went silent as he concentrated on the code.

"I think we might have something," Ethan said with excitement. "Starting with an offset of six and following the pattern, the message would be *Iter magis latet secretum.* I don't know much Latin, but I'm pretty sure that last work is secret."

"Let me type it in the translation app on my phone." Chloe double-checked the spelling as she carefully typed in the Latin phrase. "Bingo. The phrase translates roughly as *The journey of the Magi hides the secret.*"

She pulled out a copy of the other parts of the coded message that Ethan printed off his computer the previous night.

"Since this new message started with a six-letter offset, it should go in between 'If I should pass from this world, proof of my claims are hidden for one worthy to continue this quest' and 'Young Lorenzo rides over the concealed location. May God grant you success.'"

"Does this help? Do you know anything about

the journey of the Magi?" Ethan asked.

Chloe scrunched up her nose and absent-mindedly chewed on the inside of her lip as she thought through the decoded messages. Within moments, her head cocked to the side and her eyes widened. Her finger began tapping a quick rhythm on the tabletop as she turned to lock eyes with Ethan.

"I know what this is saying," she said a bit too loudly for a library setting. Dropping her tone, she repeated, "I know what this is saying. I know where the message is sending us."

Ethan let her take a few deep breaths, hoping she didn't hyperventilate. "Where is it?"

"Okay. Have you been in the Palazzo Medici?"

"Of course."

"One of the special rooms in the Palazzo is a chapel. Have you seen that?"

"Yes, I went through it on a tour about a month ago."

"That chapel is sometimes called the Magi Chapel and it's decorated with a large fresco painting on three of the walls. Do you remember that?"

Ethan nodded.

"That painting is called the *Procession of the Magi* by Benozzo Gozzoli, but is often referred to as the Journey of the Magi."

"That matches the message we found, but how can a painting hide what we're looking for?"

"I don't know exactly," Chloe admitted. "But there's more. The part about Lorenzo riding over the location gives us another clue. Many of the characters Gozzoli painted into the fresco resembled members of the Medici family. That included one of the Magi who has always been rumored to be a depiction of Cosimo's grandson Lorenzo. That character is dressed in white and riding a horse."

"So you're suggesting that the documents Cosimo Medici hid away over five hundred years ago could be hidden somewhere underneath the likeness of Lorenzo in this painting? In a room that's visited by hundreds, maybe thousands, of people each year?" Ethan sounded skeptical.

"Sounds crazy, but I'm convinced that's where the messages are leading us."

"So what do we do now? We can stay here and look through more books or we can try to follow this lead."

Chloe stood up and gathered her things, answering Ethan's question by her actions. They went to return the book to Mario and found him standing right outside the door, nearly running into him as they exited in a rush.

"Mario, you certainly are attentive to our needs," Chloe said, handing him the volume.

"Yes, signora. Can I get you another book?" Mario said, his eyes magnified behind his thick glasses.

"Not at this time." She answered as they passed by. Chloe stopped and turned. "I do have a request, however."

"I'll do whatever I can," replied Mario.

"Would it be possible to extend my research pass for a couple of days? We might need to complete our project and my pass expires today."

Mario looked up and down the hall, checking if anyone else was around. "Signora Conrad, there is a way to do research without coming to the library. All the volumes can be viewed online. However, this is a new system and is not known to anyone outside of our office. It could cause me much trouble if I gave you the address. Though for a small fee, I might be convinced to help you out."

"A small fee? What are you talking about, Mario?"

"I think he means a bribe," inserted Ethan.

Mario smiled and nodded in acknowledgment.

Chloe turned to Ethan. "We could be anywhere and do more research if this website is what he says."

Ethan pulled out a fifty Euro note and held it up to Mario. "Is this fee sufficient?"

"I believe it is, Signor Ethan." Mario slipped a business card out of his wallet and wrote an online address on the back. He handed the card to Ethan, who snatched it.

"This better be for real," said Ethan, in his best Army voice as he stood over the diminutive Mario. "If not, I'll come back for a refund."

The smile—and the color—drained from Mario's face.

———•●•———

Mario stuffed the money into his pocket once the American couple left. The man named Ethan intimidated him, but Mario was still fifty Euros richer and could now place a solid wager on the ACF Fiorentina soccer match tonight. There was also the chance for some additional cash from Adolfo once he passed on the new information he overheard.

He went back to his office and called his childhood friend. As long as Mario put in the right information, Adolfo would dispense a monetary reward; much like a human vending machine. The easy exchange of information for cash was becoming addicting, much like his gambling. Mario just needed one big wager to come through and he would be free.

"Adolfo, I have information I think you'll want," Mario said once his friend answered.

"This better be good. I'm busy."

"The Conrad woman and her friend Ethan were back at the library today and I heard them talk about a breakthrough in their research."

"Okay, you have my attention."

"Before I tell you, I think I need a bigger fee for my services."

"Is that so," said Adolfo, in a sarcastic tone. "How about this? If I like your information, I'll give you a bonus. But if I don't, I get to visit you later tonight in your little apartment off the Via di Mezzo."

It never occurred to Mario that Adolfo knew where he lived, or that his old friend might be dangerous. He swallowed the lump in his throat and tried to sound confident.

"I couldn't hear all the details, but they examined one of the old Medici books and then spoke about some documents hidden in the Palazzo Medici. I believe they mentioned something about the chapel."

"Hmmm. Very good Mario. That might be enough for a small bonus. Were they going straight to the Palazzo?"

"That I don't know, but they did leave the

library in a hurry."

"How long ago?"

"No more than ten minutes."

The line immediately went dead.

What about my fee? thought Mario.

Chapter 7

A two-minute walk took them from the Laurentian Library to the Palazzo Medici. Ethan and Chloe stood looking up at the three-story residence designed by the architect Michelozzo in 1444. Brunelleschi, who devised the plans for the great dome on the Duomo, submitted drawings for the palazzo, but Cosimo considered them too extravagant. Rough stone brick covered the first-floor edifice, while each successive floor had progressively refined stonework, giving the structure a sense of being taller. A massive cornice circled the top floor.

The building had turned into more of a museum and less of a former residence during the last century. What started on the lower level as the stables for the Medici family had been converted into a showroom for archeological pieces and works in marble. Other areas of the structure featured exhibits from various artists. Tours of the building took visitors through the museum sections and a guided walk through the former family areas, including the Magi Chapel.

Ethan remembered from his previous visit that small groups entered the chapel on a regular schedule, but remained in the room only a few minutes until ushered into the next part of the tour. There would be very little time or opportunity to look for a five-hundred-year-old hiding place.

Ethan nudged Chloe from the line of tourists that snaked up to the entrance and guided her away from the crowd.

"We are not going to get the time we need on a regular tour to examine the painting in the chapel, much less hunt for a secret manuscript," he said. "But I have an idea. Give me a few minutes to make a call and I'll be right back."

— • ● • —

Ethan left in search of a quiet place to make a call, while Chloe leaned against the stone façade of a hotel across the street from the palazzo. The streams of people walking along the sidewalk helped to make her somewhat invisible to the masses. Nevertheless, she tried to stay aware of her surroundings. Only yesterday, a bearded man had held them at gunpoint, a memory for her that wouldn't fade.

"Success," Ethan said, appearing suddenly five minutes later. "We will have the chapel all to ourselves this evening for fifteen minutes."

"How did you manage that?" she asked as they began to walk north along the Via Cavour, opposite the direction Ethan walked two days ago for their original meeting.

"I remembered that one of the locals in my architecture class said he had a part-time job as a guide at the Palazzo Medici. I called and said I wanted a private tour of the Magi Chapel, and he said that he could make that happen."

"You just asked for a private tour, and he agreed that quickly?"

"Well, I might have mentioned that I wanted to impress a girl. You know how the Italians love romance."

"In other words, you lied."

"I would call it expounding on the truth. I just told him a friend of mine wanted to see the Magi Chapel and that she would be impressed if we could go in alone. I never said anything about romance."

A sly smile creased Chloe's lips. "You are a clever one, Mr. Montgomery."

"I guess six years in the U.S. Army taught me to be creative."

As they walked, Ethan explained that they needed to meet his friend Mateo outside the entrance of the Palazzo at exactly seven-fifteen tonight. Mateo would get them into the chapel between two other evening tours.

"So what do we do until then?"

Ethan checked his watch. "I suggest we find something for lunch and then lay low until this evening."

They walked straight for several blocks, passing the Piazza San Marco and found a small café catering to locals and college students. Neither was extremely hungry, so they settled on Tuscan soups—Carabaccia for her and Ribollita for him—with thick slices of fresh bread and bottles of water.

The talk as they ate bounced from Ethan's military experience to Chloe's time in a boarding school, to plans for their futures. A normal conversation among new friends was a welcome break.

Both avoided any mention of the Medici, epistles of Paul, and secret messages—at least for a short time. Those topics had dominated Chloe's waking moments for most of the last two weeks. Ethan was a relatively new factor in the equation, but the past forty-eight hours had served as a trial by fire for him. He was now fully involved.

Chloe admitted that she needed some additional clothes and other items from her apartment, so they headed in that direction after lunch. Ethan made her wait safely inside a corner grocery store a block from the apartment while he did a brief surveillance run. Not seeing anything suspicious, they spent twenty minutes inside the apartment, leaving with a backpack and a small duffle full of Chloe's things.

———·◉·———

Both of them failed to notice a young man watching them from a bus stop down the street. Adolfo rushed to the Medici Palace after the tip from Mario and scouted the area for an hour with no success. Frustrated with missing them or having been given bad information, he decided to take a chance on watching the Conrad woman's apartment. A few minutes after finding an inconspicuous spot at the bus stop, his plan produced a result. The woman, along with her friend Ethan, walked out of the apartment, each carrying a bag. He followed at a distance, hoping they would lead him to whatever they had discovered.

Signore Morelli would be very pleased if Adolfo got his hands on the discovery and took care of the two Americans.

———•●•———

The skies grew dark and a stiff breeze whipped against their backs by the time Ethan and Chloe returned to his apartment. They managed to get inside and deposit their bags on the floor before the rain began falling.

Ethan excused himself to contact his professors and make arrangements for missing the remaining classes of the semester. The professors wouldn't be happy, but Ethan had completed all his projects and performed well in his classes, so should receive high marks. He had until the end of the month to submit his final thesis to his advisor back in the States.

Chloe opened Ethan's computer on the small dining table and took the time to double-check their research from earlier in the day and confirm her original deduction about the hidden manuscripts. She also checked out the web address from Mario and found that it did lead to a site where all the volumes from the Laurentian Library could be viewed. She would certainly have time to explore more thoroughly in the days to come.

For now, Chloe pulled up all the available information about the Palazzo Medici, its long history, and a reminder of its overall layout. So much had been done to the building since the days of Cosimo Medici, it was difficult to believe that anything hidden in the 1400s could still be found.

The Palazzo served as host to Michelangelo and Leonardo da Vinci and saw the births of Giovanni and Guilio Medici—who went on to be Pope Leo X and Pope Clement VII. It had even hosted an infamous meeting between Adolf Hitler and Benito Mussolini in 1938. It seemed right out of a movie script that something as sacred as an original writing from the Apostle Paul might be hidden in such a storied structure.

"Have you talked to your father recently?" Ethan's question startled her.

"I called him the evening we first met," replied Chloe." I guess that was just two days ago. He's pleased that you are helping me out."

"So you didn't tell him about getting robbed at gunpoint?" Ethan sat down across from her.

Chloe closed the laptop and organized some papers on the table. "No," she said hesitantly. "I know I should have, but thought he would lecture me and then spend far too much time worrying about me."

"If he knew I was with you," Ethan said, "I can imagine him calling to tell me to stand at attention while he chewed me out over the phone."

"Yep, that's my dad. I think he's always been harder on the ones he liked the best. I know he was hard on me, but I never doubted how much he loved me."

Ethan saw a hint of Colonel Conrad in Chloe's face but assumed she looked more like her mother. He saw some of the Colonel's toughness in her, though. Despite the intensity of the past couple of days, she was still moving forward when many people—men and women—would have given up.

"Tell me more about your parents," she prodded. "What was it like growing up in the Midwest and living in the same town all your life?"

"My parents could be on a poster for the Midwestern life. They met in high school, got married during college, and then had me a few years later," Ethan explained. "Mom had some complications during my birth, so couldn't have any more children. Most would say they spoiled me, but they also made me work hard and I'm thankful for that. They've lived in the same house for most of their married lives and they sit in the same pew at church every Sunday. Dad is still in the same teaching and coaching job he started right after college. My mom has been teaching third grade for about ten years—ever since I graduated from high school.

"My hometown has less than twenty thousand people but was big enough to supply a decent education and a lot of opportunities. Many kids, like myself, leave town after high school, although I know many of my former classmates have moved back and started families there. I don't know if I would ever move back permanently, but I'll always enjoy visiting."

"So, were you in church with your parents every Sunday?" asked Chloe.

"Yeah, I was. Church was a big part of my life growing up and some of my best friends were in youth group with me. I guess I kind of inherited my parent's beliefs, though I never felt it was forced on me.

"What about you?" Ethan returned the question. "Were you a church-going girl?"

"I was, believe it or not," she replied. "My experience was much different than yours. We had to go to chapel on the bases where my dad was stationed or sit through services in churches that sometimes conducted the service in a different language. I never had a youth group or ever felt that I was a member of a particular church, but my mom made sure we kept it a priority."

"You know, the more I think about it, I might remember you sitting next to your mom and the Colonel in a chapel service in Vicenza. You were a teenager at the time," said Ethan.

A sentimental look crossed Chloe's face as she looked past Ethan.

"I really miss my mom," she admitted. "Even though my dad was this tough Army commander, my mom was the rock of the family. When she first received the diagnosis of breast cancer, she and I could have easily remained in the States while my dad served at various posts. But she insisted that the family stay together and worked hard to make sure at least a part of our lives was as normal as possible. When I attended boarding school in Geneva, my mother managed to make frequent trips on the train to see me. I also tried to make it back to the base as often as possible.

"I know my mom's faith gave her strength despite all the moves and the difficulties of fighting the disease. During the last months of her life, she often talked to me about her joy, even amidst pain. Honestly, I feel my dad is only a portion of himself since she died. I worry about him as much as he worries about me."

Ethan sensed the emotions welling up in Chloe. He stood and walked to the window to give her a moment to compose herself.

"I hope this rain stops before we have to go out tonight," he said, almost to himself.

Ethan watched as the colorful umbrellas passed by on the sidewalk below his apartment. Each pedestrian looked to be in a hurry to get to some place dry. He wondered why one man—a drooping black umbrella blocking his face—stood motionless across the street in the steady rain.

Chapter 8

You realize that if we find something tonight, this ordeal will take on a whole new meaning," said Ethan as he and Chloe left the apartment. They were pleased that the rain had moved out and the early summer sun still provided some light. "Until now, all we've done is research and some speculation—nothing illegal or even the least bit dishonest. Taking something from that chapel tonight, though, puts us at the point of no return. Are you ready for that?"

Chloe carried an almost empty backpack on her shoulders, planning for somewhere to hide any potential find. She continued to walk side by side with Ethan for most of a block before stopping suddenly and pulling him into the shaded entryway of a bank, already closed for the day.

"Two days ago I would have gladly passed on anything we might find to the proper authorities," she said with a bit of fire in her voice. "But after being followed and held up at gunpoint—not to mention Pietro being murdered—it's obvious that we are not alone in this little quest. Someone is willing to do about anything to find this writing from Paul or whatever it might be that the Medici hid away."

Chloe continued after a deep breath. "You know as well as I do that if we discover something tonight and take it to a museum, a historian, or whoever, there will be a big hullabaloo in the antiquities world. Then it would be weeks—if not months—until someone kept following the clues to see if there was another important find out there." She stood up on her toes and moved into Ethan's face, her cheeks red and eyes wide. "I'm not willing to let whoever killed Pietro and stole my computer get there first. Are you?"

Ethan kept calm and then raised one finger before speaking. "Can I just ask one quick question?" Chloe took a small step back. "Did you actually use the word hullabaloo in a sentence?"

They both laughed and the slight tension relaxed.

"Sorry," she said. "I get a little worked up sometimes. My dad always said I should have been an officer in the military; I'm stubborn and I like to give orders."

Ain't that the truth, Ethan thought as they continued walking down the Via San Zanobi. *But she is kind of cute when she's riled up.*

The two discussed various scenarios in case they had success during their fifteen minutes inside the Magi Chapel. The specter of an unknown assailant stalking them factored into their planning. Both voiced a commitment to make sure they protected any discovery, even if that meant sneaking out of Florence to conduct further study or follow additional clues.

A few people milled about the area of the

Palazzo Medici as they approached. The earlier rain and the fading sunlight combined to drive most locals home for dinner and most tourists into the welcoming arms of eager restaurateurs.

Ethan and Chloe arrived a few minutes early at the designated spot where Ethan's friend Mateo would meet them. They stood with nervous anticipation until a small group of stout, chiseled-face people exited the Palazzo, speaking among themselves in an indecipherable language. A dark-haired young man followed a step behind the group, his friendly smile and exuberant stride aimed at Ethan.

"Ciao, my friend Ethan," the man said, grasping Ethan's hand and pulling him in for a quick hug. Stepping back, the man turned to Chloe. "And this must be the lovely lady you told me about."

"Yes, this is my friend Chloe," Ethan said in introduction. "And Chloe, this is Mateo."

Chloe also received a brief hug from the very outgoing Mateo.

"I am pleased to be able to help out such a striking couple," Mateo said in his best tour guide voice. "Follow me. We don't have much time until the next tour begins."

They fell in stride behind Mateo as he led them into the Palazzo through the long vestibule and then turned right once they reached the courtyard.

"I'm going to take you up a small stairway that is rarely used anymore," said Mateo. "It will take us to a side door that opens into the chapel. The Medici family would have used this for a private entrance."

The trio opened a nondescript wooden door and

entered a narrow, stone stairway lit by only two small lights. The passage felt claustrophobic once the door closed behind them. They ascended without conversation to a small landing that provided just enough space for the three of them to stand. Mateo removed a key from his pocket and placed it in a modern lock on an otherwise centuries-old, handmade door. The key turned with a soft click and Mateo pushed the door inward. The entryway stood less than six feet tall, forcing Ethan to stoop as he entered.

Coming out of the rough stone stairwell and into the illustrious chapel was like stepping into a different world. The surrounding fresco painting dominated the space, but the mosaic marble floor, the elaborate inlaid ceiling, and the intricately carved wooden seating stalls added to the aura of wealth and piety.

"I'll leave the two of you to enjoy the chapel for a few minutes. Please don't touch the fresco or other artwork," instructed Mateo. "I'll be back to lead you out before the next tour comes through."

Ethan pulled out a couple of twenty-euro bills and slipped them to Mateo. "Thanks for your help. I hope I can repay the favor sometime."

Mateo nodded and disappeared through the small doorway.

Ethan and Chloe stood in the center of the chapel, rotating slowly, trying to take it all in. It was like being inside a piece of art, as almost every square inch—floor, ceiling, and walls—showed impressive design and precision craftsmanship.

"We don't have much time, so let's get started,"

Chloe said as she moved toward the east wall of the room. She pointed to the figure riding a white stallion, clothed in a golden robe and wearing a jeweled crown. "This is the portion of the fresco I told you about. The boy on the horse represents Caspar, the youngest Magi, but has long been believed to be a likeness of Cosimo's grandson, Lorenzo."

The depiction of Lorenzo appeared near the bottom of the fresco, with only a small dog and the rocky path illustrated below the white horse. The top edge of the seating stalls met seamlessly with the lower portion of the painting. The wooden stalls boasted beautiful carvings, with geometric patterns and designs repeating the length of each section on the arms, backs, and even the seats.

Ethan knelt on the floor to look under the seat, remembering the clue that said *Lorenzo rides over the concealed location.* He tapped on the wooden floorboards below the bench, hoping to hear a hollow sound, but with no success.

"I guess the Medici were smarter than me," quipped Chloe about the hiding spot in her apartment.

"Well, let's hope they weren't too smart," retorted Ethan as he felt around the wooden seat and back of the stall for some type of hidden compartment.

They took turns exploring every minute detail of the painting, the stalls, and the floor along the east wall. They tried the same on the opposite wall, reasoning that the eyes of Lorenzo in the painting looked straight across the room. Frustration mounted as the minutes ticked by.

"Maybe we're on a wild goose chase," said Ethan as he plopped down on the marble floor. "If anything was ever here, there's a good chance it would have been found before now."

Chloe continued to walk back and forth, staring at the wall. "I find it hard to believe that the coded messages we found were put in those old books to send someone on a fruitless chase. That doesn't make any sense. Plus, if someone found a manuscript ascribed to the Apostle Paul—even a couple of centuries ago—I'm sure the discovery would have been documented."

"I agree," said Ethan. "But I don't know what else we could do short of tearing out these stalls."

Chloe made one more pass around the entire chapel, her eyes looking down at the seats of the wooden stalls.

"Hey, take a look at this," she said pointing to a section of the seats. Ethan jumped up to see what she might have found. "Each seat around the entire room has one of two different designs. One is a fleur-de-lis and the other looks like a torch and flame, both of them over a shield. But the one directly below the painting of Lorenzo is different. There is a shield, but it has the Medici crest represented by the six balls. I guess there were so many details to look at in this room that we never noticed this bench is different."

Ethan wasted no time as he knelt and examined the bench and the stall again. He pressed and poked on all the ridges and carvings, hoping for something to happen. Nothing moved. Nothing magically appeared.

"There has to be a reason why this bench is different," said Chloe. "Let me take a look."

She ran her fingers over the Medici crest and felt that the carved grooves around the six balls seemed a little deeper than the other etchings. She pushed on each one of the six circular carvings without any result. Then she used both hands and fashioned her fingers in a way to depress all six balls at once.

The balls moved inward a fraction of an inch and a latch released. Ethan and Chloe stared with open mouths as a square section on the back of the stall inched open. Neither of them moved for several seconds, frozen in place by both anticipation and disbelief.

"We found it," Chloe said, almost with a reverent tone.

Ethan knelt and cautiously pulled the wooden section open, seeing it functioned as a small door. The precise carving around the edges allowed the door to escape detection for more than five centuries. He reached in and found a flat wooden box the size of a large mailing envelope and about two inches thick. A waxy substance covered the seams— probably to make the box airtight. The box, itself, showed impressive decoration. It included a carved shield on the lid, complete with five round rubies and a sapphire to represent the Medici crest.

They heard footsteps and a key scraping into a lock. Ethan hurried to push the panel shut, thankful that it latched back in place. He spun Chloe around, unzipped the backpack still on her shoulders, and slid the jeweled box carefully inside. As the door began to open, he turned her back around and leaned in for an impromptu kiss. He felt her surprise at first but also noticed she played along with little hesitation.

"Aahh. I see that your time in the chapel has been productive," joked Mateo, stepping through the small door. "It's unfortunate, but this part of your romantic evening has to come to an end."

Ethan stepped away from Chloe, hoping she wouldn't slap him. Instead, she slid her arm around his waist—showing no embarrassment. They followed Mateo down the cramped stairway, around the courtyard, and out onto the street.

A slim streak of blue sky was still visible on the western horizon, but a clear, moonlit evening would soon descend on Florence.

They walked without speaking, both filled with a sense of euphoria as they took a circuitous route away from the Palazzo. They remained on major streets, using the openness to allow clean sightlines and make it difficult for anyone to approach them unseen. Carrying around a potential historic artifact in an old backpack wasn't the smartest idea, but it would keep them inconspicuous until better arrangements could be made.

Both had the strong desire to stop and rip open the backpack to see what the box held, but they knew that a safe and sterile location was needed before exposing the contents.

"I still can't believe it," said Ethan, a huge smile of satisfaction on his face.

"What? You can't believe that Mateo bought that sloppy kiss you laid on me," said Chloe, laughing at her own joke.

"Hey, I didn't hear you complaining."

"Just playing my part."

And you played your part very well, thought Ethan.

The pair continued to walk in silence—letting the tension from the evening's activities dissipate—and soon reached the area of the city where Ethan attended his classes. Foot traffic was sparse on this one section of their path back to Ethan's apartment. The headlights of only an occasional car illuminated them as they walked. The two turned on a small side street for a one-block detour that would bring them out at the Piazza San Marco. From there it was a short distance to the apartment.

Halfway down the darkened street, Chloe suddenly turned.

"I think I heard something."

Footsteps became more noticeable before either could see anyone through the deep shadows that enveloped the area. A hooded figure abruptly appeared seconds later with a gun pointed in their direction. Ethan stepped in front of Chloe, much as he had two days earlier. The figure stopped a few feet away.

"It looks like we meet again." The man pulled off his hood, revealing dark hair and a smooth, but still bruised face. It took Ethan a second to realize it was the same man—and the same gun—from the previous confrontation. The lack of a beard made the man look even younger.

A flick of the gun indicated that the man wanted them to walk through a pair of huge wooden doors to their left. Ethan passed by these doors often and knew they led to a tunnel-like entryway for a series of university classrooms. There must be a class going on somewhere inside or the doors would be shut and locked. The tunnel was empty, though, with only a faint light at the far end confirming a class in session.

"I've been anxious to cross your path again," the man said while prodding Ethan forward with the gun in his back. They stopped a few strides into the space and Ethan began to turn around. "No, you face away. Signora Conrad, you can remove the backpack and set it on the ground."

Chloe stole a glance at Ethan and he gave a slight nod. She slipped the backpack off her shoulders and set it at her feet with care. Ethan sensed the man bending to reach for the backpack, the gun wavering as it pressed against Ethan's spine. With surprising speed, Ethan pivoted at his hips, his left hand reaching back to grab the barrel of the gun before it fired. His right fist gained momentum during the spin and landed a perfect knockout punch to the man's jaw. The young man's legs crumbled as he collapsed in a heap on the stone floor.

Ethan still held the barrel of the gun in his left hand and attempted to shake out the sting in the knuckles of his right as Chloe retrieved the backpack. She looked up at him with a certain amount of admiration and just mouthed the word, "Wow."

Ethan reached out to grasp Chloe's hand and prayed she didn't feel how much he was shaking. They took off walking as calmly as possible, leaving the man sprawled unconscious on the ground. Ethan tossed the gun into a trash bin near the end of the street.

Chapter 9

Dinner was long finished, and the two children finally gave up arguing about going to bed. Giancomo Morelli poured himself a large glass of wine and escaped to what the Americans would call a man cave. Instead of sports memorabilia and a wall-sized television, he enjoyed being surrounded by the spoils of his trade: a small Renaissance painting that was part of a massive burglary from a museum in Rotterdam; an ancient Greek amphora vase made around 300 B.C. and acquired from a contact in Sicily; and a fifteenth century Bible stolen in Germany by a group of Dutch thieves. All would leave Morelli's hand in the future, but not until the time was right and buyers emerged. Any buyer would need a large sum of money and a small amount of scruples.

Before settling into a comfortable chair, Morelli stood by his vintage Victrola record player—a gift from a satisfied buyer—and put on an album of Beethoven's Symphony No. 5 in C minor. He sipped his wine and enjoyed the time to think while being enveloped by the strings, horns, and percussion of the music. During the crescendos of the symphony's second movement, Morelli's phone chimed, almost in pitch and timing with the orchestra.

A text appeared. He clicked the icon and saw it was from Adolfo in Florence. The message was enough to ruin the evening.

Ho fallito it said. I failed.

Morelli resisted the urge to throw the phone against the wall. He closed his eyes and let the music calm him. It worked for a few moments, but soon he stood and paced the floor. The last word he received from Adolfo was that the woman and her friend discovered some type of clue and were headed to the Palazzo Medici.

Did they find anything? Could they have found a manuscript of the hidden Pauline epistle?

Many questions sprinted through Morelli's mind, but no answers appeared in their wake. That was Adolfo's job: find out what the Conrad woman knew and what she had discovered, if anything. The young man in Florence had initially shown promise. Too bad his failure would need to be dealt with harshly.

Morelli proactively hired researchers earlier in the day to aid with the pursuit of whatever the Medicis had hidden away. The pair—a retired history professor and a former detective with some skeletons in their respective closets—assisted Morelli in the past and he knew they were thorough. More importantly, he knew the cash he promised would ensure their silence.

The researchers remained busy digging through the notes on the stolen computer and looking online at the Medici books for more hidden clues.

Morelli planned to stay in the hunt, even after

Adolfo failed in Florence. If Chloe Conrad found an artifact or manuscript worth owning, Morelli knew someone who could track her down and take it away. No more fooling around with hiring young thugs. It was time to call in the big boys.

———•●•———

The wooden box sat on the table between them, the rubies and sapphire reflecting the room's light into small, bright pinpoints on the walls. Ethan and Chloe spent the last twenty minutes staring at the box, torn with indecision on how to proceed. There was an almost irresistible urge to open the box and discover its contests. That came with an equally strong fear that they would be disappointed—or worse—that they would somehow permanently damage whatever was in the box. Those contrasting thoughts tempered the realization that someone out there knew what they were doing and had twice tried to intervene. The loss of Chloe's computer and Ethan's sore knuckles were the only consequences so far, but personal safety had to be considered.

"What if we turned the box over to a museum? They would have the personnel and the knowledge to know how to deal with whatever's inside. It would take us out of the loop so we wouldn't have to worry about being held up at gunpoint again."

Chloe glared at him. "You know my thoughts on that. Didn't I make that clear this afternoon?"

"Yes, you did, but I had to ask." Ethan took care as he rotated the box on the table, examining the seal around the edges. "Whatever was used to seal this box hardened over time and looks brittle in places. I think we can remove it easily without damaging the box."

Chloe looked around the room and noticed dirty dishes in the sink, dust on several surfaces, and an overflowing trash can. "No offense to your housekeeping skills, but this isn't exactly the cleanest place to examine a potentially priceless artifact."

Ethan chuckled. "In my defense, it was Dale's week to clean. So what do you have in mind?"

"I've got an idea," Chloe replied after some thought. "Let me make a call."

She grabbed her phone and left the room for a few minutes. Ethan heard her voice through the thin walls, but couldn't make out the exact conversation.

"If we're willing to wait until tomorrow, I've found a good place to open this box in a safe and clean environment," she said upon returning.

"Okay. Where are we going?"

"Rome," answered Chloe.

Ethan looked perplexed.

"You're not the only one to have friends in key places. Mateo got us into the Medici Palace, but my friend Andrea will let us into the conservation laboratory for an art gallery in Rome."

"How did you swing that?"

"Andrea and I were in college together and were part of a study trip to Rome a couple of years ago. I knew she had an internship in a conservation department, so just asked if we could use one of the secure areas. She said we would normally be out of luck, but that one-half of the Galleria Corsini museum where she works is closed for renovation. The museum won't be as busy as normal, so she can get us in. If we can be in Rome tomorrow, there will be less staff around since it's a Saturday. I told her we would be there."

"Did you mention what we were bringing to examine?"

"I was pretty vague. I just said it was a piece of art we wanted to look at in a clean environment," explained Chloe. "I think Andrea wanted to know more, but she didn't press me for an answer. We should come up with a good explanation by the time we see her."

The sound of the front door opening startled them as Dale entered the apartment.

"Hey, guys. What's going… whoa," Dale said, noticing the wooden box on the table. "What's that you're looking at?"

"Um…we found this at a souvenir store and Chloe bought one," Ethan improvised.

"That's a pretty cool box," responded Dale. "Those jewels almost look real."

Dale grabbed a drink out of the refrigerator and headed back to his room.

Chloe watched Dale leave the room, then looked at her watch. "We can't stay here. Is there time to catch a late train to Rome?"

Ethan was already pulling up the train schedule on his phone. "There's one more train in about forty-five minutes, but it's a regional train that makes several stops. We wouldn't arrive until after midnight."

"I'm going to have a hard time sleeping anyway,

so let's go for it. I'll call Andrea back and let her know we're coming."

Most of the clothes Chloe picked up at her apartment earlier in the day were still in a bag. Ethan hurried to throw some stuff together and they left for the short walk to the Santa Maria Novella Station.

The wooden box was secure in the backpack strapped onto Chloe's shoulders.

"As I mentioned earlier, a backpack isn't the safest place for carrying around something as valuable as that box," Ethan said. "But I'm sure we would stick out more if I had a metal briefcase handcuffed to my wrist."

"You're right, but we need to secure this box and whatever's inside after we get a chance to open it."

Most of the train cars were less than half-full for the evening departure for the Termini Station in Rome. Ethan and Chloe found seats near the rear of the train and had most of the car to themselves. A young couple, who appeared to be tourists exhausted after a long day in Florence, sat in the front of the car and fell asleep within minutes.

Sleep escaped Ethan and Chloe as the train chugged on, making stops in such places as Arezzo, Cortona, and Orvieto. The backpack rested between them, the contents never far from their thoughts.

"What are the odds that there's an original copy of one of the Apostle Paul's letters?" asked Ethan. "Regardless of what someone believes about the Bible, could a letter written in the first century survive?"

"Biblical texts weren't exactly part of my art

history major, but I've done some basic research in the past few weeks," said Chloe. "The oldest confirmed portion of the New Testament that's been found is a fragment from the book of John. It's dated to sometime in the early second century. Then there are the Dead Sea Scrolls, found in a series of caves near Qumran in Israel. Some of the Old Testament texts in the find are thought to be from as far back as two hundred B.C. That would make them well over two thousand years old."

"Even though I spent a lot of time in church growing up, I guess I never considered exactly where the books of the Bible came from, at least in a literal sense," said Ethan. "We were taught to believe that the Bible was inspired by God, but someone had to write it all down and then pass it on through the years."

"I read somewhere that there are far more early copies of the Bible—both the Old and New Testament—than any other works of antiquity; books like Homer's Iliad and writings by Plato," commented Chloe. "There's something like twenty thousand examples of the New Testament written within a few hundred years of Christ. None of them claim to be the original manuscripts, but discoveries are made every year."

"So, let's assume that we open the box tomorrow and find a page from an authentic writing of Paul," Ethan speculated. "What would something like that be worth?"

"First, the find would have to be verified and dated. That process would take a while," said Chloe. "If experts agreed that any manuscript was from the first century and could have been written—or at least dictated—by the Apostle Paul, my guess is it would be worth millions. Maybe tens of millions. It would be the oldest piece of the New Testament ever discovered; probably considered the find of the century."

Both remained silent as they let that sink in.

"I guess that explains why someone would want to steal your notes and keep us from finding out more," said Ethan.

Chloe rested her hand on the backpack and looked at Ethan. "That also explains why we're taking this late-night train to Rome and plan to open this box in secret. If we find something extraordinary, we have to keep it safe and can't let it fall into the wrong hands."

"Maybe a safety deposit box would work."

"Do you think we can rent one in Rome?"

"I will look into it first thing tomorrow," he said.

Ethan's watch said it was 12:45 a.m. when they finally arrived in Rome. Weariness began to drain their reserves of adrenaline as they walked to another part of the Termini Station and caught a Metro train, still running with late weekend hours of operation. The underground transport would take them near Andrea's apartment, where they would grab a few hours of sleep.

A group of rowdy students joined Ethan and Chloe on the Metro ride to the Batitstini Station, the last stop on the Blue Line. If their Metro car had been traveling above ground, they would have passed close enough to the Vatican to see the dome of St. Peter's Cathedral.

They trudged up three flights of narrow stairs to reach Andrea's small apartment. Their host opened the door in a long t-shirt, gave Chloe a quick hug, and then disappeared sleepily into her bedroom. There were two pillows and blankets placed on a chair in the sparsely furnished front room. With no couch or even a comfortable chair in sight, Ethan took off his shoes, snatched a pillow and blanket, and claimed a spot on the floor. Chloe did the same a few minutes later. The effects of a very long and eventful day washed over both of them, bringing some needed sleep.

Chapter 10

A pot of strong coffee proved vital after only a few hours of sleep. The aroma pulled Chloe off the uncomfortable floor, and she followed her nose to the tiny kitchen. Ethan was already up, showered, and ready for the day. He held his cup of coffee in one hand and held out the other with a cup for Chloe.

"Thought you might need this to get going this morning," he said.

Chloe accepted the steaming cup and took a quick sip. "Thanks. What time is it anyway?"

"It's almost nine. Andrea said we need to meet her at the gallery by ten o'clock and it takes about thirty minutes to get there on the public buses."

"She already left?"

"Yeah. She stepped right over you while you were sleeping. I guess she had an early meeting."

"This coffee better have extra caffeine," said Chloe as she picked up her bag and went to take a shower.

During the brief walk to the bus station, Ethan informed Chloe that he found a safety deposit box facility in Rome that would be open on a Saturday afternoon.

"The facility isn't associated with a bank, so there's no requirement for having an account. From what I read online, a passport and another form of identification should get us in."

"I hope we find something valuable enough to need it," said Chloe.

<hr>

They caught the correct bus and two changes later stepped off within sight of the Galleria Corsini. The massive palace in the Trastevere area originally served as home for Queen Christina of Sweden, who abdicated her throne in 1654 and lived out her final thirty-five years in Rome. The building changed owners and went through expansion under the Corsini family when Lorenzo Corsini became Pope Clement XII in 1736. Corsini descendants sold it to the Italian state in the late 1800s, along with the large Corsini family art collection. That collection was still intact at the Galleria, along with masterpieces by Caravaggio, Ruben, Van Dyk, and others.

Chloe told an attendant at the entrance that they were there to see Andrea Russo. A few minutes later Andrea appeared and guided them through an immense hall of marble floors and priceless artwork. She showed them a two-story banquet room with a trio of chandeliers the size of small cars suspended from the hand-painted ceiling. In another smaller room, the feature was a 2000-year-old carved marble throne discovered in 1732 in the Laterano area of Rome.

Despite the opulent surroundings, Ethan and

Chloe anxiously awaited the chance to get to work on the wooden box. Thankfully, Andrea's mini tour came to a close and she ushered them into a modern elevator. With a quick swipe of her employee ID card, the elevator descended, coming to a stop with a small jolt. Once the doors opened, plain white walls and glass partitions surrounded them, a different world than the palace above. Andrea pointed out the array of machines in the facility, including an extensive exhaust system to remove dust particles and noxious odors. There was also an infrared reflectometer and a vacuum hot table; all specialized equipment to protect, study, and restore various forms of artwork.

Andrea led them to the end of the hall and then used her card to open the final door. It was a square room with bare walls and a rectangular, counter-height table. They heard the exhaust system pushing in clean air while cycling out any impurities. Lighting options ranged from a soft glow to an intense spotlight, depending on the examination needs.

"This room is used for the initial exam of paintings and other artwork," Andrea explained. "It's clean and airtight. Will this work for you?"

"Absolutely," replied Chloe. "We are so appreciative that you've worked this out for us."

Andrea made them aware of some of the items available to assist them in the drawers underneath the counter: small tools, magnifying equipment, and the like. She started to leave but turned back to Ethan and Chloe. "So, are you going to tell me exactly what you're going to do? What kind of artwork do you need to look at in a room like this?"

Ethan and Chloe glanced at each other, conveying a silent agreement.

Chloe spoke. "We came across an item that we believe is extremely special and has some historic significance. It might even lead to further discoveries." She was being as truthful as possible without giving any specifics. "But, we need to examine it more closely in a safe environment before we make any claims or release more information. I'm sorry we can't tell you more."

"I guess I'll have to trust you. Just remember, if you guys make a million-dollar find, I want a small cut," Andrea quipped while pulling the door shut.

"If she only knew," whispered Ethan.

Chloe opened the backpack, gently pulled out the wooden box, and set it in the center of the counter. Ethan and Chloe remained still and stared at it for a few moments, the only noise in the room coming from the constant hiss of the air filtration system.

The mix of tension, travel, and lack of sleep, along with a big portion of anticipation made the time slow to a glacial-like pace. For Ethan, this entire saga started only three days ago, but he became consumed by it rapidly. He knew Chloe had been wrapped up in this mystery or quest—or whatever it should be called—for weeks. He admired her strength and patience because his own patience was about to reach its breaking point. All Ethan wanted to do was grab a hammer and bust open the box, but he resisted the urge.

Chloe looked through the drawers below the

counter until she located some tools that might help open the box. She came up with a small precision hobby knife and a rounded scraping tool, similar to something a dentist might use to clean teeth. Her hands shook as she placed the items on the table.

"Are you ready to do this? You've earned the right to open the box," said Ethan.

"I want to. I mean, I want to in the worst way." Chloe held out her hands and tried to calm them, without success. "But I also don't want to damage something in the process, so if you're willing, I'll let you try."

Ethan picked up the knife and slid the box to the edge of the table. He ran the knife down one side of the box, over the hardened substance that sealed the lid. A few flakes broke off on the first pass. He did it again, with a bit more pressure. Additional pieces of the sealant crumbled. Ethan exchanged tools and scraped down the same side, seeing a noticeable gap emerge. He repeated the process on all four sides of the box, wiping perspiration off his forehead between each effort.

Chloe paced back and forth in the small room, stopping often to inspect the process. Seconds turned into minutes and the minutes multiplied while Ethan continued to cut and scrape off portions of the seal. When satisfied that the initial job was complete and the box should open, they both took a step back.

"If we open this and it's just a copy of the Medici family Christmas letter, I'm going to be bummed," joked Ethan, trying to disperse some of the nervousness.

Chloe gave only a slight nod, her focus intent on

the box. She breathed deeply and shook out her hands—attempting to end the trembling—as she moved toward the counter. She placed her fingers lightly on each end of the box and pulled up on the lid. At first, nothing moved. Then a small section of the seal missed by Ethan crumbled off a corner and the lid came free. Chloe laid the jewel-filled cover off to the side, almost afraid to look inside.

Ethan slid forward to be by her side, close enough to smell the lilac scent of her shampoo and hear her rapid breathing. Two pairs of eyes locked onto the open box, fueled by expectations, but wary of disappointment. A piece of parchment filled the rectangular opening but showed no obvious writing.

Chloe stopped Ethan as he reached out to inspect the parchment. "Don't touch it with your bare hands." She opened several drawers under the table and came out with two pairs of cotton inspection gloves. "Here, put these on."

With the gloves on his hands, Ethan took great care in lifting the parchment out of the box. He noticed writing on the side that was facing down. He turned it over and laid it on the counter so that the writing was visible. Under the parchment was a small scroll, tied with a faded and deteriorating red ribbon. Next, was a folded letter kept together with a crumbling wax seal that appeared to be stamped with the Medici crest.

Chloe removed the items and placed them next to the parchment. A fine silk cloth lined the bottom of the box. When Ethan moved the cloth, he saw another parchment below, this one looking older and more fragile than the other documents.

"That parchment looks like it will fall apart if we try to move it," said Chloe, pointing to the final document in the box. "The writing is faded, but most of it's visible. Maybe we just leave it where it is, for now."

"Probably a good idea." Ethan bent down and studied the parchment remaining in the box. "The writing looks to be some type of Greek."

Chloe nudged Ethan aside and looked for herself. "Oh, my gosh, Ethan." She was practically bouncing on her toes, now. "The Apostle Paul primarily ministered to people who spoke Greek, so his letters would have been written in Greek. Could this be what Cosimo Medici was talking about?"

"You're asking the wrong guy," answered Ethan. "I struggle some days with writing English. I can speak passable Italian, but Greek is a whole new alphabet." He looked back at the first parchment that came out of the box. "This one looks to be written in Latin. We'll have to open the scroll and the other letter to see if we have two or three different languages to translate."

They both contemplated the next move. The excitement that spurred them to this point still existed, but they now needed to move from a general *What if?* to a more specific *What now?*

"Can we get clear enough pictures to download onto a computer so we can translate the text?" asked Chloe.

"My cell phone takes quality photos and there should be plenty of lighting options in here. It's worth a try."

Both were initially hesitant to remove the wax

seal on the folded letter and unroll the small scroll but accomplished those tasks without damaging the documents.

After an hour of arranging the artifacts, shifting lighting, and snapping dozens of pictures, they were confident that the photos were clear and could be enlarged enough to decipher the writings. They sealed each manuscript inside clear, protective envelopes found in the drawers of the table and slipped the envelopes inside the jeweled box. Once the box was loaded into the backpack, it was time to go.

Ethan led the way to the elevator before remembering it took an employee ID card to operate.

A young woman walked by in a white lab coat, boasting jet-black hair, multiple ear piercings, and a nose ring. Ethan engaged her in Italian. The short conversation ended with her swiping her ID with a tattooed hand and pushing the button to return the elevator to the main floor.

"Grazie," said Ethan as the elevator doors slid shut.

"What did you say to her?" inquired Chloe.

"I just complimented her piercings," he replied. "I also might have mentioned she had nice eyes."

"Smooth. Very Smooth."

Giancomo Morelli spent much of his life on the phone. Whether it was his legitimate business in buying and selling antiquities through his company known as Antichita Della Citta Eterna—Eternal City

Antiquities—or his more elicit endeavors, most of his deals transpired via the phone. Some on the more dangerous side of the business used the dark web to avoid detection and operate in complete anonymity. Morelli was just old enough not to put all of this trust in computers, though he realized that phones could be compromised, as well. He kept several burner phones on hand at all times and usually had more delivered to his office each month. The one phone that always remained within easy reach was a state-of-the-art, heavily encrypted device that served as his primary source of communication.

Several bars of music from the Raiders of the Lost Ark theme song rang out from the device, indicating a call from a trusted associate.

"It's me," said the man on the other end of the line, not needing to give a name. Very few knew his real name. He was simply known as the *cercatore*—The Seeker.

He had better be the best seeker for as much as he charges for his services, Morelli thought.

"Have you been able to find anything?"

"First of all, I need to inform you that your boy Adolfo showed an impressive amount of sorrow for not completing the job you gave him. He will not be available for any more work for quite some time. His legs are not working properly."

Morelli winced. While he never had qualms about dishing out punishment, he rarely asked for details. He didn't want visuals of the physical consequences floating around in his head.

The man continued. "The boy did tell me, however, where the Conrad woman lived, so I'm making progress. I tracked down her property owner and used some gentle persuasion to convince him to give me the woman's contact information. Once I had her cell number, an associate of mine who works for the Telecom Italia network was able to track her device. He can't get an exact location unless she's on a call, but said the phone is currently in the vicinity of Rome."

"Then you need to get to Rome as soon as possible," Morelli demanded. "Will you be able to find her?"

"I will be there in a few hours, but Rome is a big city and there's no guarantee that the woman stays in place. If she remains in Rome, I'll find her. But, it could take some time."

"As much as I'm paying you, I hope it doesn't take too much time." Morelli felt some excitement that Chloe Conrad was somewhere close, but his patience was wearing out. He already had a good deal invested in this search and still had dreams of a huge payoff. "Keep in regular contact and call me as soon as she's found."

Morelli hung up and dialed his two researchers for an update. They reported having found some additional coded text in the early Medici books. Added to the initial notes they received, the researchers believed the new clues confirmed something could be hidden in the Magi Chapel at the Palazzo Medici.

"I already knew that," Morelli exploded. "I need something more!" He assumed that the Conrad woman and her friend had already been to the Palazzo Medici and found whatever might be hidden there. If not, she wouldn't have left Florence.

"We have hundreds of books to go through page by page, Signor Morelli. We are moving as efficiently as we can," said the researcher in defense.

"Then move quicker," he shouted.

There was a brief pause and then the other researcher on was the line. "We did find one additional message in a different set of books."

"What was it?" Morellis said a bit more calmly.

"The message was in a book added to the library around 1490, which was twenty-five years after Cosimo Medici died."

"What did the message say?"

"So far we've found two short sentences," said the researcher, who began to speak with more confidence. "Together they say that Sultan Mehmed died and that his son Bayezid took over the throne."

"That's it?"

"Yes, Signore Morelli, but we'll keep looking."

Interesting, thought Morelli. If there are more messages, it most likely means that whatever was in the Palazzo Medici was just the beginning. Chloe Conrad hasn't found everything yet.

Chapter 11

Careggi, Italy 1492

He laid in bed confident that his days among the living were dwindling. As his strength ebbed away, Lorenzo Medici vividly remembered the mandate he received in this very room from his grandfather Cosimo. Like his grandfather, Lorenzo knew he would likely die before recovering the sacred writings from the ruler of the Ottoman Empire.

Thirty-four combined years of effort had regrettably produced little progress in the search for the letters from the Apostle Paul boasted about by Sultan Mehmed in his long-ago message. To do his part, Lorenzo sent a variety of scholars, politicians, and spies to Constantinople each year for two decades with hopes of acquiring the original epistles. His envoys tried using convincing rhetoric, significant financial offers, and even stealth, but none of those strategies were successful in wrenching the manuscripts away from Mehmed—or after the Sultan's death—his son, Bayezid.

The one thread of optimism came from a rumor passed on to a Medici spy from a cook in the Sultan's palace.

Within months after Bayezid took the Ottoman throne, his younger brother Cem challenged for control and a family skirmish ensued. Cem lost the showdown, forcing him to leave Constantinople and escape first to Egypt and then to the island of Rhodes. There was talk that Bayezid became incensed days after Cem's escape when he discovered his younger brother might have secretly removed valuable manuscripts before leaving the country. Bayezid ordered the entire palace searched and threatened severe punishment for failure to find the missing texts. At least two servants who participated in the search were never seen again.

The window in Lorenzo's room stood open, letting in the cool air of an early spring evening. He heard the rustle of the leaves just outside as a gentle breeze seemed to push the daylight away. The anguish of failure and the pain of illness caused him to stir, something close to a moan escaping his lips.

"Father, can I help you?" asked his daughter Louisa, who spent most of the day by his bedside. Her mother and Lorenzo's wife, Clarice, passed away four years earlier, adding additional heartache to the Medici family.

"Louisa, please get my son," said Lorenzo, his scratchy voice straining to be audible.

"Which son, father?" She wondered if her father was lucid. "You have four sons."

"The oldest," he said. "Piero."

Louisa left the room to summon her older brother, who was staying at the Careggi home while his father was ill. Named after his grandfather, Piero would take over the Medici family upon the death of Lorenzo.

Piero entered the bedroom minutes later, noting it already felt like death. The tapestries on the wall needed cleaning and the paintings were not quite as vibrant as in years past. The fading light and the smell of decay added to the feeling of gloom.

Lorenzo raised a feeble hand, directing his son to sit by his side on the massive bed. The dying man spoke at length in a hushed tone, stopping occasionally to rest and for Piero to confirm his understanding with a nod.

"Your sister Louisa has a letter that I wrote and sealed several days ago. I will not make it back to our palace in Florence, so I am asking you to take the letter and secure it in the secret place. You must also continue the search. Can you do that?"

"I can father," Piero said through tears. "I will not fail you or this family."

The conversation ended when Lorenzo, sapped of strength, could talk no more. Piero laid his head on his father's chest and wept.

Lorenzo, often called *The Magnificent,* would be buried the following week in Florence, near his father and grandfather in the family tomb.

Days later, Piero fulfilled the first part of his father's wishes. The newly elevated Lord of Florence visited the Magi Chapel late one evening, finding the seat with the Medici crest and opening the hidden compartment. He took the jeweled box to his office, placed the letter from Lorenzo inside, and sealed the edges before returning it to its hiding place.

Piero had no way of knowing at the time that the

Medici would be forced out of Florence within two years and the hidden wooden box forgotten. Piero—nicknamed *The Unfortunate*—would die before ever passing on the secret.

Chapter 12

Present Day

After leaving the Galleria Corsini, Ethan and Chloe hailed a taxi and traveled to central Rome with hopes of renting a safety deposit box at a facility called Roma Caveau – Roman Vault. They decided on a joint account, so both filled out the necessary information, presented their passports, and had fingerprints taken to use in a biometric scanner to gain future access. Ethan offered to pay the initial fee and an employee guided them to one of the vault rooms, where they were left alone to deposit their valuables. Ten minutes later, they were back on the street feeling lighter without the pressure of carrying around a box of manuscripts possibly worth millions.

"So, where can we go to study the pictures we took of the manuscripts?" asked Ethan.

"Maybe a public library would work. I'm sure we would have Wi-Fi and a library would also give us some anonymity while we work."

Chloe did some quick research on her phone and settled on the Biblioteca Angelica. The library opened its doors in 1604, thanks to the work of its founder, Angelo Rocca, an Augustinian bishop. Main collections in the 200,000-volume library include texts on the thoughts of St. Augustine, the history of the Reformation and Counter-Reformation, and rare editions of works by Dante and Petrarch. Unique volumes of Italian literature and theater from the fifteenth to eighteenth centuries were also among the library's collections.

A fifteen-minute walk allowed them to stand in front of the secluded doors of the library that first opened more than 150 years before the United States officially became a country. A soaring main room served as the heart of the building, highlighted by thousands of volumes held in three levels of stacks. The main room had a vaulted ceiling and a series of arched windows to provide a greater feeling of openness than in most darkened libraries. Ethan pointed out a pair of open seats and Chloe followed him to a handcrafted wooden table with stout chairs.

The Wi-Fi strength was good, allowing the pictures from Ethan's phone to transfer rapidly to his computer. They started with the manuscript that had been at the top of the box and initiated their study by enlarging the Latin script on the computer screen. After Ethan identified each word, Chloe typed it into a translation app on her phone. They realized within minutes that they were reading the same words as the clues in the Medici books.

"It looks like we had most of the original letter. We only missed a couple of sentences," Chloe said after completing the entire translation.

They each read through the English version.

I, Cosimo Medici, have been blessed to see a

portion of a letter from the Apostle Paul to the Ephesians, written by his own hand. Sultan Mehmed claims to hold the complete letter in his possession and another from Paul to the Colossians. I long to acquire the full letters and reveal them to the world, but the Sultan will not relent. He holds them to prevent the Holy Father from leading a crusade against his territories. I pray that a solution will be found before my time on earth is complete. If I should pass from this world, proof of my claims is hidden for one worthy to continue this quest. The Journey of the Magi hides the secret. Young Lorenzo rides over the concealed location. May God grant you success.

"Not much new information that helps us," said Chloe.

"No, but we learn that the second writing of Paul is the letter to the Colossians, which is amazing to think about," replied Ethan. "Also, the reason for Mehmed to hold onto the letters was to prevent the Holy Father—which I assume refers to the Pope—from forming a crusade against the Sultan."

"When I decoded the original message and saw the name Mehmed, I looked into the story," claimed Chloe. "Sultan Mehmed conquered Constantinople and continually threatened to expand his empire, including the possible targets of Venice and other seaport towns on the east coast of Italy. Pope Pius II tried to form crusades against the Sultan, but could not get enough armies involved. Pius died while attempting to raise the morale of the potential crusaders."

They agreed that the letter penned by Cosimo Medici before his death was a startling document on its own. The value multiplied because of where the clues in the letter guided them.

But there was more to look at.

The pictures of the scroll found in the wooden box were not as easy to interpret. First, the message was written in Greek—a tough language for most non-Greeks to decipher. Despite being enlarged, the writing was also faded and difficult to read. The process proved tedious and involved much trial and error before any success became apparent. An hour into the effort Chloe felt they finally had the basic outline of the content.

"Looking at this on a computer screen kind of takes away the impact of reading a never-before-seen letter written by an Ottoman sultan in the fourteen hundreds," said Chloe. "But, here's what we have." Once she jotted down the translation, she slid it in front of Ethan.

After carefully reading the text, he said, "It looks like Mehmed is boasting of having possession of the letters from Paul, acquired from the churches in Ephesus and Colossae for the ancient Library of Constantinople. Then he states a warning that the letters will be destroyed if the Pope attempts any type of aggression with the Ottomans. From what you just said, the Pope at least tried to mount a war against the Sultan. I wonder if Pope Pius ever read this letter."

"That's something we'll probably never know," stated Chloe. "We only know that any type of significant crusade never happened. So, if what Mehmed said was true, we can hope he didn't destroy what he claimed were letters written by the Apostle

Paul."

Ethan nodded in agreement before glancing at his watch. "I think this library closes in less than an hour. I say we work on the final manuscript until they kick us out."

If Ethan and Chloe were honest with each other, both were anxious to examine the photos taken of the oldest item in the wooden box. The manuscript's age, combined with the fact that the writing was in Greek, heightened their anticipation.

"I'm with you," Chloe said. "You keep deciphering the Greek letters and I'll keep working on the translation."

Ethan pulled up the pictures taken of the manuscript and started the process. He thought the scroll from Mehmed had been difficult to interpret, but the handwriting on this document was not as uniform and orderly; the script of the Greek symbols was not as consistent. The result was even more trial and error with Ethan blowing up each word as large as the computer screen allowed. Still, he had to guess on a few of the letters; guessing incorrectly as many times as he was correct.

Their final minutes in the library ticked away as several pages of Chloe's notepad filled with penciled-in letters and crossed-out mistakes. Her writing looked more like a five-year-old's doodles than the results of a possible historic attempt at translation.

Ethan had his face almost up against the screen in an attempt to confirm the next letter when Chloe reached out and grabbed his forearm. "Stop," she said in a voice louder the necessary, causing a few of the remaining patrons to look their way. "Stop," she said again, quietly. "I think we have enough. I could have stopped after the first word, but I wanted to get through a few sentences."

The Greek letters Ethan called out appeared haphazardly on one sheet of Chloe's notepad. Amidst a few cross-outs and erasures, they made four lines.

Παύλος, απόστολος του Ιησού Χριστού με το θέλημα του Θεού,

Προς τους αγίους που είναι στην Έφεσο και πιστούς στο Χριστό Ιησού,

Χάρη να είναι σε σας και ειρήνη από Θεού Πατρός

ημών και Κυρίου Ιησού Χριστού.

"I know my depiction of Greek letters is not the best, but I think I'm close," she said. She then flipped to the next sheet where four lines of English appeared, surrounded by more notes and scribbles.

Ethan read the lines. He turned to Chloe, not knowing what to say. "Could it truly be...?" He couldn't bring himself to say it aloud.

Paul, an apostle of Jesus Christ by the will of God,

To the saints which are at Ephesus, and to the faithful in Christ Jesus:

Grace be to you, and peace, from God our Father,

and from the Lord Jesus Christ.

"Yes it could," Chloe said. "Those are the first two verses of the book of Ephesians."

"It's hard to believe that we found a first-century manuscript from the Apostle Paul."

Chloe agreed, but added, "All we know is it looks to be extremely old. We're a long way from confirming when it was written." She was as excited as Ethan, but was trying—semi-successfully—to keep her emotions under control.

"There's much more on this page of the manuscript, maybe the entire first chapter of Ephesians," noted Ethan. "Should we keep going?"

"We'll have to do it later," said Chloe, as she noticed the time.

They gathered all the notes and Ethan's computer and headed out as the library staff prodded any remaining visitors toward the exit. Pleased with what they found so far, but still short on direction, both knew some tough—and more importantly—wise decisions were going to be vital shortly.

Where should they go next? Who could be trusted with the documents and were there more to find? And maybe the most concerning question: Was there more danger coming from others involved in the search?

It was late on Saturday afternoon when they walked out of the library. They turned left on the Via di Sant'agostina and then took another left on Via della Scrofa to walk toward the nearest Metro station. The streets were starting to fill with tourists and locals, alike. The early summer weather was perfect for a stroll to enjoy the many historic sights of Rome before finding seats at one of the city's stellar restaurants.

Chloe's phone rang. She didn't recognize the number but answered and stopped walking to speak with whoever was calling.

Ethan watched and listened as the conversation lasted for several minutes with Chloe giving mostly '*Yes*' and '*No*' answers. She appeared to be ready to end the call a few times, but would then begin her brief replies once again.

"That was strange," she said after finally hanging up.

"Who was it?"

"The man said he was calling for my landlord and needed me to confirm some information. He kept reading off facts that were on my rental agreement and asked me if they were all correct. In the end, he was just talking like he didn't want to hang up. He never really said why he needed my confirmation."

"He's probably hoping you'll become annoyed and move out so he can charge double for the summer tourists."

"Maybe. It was a strange conversation, though."

They continued to walk along the Via della Scrofa for several blocks, seeing the Tiber River appear on their left as it wound its way through the city. They crossed a road near the Ponte Cavour and soon came to the Mausoleum of Augustus. The site recently reopened to the public after many years of restoration. The Roman Emperor Augustus built the circular structure in 28 B.C. to honor his accomplishments in war and serve as the resting place for himself and members of his family.

"You know we've never been able to have a decent meal together," Ethan said as they peered through an iron fence at the mausoleum. "It seems we're always in a hurry or too distracted. I doubt that we will get anything more accomplished tonight, so what about joining me for dinner?"

"Are you asking me on a date Mr. Montgomery?" Chloe faked a shy smile.

"So far, you've pulled me into an intriguing mystery causing us to be held at gunpoint, not once, but twice. However, we've also uncovered documents not seen by anyone in a few centuries," quipped Ethan. "I guess I can repay you in this small way for bringing some excitement to my life."

"In that case, I accept," she replied, keeping the mood light with a girlish curtsy.

"Great. I think there's a McDonald's around he somewhere," he joked. Chloe responded with a punch to Ethan's shoulder.

"Ouch. No need for violence. I'll find a quality eating establishment that will live up to your high standards.

Less than a block away stood the *il vero Alfredo* restaurant, which Alfredo de Lelio established in 1908. "Will this do?" Ethan asked as they passed by the large double doors of the historic establishment.

Chloe pretended to contemplate the choice but soon ended the act. "This looks like an awesome choice."

Before their food arrived, Chloe received another call. She left the table, returning minutes later with a confused look on her face. She commented to Ethan how strange it was to have to answer additional questions again about her apartment lease.

They settled in and shared a bruschetta appetizer and a first course of the namesake Fettuccini Alfredo. Ethan chose a veal dish for his main course, while

Chloe went for the grilled salmon. They split an order of tiramisu for dessert. Both were way beyond full when they finally stood to leave.

Their overall weariness, combined with the sluggishness that comes after a large meal, served to lower Ethan and Chloe's attentiveness. As a result, they failed to notice a trio of men following them as they left the restaurant and walked the final blocks to the Spagna Metro Station.

The trip back to Andrea's passed without incident. The cooler evening air during the walk from the Metro stop to the apartment managed to pump a little energy back into their bodies. Upon entering, they found a note from Andrea letting them know that she was out with a friend for the evening and hoped to be home by midnight.

Despite being tired, neither felt like trying to sleep.

"Do you have the energy to check out the final document, the one sealed with wax?"

"I'm willing to try," Chloe answered. "I can't promise how sharp I'll be, but the thought of sleeping on the floor again isn't exactly enticing me to go to bed."

Ethan put his laptop on the only table available, a round bar-height counter with just enough space to serve a meal for one. There were two stools, so Chloe scooted up close as the computer came to life. She realized for the first time that Ethan's screen saver was a picture of his family. He appeared dressed in his Army uniform with his mom and dad standing on each side. Ethan wore a big smile on a face that looked younger and more innocent. Dad looked proud; Mom looked worried.

Ethan noticed Chloe checking out the photo. "That was the day I left for basic training, only a few weeks after I graduated from high school. My dad tried not to cry, but I knew he was proud of me. Mom was a mess. I think she went through an entire box of tissues that day. I was excited for whatever was ahead."

"What do you think of that decision now? Did your Army experience help you *be all you can be?*"

Ethan wondered how to reply. He hadn't told Chloe about the real reason he left the Army. Now wasn't a good time to get into it.

"Let's get to work before I'm too tired," he said, ignoring her questions and mimicking a yawn.

He pulled up the pictures of the last document left to examine. The creases created from the letter being folded for a few hundred years made some of the writing difficult to read, even in an enlarged photo. A short time was all it took for them to discern the letter was written in Latin and that it was different handwriting than the letter from Cosimo Medici. Despite their fatigue, Ethan and Chloe fell back into the routine of him calling out the letters and her translating the completed words. The letter was not long, so the process moved quickly.

"What do we have?"

Chloe typed the final words into her translation app and scribbled out the results.

"The letter is signed by Lorenzo Medici and dated in March of 1492," she said. "I think this will give us something to think about." She handed him her hastily written notes.

Sultan Mehmed has died. The Sultan's eldest son Bayezid took the throne. Younger son Cem was forced into exile and sought refuge with the Knights of Saint John on the island of Rhodes. Our spies learned that Cem removed valuable manuscripts from the palace before leaving and believed the manuscripts were the holy letters of Paul.

"This just keeps getting stranger," said Ethan after reading the message. "We've gone from a secret code left in books at a library in Florence to a letter from a Sultan of the Ottoman Empire. Now there's the possibility that the clues lead to an island that's somewhere—I think—in the Aegean Sea."

They rechecked the translation for any mistakes before Ethan backed up his files. Their discussion of the new information kept them awake for another hour, but the urge to sleep finally took control.

Chloe whispered, "Thanks for the dinner date" once they settled in with their pillows and blankets on the floor. The only reply she heard was Ethan's rhythmic breathing.

———•●•———

"Wake up Giancomo." Morelli felt a stab in his side. He soon became aware that not only was his wife elbowing him, she was saying that his phone was ringing.

He rolled over and grasped for the buzzing device on the nightstand. Through groggy eyes, he managed to push the green icon and answer the call. "Give me a minute," he said to the caller, then pulled on a robe and left the bedroom.

"This better be important," said Morelli once he entered his private room and sat in his favorite chair.

"We found them," said the man known as The Seeker.

The Seeker went on to describe to Morelli how he called Chloe Conrad and kept her on the line while his contact in the phone company traced the call. A second call an hour later helped to pinpoint her location at a restaurant.

"We followed the woman and the man with her back to an apartment on the west side of Rome. There are three of us set up for surveillance, but I need to know how you want us to proceed."

Morelli and The Seeker discussed various options.

"Follow them tomorrow and report back where they go and who they see," instructed Morelli. "If we don't learn anything, I'll let you get a little more personal and speed up the process."

Chapter 13

Ethan suffered through a reoccurrence of his troubling dream in the middle of the night, waking suddenly, covered in perspiration. Having the dream multiple times in a week was more unsettling than normal. He managed to rise and find a glass in the small kitchen without turning on a light. After drinking the cool water and calming his heartbeat, he returned to the uncomfortable floor, trying not to wake Chloe.

Three hours later, Ethan was still asleep when he felt a hand on his shoulder. He bolted upright, temporarily confused by his surroundings.

"Easy there, big boy," said Chloe. "I made the coffee this morning and thought you might want a cup."

Ethan accepted a warm cup, finally getting his bearings. He saw that Chloe was dressed and looked ready to face the day.

"I slept well, but woke up early," she said. "I guess there are too many things rolling around in my head to stay asleep. Plus, I have an idea."

Still sipping the coffee, a raised eyebrow signaled Ethan was paying attention.

"There's an English-speaking protestant church

in Rome near where we were yesterday. I thought with everything going on, it might be nice to take a step back and spend some time in a worship service. What do you think?"

Ethan looked down at himself, seeing an old t-shirt and gym shorts. Chloe dressed in light-colored Capri pants and a bright blue top, similar to the first time they met. "Maybe I should shower and change first. How much time do I have?"

"We need to be at the Metro stop in about thirty minutes."

"Here comes the five-minute Army shower and shave," he said, picking up his bag and heading to the bathroom.

They made it to the Metro stop just in time and walked onto the platform as their train arrived. Not many people were up and moving on a Sunday morning. The station would be shoulder to shoulder with commuters on a weekday, but now held less than a dozen people. Besides Ethan and Chloe, a group of three—who appeared to be food service workers—and a couple with a young child boarded the train. The final travelers were a pair of hard-looking men in dark clothes, both staring blankly ahead.

The church was less than a quarter mile from the library they visited a day earlier, which required them to get off the Metro at the Spagna stop. Ethan and Chloe entered the Rome Baptist Church just as the first hymns were starting. A greeter handed them a bulletin, which listed the order of service and provided some basic information about the church. They slipped into the pew near the back and tried to join in the singing, both a little self-conscious. Despite all they had been through in recent days, sharing in a worship service felt more personal; like they would be opening up new parts of themselves.

Coincidently, the sermon for the morning centered on the first chapter of Ephesians. Ethan and Chloe looked at each other as the pastor read the opening verses of the passage. They both had thoughts that the portion of the manuscript in their possession could have been the first time Paul put the words they were hearing on paper.

The pastor concentrated on the first half of the chapter, pointing out that eleven of the early verses were all one sentence in the original Greek; a section described by one commentator as *'a cascading waterfall of grace.'* The sermon dug into the key points of the passage, focusing on the blessings that God bestowed on mankind through his son Jesus Christ and how the Apostle Paul emphasized the importance of grace, redemption, and the eternal inheritance believers can receive.

The idea of grace had always been a tough concept for Ethan to accept. Getting something that was unmerited and unearned went against the way he wanted to live his life in the real world. People needed to work for what they wanted; nothing should be given away for free. The first steps of becoming a Christian—admitting his sin and asking God for forgiveness—came naturally for Ethan in his early teens. The daily process of accepting God's grace was not as easy. He constantly felt the need to earn his salvation, and any failure on his part put him in eternal peril.

Letting down a friend who died unexpectedly was a tough failure to overcome—at least in Ethan's mind.

"So, what did you think of the service?" asked Chloe as they left the church.

Ethan didn't answer right away, not sure if he wanted to admit his inner theological turmoil. "Other than being a bit freaked out by the coincidence that the message was on Ephesians, I thought it was good. I guess I struggle sometimes with the concept of God's grace, so any passage that mentions the subject always gets me thinking."

Chloe asked some more questions and Ethan tried to explain his thoughts on the idea of grace.

As they walked toward their Metro stop, they took a slight detour to sit on the famed Spanish Steps and continue their discussion while enjoying the late morning sun. The Trinita dei Monti Church was at their backs and they viewed the Barcaccia Fountain at the bottom of the steps. The crowds of tourists expected later in the day had not yet materialized.

"The best way I've heard grace described is that it's God's unmerited favor," said Chloe. "We can't earn it by good deeds, but the fact that God's favor is on us should guide our actions."

"I have a hard time with the thought that we don't have to do anything," said Ethan. "My whole life has been about earning something, like an award or a rank. The acceptance of God's forgiveness and His love without any work on our part just doesn't compute with me. Or the idea that we can do anything we want—right or wrong—and then grace covers us."

Chloe thought for a moment before she replied. "I don't think grace is a free pass to do anything we want. While we can't work our way to grace, it should cause a change in our behaviors and possibly the path of our lives. There's a verse somewhere, I think in Romans, that says something like, *'Should we go on sinning so grace can increase?'* and Paul answers his question with an emphatic, *'No.'"*

Time flew by as their conversation continued. The sun soon became more direct, and the crowds picked up, putting an end to their comfortable and quiet surroundings. They found a small restaurant on the nearby Via della Croce to eat a quick lunch. The Metro then carried them back to Andrea's apartment by two o'clock.

Ethan swore that one of the men in their car looked familiar, but couldn't place him.

Andrea was home when they arrived, so Ethan let the two women spend some time together while he continued to do research. The clue that a son of Sultan Mehmed might have taken original copies of Paul's letters to the island of Rhodes was intriguing. However, he wasn't sure how that information would help, since even if it were true, there was no hint as to exactly where the manuscripts might be hidden. Rhodes was small in overall landmass, but it's not like they could just arrive on the island and start looking for a centuries-old hiding place. There had to be somewhere to begin the search, some type of clue or starting point.

The lack of Wi-Fi in the apartment slowed the search process, but Ethan used his phone as a hotspot, allowing his computer to connect to the internet. He looked up information about Rhodes, the Knights of St. John, Mehmed, and his two sons Bayezid and Cem. Cem spent several years on the island, protected and held captive at the same time. It seems that Bayezid worried that his younger brother might build an army and return to battle for the Ottoman throne, so paid the Knights to keep Cem on Rhodes. The history was interesting, but after two hours, Ethan failed to find any details that might help.

Frustrated, he went for a short walk and found a gelateria around the corner. The dense and flavorful gelato dessert popular among Italians—and visitors—hit the spot and revived his mood. He chose the Gianduia flavor, which mixed chocolate and hazelnut. Ethan felt bad that the two girls would miss out on the treat, so ordered one coffee flavor and one wild strawberry flavor to go. He returned to the apartment before the gelato could melt. Chloe and Andrea appreciated the gesture and savored the cool desserts.

Andrea asked them several questions about their research, which Ethan and Chloe deftly deflected with generic answers and claims that secrecy was still required. Not so subtly, she also asked about a possible relationship between the two. Chloe laughed it off, claiming they were only working together. Ethan shook his head and kept quiet.

"Can I borrow Chloe for a few minutes?" Ethan said to Andrea once they all finished consuming the gelato.

"No problem," said Andrea. "I need to go to the corner market to get a few things, so you two can stay here. I'll be gone about thirty minutes."

Once Andrea left, Ethan updated Chloe on his search results, or more accurately, his lack of results.

"There simply isn't enough to go on," he said. "If this Cem character took the writings of Paul to Rhodes, I haven't found any information that would help us or give us a place to start searching."

They discussed various theories and options before coming to the unfortunate decision that they might have reached the end of their search. They would catch a train in the morning back to Florence and then decide the best way to reveal the documents that were now safe in a vault.

Andrea returned and the three worked together in the small kitchen to fix a simple pasta dinner. The trio enjoyed the evening sharing stories of growing up, college, and—for Ethan—life in the military.

With work the next day for Andrea and plans to catch an early train for Ethan and Chloe, all felt the need for a good night's sleep. They were in bed by ten o'clock.

An hour later, the apartment was dark and silent, but Ethan still couldn't get to sleep. The decision to end their search didn't sit well with him, especially with all the progress made in the last few days. The infusion of adrenaline—even with the fears involved by being held at gunpoint a couple of times—awakened something in him that he thought he'd lost; something that he wasn't ready to give up again so soon.

With thoughts of manuscripts, sultans, and island fortresses rolling through his mind, some unique combination of synapses fired suddenly in

Ethan's brain. An idea materialized.

He stood from his makeshift bed, went to the corner of the small room, and started up his laptop. His charged phone was ready to serve as a hotspot again, giving him a chance to run a search. Ethan typed in the address for the Laurentian Library site that Mario Ranallo had turned over to them. The process inched along with a shaky internet connection. There were thousands of books on the site and Ethan was searching for one particular author in one specific period of time.

Once he set the parameters, the hourglass icon turned over repeatedly as the search function worked its way through the online listings. It finally stopped, showing only one result for the request.

Ethan looked at the title and author of the lone book shown in the results and smiled. "Bingo," he whispered.

He clicked on the link to the book and glanced through each page. The writing was different from any they had translated so far, but he had a good idea of what language he was looking at. Though there was no guarantee that the text would help continue the search for Paul's letters, Ethan felt confident he was looking at a new clue. Only an accurate translation was standing in the way.

We're back in the game, Ethan thought as he peered over at Chloe asleep on the floor. He decided not to wake her and would wait until morning to fill her in. He knew sleep for himself would be tough to come by, and he was okay with that.

Chapter 14

A brief discussion took place while Ethan and Chloe were packing up their few belongings the following morning. They decided to leave the Medici manuscripts in the safety deposit box, which would relieve the pressure on them to keep them secure. No more carrying the box in a backpack. In the meantime, the many pictures they took should be enough to convince someone of their find.

Andrea departed early for work but left a spare key and asked Ethan and Chloe to slip it into her mail slot on their way out of the building. As they started down the stairs, Ethan remembered his phone charger was still in the apartment.

"Go on down and I'll meet you outside," he told Chloe.

He turned the key in the lock and stepped inside, finding his charger still plugged in near the spot on the floor where he slept. He secured the charger in his bag before re-locking the apartment's door.

Just as he twisted the key to engage the door's deadbolt, Ethan heard a commotion at the bottom of the stairs. It sounded like a muted scream and some type of brief struggle. Ethan peered down the gap made by the winding stairway but didn't have the best angle to see anything in the cozy lobby. He took a few tentative steps downward until reaching the midway landing. A look around the corner allowed him to view the front door of the apartment complex. Seeing nothing, he took the final steps to the bottom and nudged open the entry door.

Turning to look to his right, the activity in front of Ethan caused his breath to catch in his chest. His fight-or-flight responses instantly began an internal battle. Since his tendency to fight usually won out, he dropped his bag and bolted out of the door toward Chloe, who was being dragged away by two large men.

Chloe turned her head and saw Ethan as he emerged from the door. "Ethan. Run!" she screamed.

A third man stepped out from the sliding side door of a van parked along the street, a gun in his hand. The man's attention locked onto Ethan and the gun came up, causing Ethan to stop in his tracks. He dove to the ground just as two shots rang out. Ethan managed to roll away, the impact of the bullets producing fragments of brick dust that rained down from the building's facade. The man continued to approach with the gun aimed in Ethan's direction.

At the same instant, another apartment resident exited the nearby door. The young man had a mop of unkempt blonde hair and bright red headphones on his ears, which served to render him oblivious to the gunfire. The new person in the mix made the gunman hesitate, giving Ethan enough time to jump to his feet and slide through the still-open doorway.

Ethen flew up the stairs, taking two steps at a

time. As he approached Andrea's apartment, he realized he still had the key gripped in his hand. He steadied his shaking fingers enough to get the key into the lock and enter the apartment. He snapped the deadbolt shut and stood with his back to the door.

The sound of heavy steps coming up the stairway resonated in the apartment. Ethan's mind raced, trying to find an advantage. His military training in tactics and combat failed to discuss how to win a battle when you're unarmed, and your opponent has a gun. Ethan sped to the back of the apartment and entered Andrea's bedroom. There was a window overlooking an alleyway, but it was at least a twenty-foot drop. Out of options, he pulled open the window just as a gunshot shattered the lock on the front door.

The old window grudgingly slid open enough to allow Ethan to get his six-foot-three frame through the space. He shimmied down until his fingers latched onto the bottom sill of the window frame. With his feet hanging down, the distance to the ground was now less than fifteen feet. Not ideal, but survivable. Ethan let go and dropped as the door to Andrea's bedroom burst open. He let his legs bend and absorb some of the force of the impact and rolled to his side. Before he could take account of any injuries, a bullet ricocheted off the ground near his head. Ethen sprang to his feet and sprinted toward an opening at the end of the alley, zig-zagging to make himself a tough target.

A little out of shape, but still possessing some of the speed he used to set records for timed runs in his Army days, Ethan managed to remain unscathed and reach a safe distance from the shooter. A look back gave him a brief glimpse of the man who tried to kill him. The shooter still had his torso leaning out of Andrea's window, his menacing gaze locked onto Ethan. The man's appearance, with a bald head and thick black beard, would be seared into Ethan's memory.

Ethan frantically searched for a safe place, a place to give himself a chance to think. He found a small coffee shop and slid inside, taking a seat where he could see out the window. With everything happening so fast, the realization that Chloe had been taken began to hit him in full force. He rested his head in his hands, elbows on the table, as his body shook. Negative thoughts coursed their way through his mind, the disappointment in himself almost paralyzing. *I let her down,* he kept thinking.

He managed to order coffee when a waiter approached, not that he needed the caffeine, but to have a warm cup to hold. His body calmed itself after a few minutes and Ethan took stock of his options. He knew the authorities were most likely already at the apartment, the sound of gunshots sure to elicit calls to the police. Should he go back and report what happened? Could he give the police any helpful information? He was confident Chloe's abduction had something to do with their research, but couldn't figure out how anyone could have found them. Adding to his concerns was the realization that she might be forced to talk about the Medici documents and even open the safety deposit box. At the moment, he didn't care about losing the manuscripts. He was solely focused on Chloe's safety.

He left money on the table to pay for the coffee and looked up and down the street before exiting the shop.

Ethan decided to return to the apartment and talk to the authorities. He also hoped to get his bag of clothes and his computer, which he'd dropped at the bottom of the apartment's stairs.

He turned the corner and saw a police car parked near the entrance of Andrea's apartment building, a small crowd gathered on the sidewalk. Ethan took a deep breath and began to approach. As he drew close, his phone started buzzing in his pocket. A quick look at the screen told him the call was coming from Chloe's phone.

"Chloe, is that you? Are you okay?" he said excitedly.

There was no immediate response, only a slight chuckle. "I'm afraid that your friend Chloe is busy at the moment," said the voice, thick with an accent.

"Who is this? What have you done with Chloe?"

"You ask a lot of questions for someone lucky to be alive." The voice came across as confident and in control.

Ethan forced himself to keep his mouth closed and wait for the man to speak.

"Ethan. It's alright if I call you Ethan, isn't it?" The man paused for a few moments. "Here's what I want from you. If you hope to see your friend Chloe again, I need to know all the information you have on the Medici manuscripts and any results from your research. Your pretty friend has already given up the fact that you two put the original documents in a vault. We'll be going to retrieve them soon. But I know you have a computer full of notes and research that would be beneficial to my employer."

"I'm not sure who you are, but you better not touch a hair on her head," Ethan said with as much determination as he could muster. "I'm not telling you anything until I know Chloe is unharmed."

"Very well, tough guy. Your wish is granted."

Ethan heard some rustling through the phone before Chloe's voice came on. "Ethan?"

"I'm here. Are you hurt?"

"No. But I had to tell them about the box."

Before Ethan could speak again, he heard what sounded like a muffled scream from Chloe.

"Chloe!"

The original man came back on the line. "She will remain in our company until you turn over any information you have. I'll call you back in thirty minutes, and we'll arrange a place to meet. Don't talk to the police." The line went dead.

— • ● • —

Morelli heard the familiar ring tone of his primary phone and his heart rate kicked up a couple of notches. He anticipated good news from The Seeker and was not disappointed.

"We have the girl," were the first words out of The Seeker's mouth. He went on to give a quick description of the wooden box and the manuscripts inside—at least all the information that Chloe passed on. The Seeker told Morelli that they would soon go to the safety deposit facility and retrieve the items.

Morelli voiced his approval.

"Was there a laptop or any type of notes?" He had the Conrad woman's laptop but knew she and her friend continued to do research the past few days. He wanted to know what they'd found.

"No laptop or other materials," replied The Seeker. "The man with her managed to avoid us, and we believe he has additional information in his possession. I made contact with him and made it clear that the woman's life depended on his cooperation. I will call him back soon to set up a meeting spot."

The potential recovery of the documents excited Morelli. However, the fact that her friend escaped was troubling; a loose end that hadn't been tied off. Again.

"Once you retrieve the box and documents, have one of your associates bring them to my office right away," Morelli instructed. "Then, see what more you're able to get from the woman and her friend. If the two of them choose not to cooperate, don't play around or take any chances. Just make them disappear."

—— • ● • ——

Ethan had less than thirty minutes to decide what to do. A dozen scenarios flew across his mind, but few were realistic without time to prepare. He convinced himself that he had to meet whoever was holding Chloe and try to get her back. At this point, he could care less about the box or the manuscripts. He would be glad to pass on his thoughts about Cem, the island of Rhodes, and the deduction he'd made the previous evening.

He began by strolling down the street in front of Andrea's apartment, acting as inconspicuous as possible. He glanced inside the front door and saw his bag was still lying in the corner of the lobby. Ethan wasn't as concerned about losing his possessions as he was that his laptop would fall into the wrong hands. Even if the authorities found it, the files he and Chloe added in recent days would prompt a great many questions; questions he didn't want to answer right now. He knew that Andrea would soon be contacted and would give the police the names of her two house guests. Ethan needed to delay his name coming up until he had Chloe back.

Only one policeman was still on the street, the others were most likely up in the apartment with a busted front door. The officer was taking notes from an older woman, possibly a tenant in one of the apartments, and didn't notice Ethan slip into the lobby area and snatch his bag. Ethan was back on the sidewalk moving in the opposite direction in only seconds.

With the first objective reached, Ethan dialed the Galleria Corsini and asked to speak with Andrea. He explained in a calm, but rapid, manner that there had been some trouble in her apartment and that she should expect a call from the police. Ethan didn't tell her that Chloe was taken captive or that he was lucky to have escaped with his life.

"I realize you don't know me very well, but I need a big favor," Ethan said. "I need you to delay giving the authorities my name or Chloe's, at least for a few hours."

Andrea rightfully expressed her concerns and asked more questions that Ethan couldn't fully answer.

"I promise that we will explain everything as soon as possible and that you won't get into any trouble." He tried to soothe her, knowing it was a tough sell. He hung up without knowing if Andrea would play along or not. At this point, he didn't have any more time to worry about it.

Ethan made two more calls, putting a rushed and risky plan into place. He had time to speed walk to the Metro station and find a bench in the concourse before the man who was holding Chloe called back.

The phone began to buzz, and Ethan let it continue for several repetitions, not wanting to seem anxious. Once he clicked the connect icon, he waited for the other man to speak.

"Are you ready to make a deal?" asked the man.

"Yes, I am, and here's how it's going to work."

"I will decide how...."

Ethan interrupted, trying to take control of the interchange. "No, I have the information you want, so I make the rules. First, we meet at precisely two o'clock this afternoon, next to the fountain in front of the Pantheon."

The man tried to speak again, but Ethan kept talking.

"Once I see Chloe is unharmed, I will hand off my computer and notes. They contain all the information about our research, including new facts I discovered last night and that Chloe doesn't know about. I'll give someone time to look at the notes and start up the laptop, if necessary, but only if Chloe's released. Is that clear?"

"I think you're mistaken if you believe I will follow your orders."

"I have information that no one else knows and will help your boss find an artifact worth more money than you or he could spend in a lifetime. If you harm Chloe, I'll disappear and make the find myself. Two o'clock. The Pantheon."

Ethan hung up before the man spoke again. His body shook as the adrenaline and fear surged through him.

I pray that this works.

Chapter 15

Parts of the Pantheon have stood in Rome since statesman Marcus Agrippa started the structure in 27 B.C. After fires destroyed most of the original building, Emperor Hadrian oversaw its renovation around 120 A.D.

The bulk of the Pantheon is a circular construction of concrete and brick, with a great concrete dome that rises from the walls. The dome, with a diameter of 142 feet, is an engineering accomplishment that still stumps historians. An oculus, or eye, at the top of the dome, is open to provide light to the interior. Visitors enter through a rectangular front porch featuring Corinthian columns and massive doors made of bronze.

The structure began as a pagan temple, but the Pantheon was dedicated as the Church of Santa Maria Rotunda in 607 A.D. and still hosts Catholic services each week.

Ethan set the meeting time at 2 p.m. to give himself almost four hours to prepare. The location of the Pantheon was also strategic. The piazza in front of the structure was small—at least compared to others in Rome—so there would be less space to watch over. He would be able to stand in one place and see most of the possible lines of approach. What Ethan couldn't see, he planned to have some help to watch his back. The extra time to prepare also provided the time to get that help into place.

By one-thirty, Ethan stood next to the Fountain of the Pantheon. Pope Gregory XIII commissioned the fountain in the sixteenth century only to have it modified by Pope Clement in 1711. Clement's changes included the addition of an ancient obelisk first erected by Egypt's Ramses II in 1213 B.C.

Clear skies and a warm sun shone down on Ethan as he tried to be calm and patient. A few business executives in suits walked by, returning from late lunches, and the tourist crowd came and went in waves. The Pantheon wasn't close to a Metro station, so a series of walking tours accounted for most visitors during the heat of the day.

Ethan thought back to a previous visit to the Pantheon more than five years earlier when he was accompanied by six men from his battalion enjoying a long weekend of leave in Rome. Cam Williams had been the life of the group, always joking around and making ridiculous challenges to his buddies. Ethan won twenty bucks from his best friend for jumping into the Trevi Fountain and getting away before security got ahold of him. Another member of the group wasn't so lucky. He accepted a dare from Cam to take a rock into the Pantheon and try to throw it up and through the twenty-seven-foot-wide opening in the dome. When the rock failed to go through the target and landed near an elderly woman, security guards escorted the embarrassed Army private to the exit with a stern warning not to return.

Memories of Cam caused an ache in Ethan's heart, but also jolted him back to reality, infused with the motivation not to lose another friend. He turned slowly in place, checking every angle for a glimpse of Chloe. He hoped the man who shot at him from the window earlier in the day would be with her. Ethan would recognize him instantly. The backup he had in place had been given a basic description of Chloe and knew she was wearing blue knee-length shorts, a white top, and sandals. His spotters would also make note of any bald men with bushy black beards.

Ethan's phone chimed, indicating an incoming text message.

Possible sighting coming from the north.

Ethan turned to look in that direction, seeing a small restaurant on the corner of the piazza where the street named Via della Pantheon emerged. A bearded man and a young woman bearing a resemblance to Chloe walked together into the piazza. Ethan realized in a second that it wasn't who he was looking for.

Negative, he texted back.

Three more minutes passed as Ethan grew more worried with each tick of the clock and convinced that his plan was doomed. If the man he talked to on the phone ignored Ethan's firm demands, Chloe could already be….. *No,* Ethan said to himself. *I'm not going to believe that.*

Seconds later, his phone chimed again.

Coming up the east side of Pantheon.

A bald head and bushy beard first caught Ethan's attention as two people strolled side by side into the piazza. The man's arm was around Chloe's waist, pulling her in close. The pair stopped near the entrance to the Hotel Pantheon, the man scanning the area through dark glasses. Ethan could tell even from a distance that Chloe's eyes were red and her frame rigid. It was obvious that she was frightened.

The bald man locked eyes with Ethan and started to move with Chloe toward the fountain. When they were still yards away, Ethan's phone buzzed. He managed a glance at the screen.

Might be a partner in the area. Will follow and neutralize.

The bearded man stopped several feet from Ethan, subtly brushing the tail of his untucked shirt aside to reveal a pistol lodged in the front of his pants. The man's face looked older up close, with hints of grey in the beard and deep fissures of wrinkles on his forehead. Chloe looked scared, but Ethan also caught hints of toughness and defiance in her eyes.

"Here we are, Mr. Ethan," the man said, his thick accent still full of confidence and bravado. "Give me your papers and computer, then you get the girl. We convinced her to be very forthcoming with information about the documents you found. She even retrieved them for us from the vault."

Ethan returned the man's menacing look, choosing not to be intimidated. He carefully slid the bag off his shoulder and set it on the stone ledge surrounding the fountain. He unzipped the main compartment and slipped his hand inside.

"Easy," the man said, using his free hand to grip the gun. "Pull your hand out slowly."

Grasping the laptop, Ethan removed his hand

and set the computer on the ledge. He next pulled out a legal pad of lined paper filled with notes and placed the pad next to the computer.

"There's all the information you need," Ethan said. "Feel free to examine it."

Before Ethan realized what was happening, he felt a slight shove from behind and a second man grabbed the computer and notes and took off. Ethan's instinct was to run after him, but the man who held Chloe now had his gun out and pointed at her side. His long shirt still obscured most of the action from others in the area.

"It seems now that I have the girl and your research," the man said with a smirk. "You are fortunate to be alive. Don't try to follow us."

Just as the bearded man finished his statement, a scream came from the direction the thief had run. The thief was now sprawled on the pavement, a bigger man standing over him with a large boot on his neck.

The commotion caused Chloe's captor to turn his head away. Ethan used the distraction to charge forward, hitting the man like a linebacker making a tackle. The gun went flying as Ethan landed full force on the man's chest, which caused an audible grunt as the air spewed from his lungs. A punch to the gut and one to his chin left the bearded man gasping for breath. Ethan grabbed Chloe's hand and pulled her away.

"We need to get out of here before the police arrive. Can you keep up?"

The toughness Ethan recognized in Chloe's eyes became more evident. "Just try to leave me," she said, matching him stride for stride as they ran down the west side of the Pantheon on the Via della Rotunda.

They took a right at the next street, slowing to a quick walk. Ethan looked over his shoulder frequently but didn't see anyone pursuing. He abruptly pulled Chloe into a small, cramped restaurant with only a few tables for inside dining. Most meals were consumed at a seating area set up outside in a circular courtyard.

"We'll sit here and wait," Ethan said, taking a seat at one of the square tables. Both were breathing hard from the last few minutes of exertion.

"Wait for what? Shouldn't we keep moving?"

"The others will be here soon."

Chloe looked confused. "What others?"

"I arranged for some men to be stationed around the Pantheon to serve as extra eyes on the situation. They were there to make sure nothing happened to you."

Ethan looked Chloe over, not seeing any obvious injuries, bruises, or signs of trauma. "Are you alright? Did they hurt you?"

"I'm fine. They pushed me around a little after getting me into the van outside Andrea's apartment. There were a lot of threats and a constant gun in my face." She lowered her eyes, looking at the floor. "I'm sorry about getting the manuscripts out of storage for them. I was scared, but more than anything, I didn't think those old papers were worth dying for."

"I would have done the same thing. I'm really glad you're safe," admitted Ethan, lifting her chin and then grasping her hands in the middle of the table. "I didn't know if I would see you again."

Ethan pulled out his phone and handed it to her. "Here, call your father. Let him know you're okay."

"My father knows about this?"

"Yes. Who do you think helped me arrange to have the extra men in the area? I called him not long after you were taken this morning, and he gave me a contact. Someone who works for Interpol. Your father helped this guy out a few years ago and allowed a group of Interpol agents to do some specialized training at the base in Vicenza. His name is Martin Scheidt, and he agreed to loan me a few of his men for the afternoon."

"Why would Interpol risk some of their men for this?"

"I told Scheidt this whole affair centers on some historical documents and that a few were already stolen. Since Interpol often works with other agencies to track down looted artwork and historical artifacts, I gave him enough details to get him interested."

"Did you tell him exactly what we've found?"

"I had to tell him about the Medici letters and the page from Ephesians we discovered. I knew it might be the only thing to secure his help," explained Ethan. "We can talk about this later. Call your father."

Chloe dialed the phone and reached Colonel Conrad, who had anxiously been awaiting word. They spoke for several minutes, tears forming in her eyes as she assured her father repeatedly that she was safe and uninjured.

She held out the phone to Ethan. "He wants to talk to you."

Ethan took the phone and listened to his former commander, replying with "Yes sir," when asked questions. "Thank you, sir," he said, ending the call.

"He made me promise to get you on a plane back to the States as soon as possible," said Ethan. "He might have mentioned a court martial in my future if you weren't headed home within forty-eight hours."

"He can't do that, can he? You're not in the Army anymore."

"Probably not, but I don't want to get on his bad side," Ethan said in jest. "Plus, I think he's right. You need to get away from here."

Before their conversation continued, three bulky men entered the restaurant and walked toward them. One was carrying a laptop computer and notepad, which he placed on the table.

Ethan rose to shake their hands and introduced them to Chloe. She stood and gave them each a hug, causing the men slight embarrassment. They were unaccustomed to being thanked in such a way— especially from an attractive woman.

"The man who snatched your belongings is now in the custody of the local police," said the apparent leader, his accent sounding British. "He's a low-level thug, so I don't expect him to know much useful information. The other man recovered from your spot-on tackle and fled the area. We followed on foot, but he had a van waiting and drove off. Marcus here did get a good look at him, though," the man said, pointing to his associate. "He recognized him as someone who's been on our radar for quite some time. We don't know his real name, but he's called The Seeker. He's a high-priced bounty hunter, working exclusively for the mafia and other criminal elements. If The Seeker's involved, someone with clout is paying his large fee."

"When they had me in the van, I heard the guy you call The Seeker make a phone call," said Chloe. "He was talking to someone named Morelli. Does that name mean anything to you?"

The three Interpol agents looked at each other and nodded. "Yes, ma'am. It sure does," said the leader. "Giancomo Morelli is suspected of being a very active dealer of stolen artwork and historic artifacts. Unfortunately, neither Interpol nor the Italian authorities have been able to pin anything on him."

Chloe added, "After they forced me to get the documents out of the safety deposit box, one of the guys in the van was told to deliver them somewhere. They were speaking in Italian, so I didn't catch everything said, but the guy took the items and left the van."

"I think we will take another look at Mr. Morelli," said the Interpol agent. "Your information has been helpful. Even though this was an unofficial operation, we need to report back to Martin Scheidt. He should contact you to follow up and get any more details that you can provide."

Ethan shook their hands again, the men silently sharing the respect that often accompanies those who have gone into battle together, even if they would never cross paths again.

Chloe gave another round of hugs.

Morelli spent a few hours on the proverbial mountaintop. There was nothing better in his line of work than taking possession of artifacts that were one of a kind and sure to attract buyers with deep pockets.

Once delivered to his office, Morelli carefully examined the box and manuscripts. The examination served to rekindle his dreams of a massive payday. He rushed to send pictures to his researchers, tasking them to complete the translation and determine if there were clues to additional pages. The items themselves would soon be on the way to a document specialist who would make an accurate—and discreet—evaluation of authenticity and age.

The highs of success soon turned into a valley of despair. A phone call arrived from The Seeker in mid-afternoon and changed the course of the foreseeable future for Morelli. The Seeker briefed him on the blown exchange at the Pantheon, the loss of the Conrad woman, and the possible involvement of the authorities. The advice of the long-time criminal was that Morelli should disappear.

"Sofia, you need to listen to me," Morelli said when he made a call to his wife. "Gather up the children and go to the home in Amalfi. Take whatever you need for an extended stay, but you need to be moving within the hour."

He listened to his wife's raised voice and answered with a harshness he rarely used with Sofia or the kids. "This is not a request. Do as I say and be on the road within the hour. I'll meet you there this evening."

She relented and agreed to pack and leave Rome with the two children for the four-hour drive. Sofia was aware of her husband's shady dealings but didn't know that the bulk of his income came from illegal activities. She also was unaware that the house in Amalfi was not listed under Giancomo's name. It was owned by a shell company that didn't exist anywhere except in an article of incorporation and on a bank account in Geneva. No one looking for Morelli would find his name associated with the vacation home on the southern side of Italy's Sorrento Peninsula.

Morelli followed the conversation with his wife with more phone calls and texts. He moved some funds around for quicker—and less trackable—access, and gave a few important people the new cell number from one of his burner phones. He also made arrangements with a trusted associate to go by Morelli's house after his wife left. The associate was to remove any incriminating items and transport them to a safe storage facility that—like the vacation home—could never be traced to Morelli. His ego caused him to keep stolen items in his home, but at least he was smart enough to have a plan in place to make them disappear on short notice.

He was also smart enough not to keep any written records of his illegal deals, so the paperwork in his office was all from legitimate business. Likewise, any artwork that hung on the walls was acquired legally. Morelli carried the Medici box, his laptop, and additional burner phones when he stood to leave. He locked the door to his office suite, hoping he would be able to return soon.

Minutes later, he was speeding toward the outskirts of Rome in his bright red Alpha Romeo Spider.

Chapter 16

By early evening, Ethan and Chloe were on their way back to Florence, this time on a high-speed train that would make just one other stop after leaving Rome. Chloe sat next to the window, still decompressing after her traumatic experience. She tried unsuccessfully to relax. Ethan remained close, only leaving her side to purchase a couple of tasteless sandwiches from the food car.

Ethan made sure that Chloe took a few minutes to call her friend Andrea. Chloe confirmed that she was safe and unharmed, still leaving out the part about being held captive for several hours. Andrea described how the police had questioned her and how she managed to leave Ethan and Chloe out of the conversation. She also professed no knowledge of why there had been a shooting in the building. There was nothing stolen from the apartment, so the biggest hassle would repairing the front door and the door to her bedroom. Chloe promised to help with the costs.

Once she hung up, they had a few brief discussions about the loss of the Medici documents, but neither was anxious to delve into that topic. Their lives had been consumed by their search, which so far had produced three harrowing encounters—two confrontations at gunpoint and one hostage situation. Those encounters outweighed, or at least balanced out, the fact that they made some amazing discoveries; discoveries that were now in the hands of someone named Morelli. They did have pictures of the documents found in the wooden box, along with research notes saved on Ethan's computer. Those, however, would not count for much if they were unable to produce the original items.

Ethan thought Chloe had finally drifted off to sleep until he felt her hand wrap around his. When he turned, she was staring at him, her features a bit worn from exhaustion, but her green eyes still filled with purpose.

"I never did thank you for what you did today," she said, squeezing his hand. "The longer they kept me in that van, the more doubts I had about them letting me go, no matter what we gave them. You came through for me, and I'm confident you saved my life."

Chloe leaned over and kissed Ethan on the cheek. "Thank you."

Ethan now felt like the men whom Chloe hugged earlier in the day, not used to any affectionate displays of appreciation. Chloe saved him from any further uncomfortableness when she turned back to the window and closed her eyes.

Chloe's words that Ethan had *"come through"* for her served as a boost to his confidence. He often swam through the swamp of self-doubt since Cam Williams died. It was an accident that Ethan convinced himself could have been prevented if he'd gone along on the fateful hiking excursion. That doubt persisted regardless of how many other experiences he handled with success. It was there, filling him with uncertainty earlier in the day as he desperately put together a plan to rescue Chloe.

The fact that she was safe pleased him the most. Her sincere appreciation was a bonus. So were his positive feelings about himself after overcoming his doubt and successfully saving a friend.

Chloe managed to sleep for the last hour of the trip.

While she slept, Ethan made contact with Martin Scheidt from Interpol and the two shared information. Scheidt confirmed that Interpol was looking for Giancomo Morelli, but that the antiquities dealer had skipped town. They would continue to search for him and The Seeker, along with the lost manuscripts. Ethan let him know that he and Chloe were on their way back to Florence. They promised to stay in touch.

Ethan spent the rest of the trip debating on whether or not to tell Chloe about the possible next clue he discovered concerning the Medici manuscripts. Colonel Conrad expected his daughter home, and Ethan wanted to live up to the assurances he made to his former commander. On the flip side, he knew Chloe would never leave if she were aware that their search might not have reached a dead end; that there might be another avenue to explore.

He remained silent on the subject once they arrived in Florence. They stopped by his place just long enough to drop off his bag, before walking together toward Chloe's apartment. She insisted that she was comfortable staying there alone. She needed a day to pack up her few belongings and plan her flight back to the States.

"Are you sure you're okay staying here by yourself?" asked Ethan. "I can sleep on your couch, or you can sleep at my place again."

"I'll be fine," she said without much confidence. "I'll get a few hours of sleep and then start packing. You're welcome to come by in the morning."

Ethan finally relented and opened the door to leave.

"Hey, I just thought of something," said Chloe. "I heard you up the other night on your computer after we pretty much decided that there was no place left to go with our search. What were you doing?"

The question caught Ethan off guard. It was one thing to decide not to share information with her. It was another to lie to her. He stood speechless for an uncomfortable minute before finally closing the door.

"I can't believe you weren't going to tell me about this." Chloe became animated and upset after Ethan admitted his thoughts on Sultan Mehmed's son, Cem, and the book he found in the Laurentian Library collection. More troubling to Ethan, she looked hurt, which was the last thing he wanted.

"Look, I'm sorry," he said, knowing as he said them that the words were not enough. "Once you were taken this morning, following more clues was the last thing on my mind. After you were safe, I didn't want to give you a reason to stay. Your father wants you home and I thought I needed to honor his wishes."

"I'm not a little girl. I can make my own

decisions." She was still angry but didn't have the same fire behind her words. Ethan hoped Chloe realized that his motives had been good, even if she didn't fully agree with his methods.

She went into the kitchen and pulled a bottle of orange juice out of the refrigerator, smelled it to make sure it was still good, and then poured herself a glass. She gulped it down in one long drink.

"So, explain your theories to me again," Chloe said, apparently cooled off from her brief spike of anger.

"We saw in the letter from Lorenzo Medici that his spies thought Cem took the Biblical letters from Paul when he escaped to the island of Rhodes. It occurred to me that Cem must have been aware that the Medicis had been trying to secure the manuscripts for years. When I read that Cem turned out to be more or less a captive on Rhodes, I tried to put myself in Cem's place. The one thing he had to bargain with was the Pauline letters, and he knew the Medicis might be powerful enough to secure his release."

Chloe nodded in agreement, as she followed Ethan's reasoning.

"Cem couldn't just send the Medicis a letter offering them the manuscripts, since he knew that anything he wrote would be monitored. I began to wonder if he ever produced any other type of writing and discovered that Cem authored a small book of poetry during his time on Rhodes. Then I logged onto the Laurentian Library site and performed a search. When a book of poetry attributed to Cem popped up, I believed there had to be a connection. A brief note on the book said it was received in Florence in the year 1494, but didn't find its way into the Medici collection until many years later. The Medici family was exiled from Florence in 1494, which explains why the book of poetry was temporarily lost.

"I haven't had the chance to work on a translation of the poems, but hope they contain a clue to the whereabouts of Paul's writings," Ethan continued. "Maybe my hopes are too high, and the book has no connection to our search. But, that would be an amazing coincidence considering all the other clues we've found and how the dates line up."

"Did you see the pages of the book? Could you tell what language the poems were written in?"

"I took a brief look at the online pictures but didn't have the time to examine each page individually. My guess is that the writing is Turkish, but most of it looks like scribbles to me. I think it'll be difficult to translate."

"I'm still not happy that you almost didn't tell me about this," she chided, "but I guess I can forgive you."

Ethan stood to leave, and Chloe gave him a brief hug.

"You need to go, so I can get some sleep," Chloe said.

"Yes, ma'am. Sleep well. I'll check on you in the morning."

* ● *

The home in Amalfi was much smaller than the main family residence in Rome. What it lacked in size, however, it certainly made up for in quality craftsmanship: marble floors, vaulted ceilings, and every modern convenience available. Morelli always enjoyed coming to the house on vacation, admiring the magnificent coastal views, and appreciating the slower—but well-appointed—lifestyle. He loved getting away from the frenetic pace of his usual schedule and relaxing poolside, surrounded by proof of his affluence. In a normal time, the second home was Morelli's favorite perk, the most prominent outward indication of his success.

This was not a normal time.

He entered the home in a bad mood, gave his wife and kids a cursory greeting, and then retreated to a small office that was always prepared for his use. He received a message from his researchers while he was driving, so he called them back as soon as he settled in the office.

"We have finished our preliminary evaluation of the pictures you sent of the items," the researcher said.

"Tell me."

The researcher spent several minutes describing the textual content of each of the manuscripts included in the wooden box. The first matched the words already discovered in coded messages in books from the Laurentian Library. The second was a letter from Sultan Mehmed threatening to destroy the original letters from the Apostle Paul if the Sultan felt the Pope was mounting a crusade against the Ottomans.

These were interesting documents and would be worth a small fortune in the antiquities marketplace, but they didn't supply any information that wasn't already known.

"What about the other two documents? The message that had been folded and the oldest manuscript?"

"The folded message looks to be the complete text of the coded lines we told you about a few days ago. The pictures were difficult to read and accurately translate, but we believe the letter was written by Lorenzo Medici. It talks about Mehmed's sons, particularly his youngest son, Cem. It says that Cem was exiled on the island of Rhodes and may have taken Paul's letters with him."

Morelli's mind was already thinking and planning. Did he know anyone on Rhodes? If not, whom could he send to look for clues?

"First, email me all the complete translations. Next, I want you to do some research into this Cem character: his history, life, death, and any relevant facts," ordered Morelli. "Finally, keep looking through the books in the library and see if you come across any other coded messages that might help.

"Now, tell me about the final manuscript."

"I think you'll be pleased to know that the writing appears to be the first chapter of the book of Ephesians from the Bible," said the researcher. "The Greek text is faded in some places, but we believe the single page contains most of the first chapter of the book."

"Very good," Morelli said, giving out a rare compliment.

If the manuscript turned out to be dated from the first century—even with no further discoveries—he would make enough money to make this entire operation worth the effort.

Now, he needed to solve his potential problems with the authorities and get back to the life he deserved.

Chapter 17

The digital clock showed 10:07 a.m. when Ethan fought to open his eyes. It didn't compute at first, the neurons in his brain failing to make the connection. He had never been a late sleeper, even in his teens. Any hidden tendencies to still be asleep when most people are at work had long since been banished by six years in the Army. He was no longer a crack-of-dawn riser but was rarely in bed past seven o'clock.

Ethan rolled out of bed, still achy from yesterday's flying tackle of the bearded man. The drain on his body after several days of tension—plus two nights of sleeping on the floor in Rome—only added to his fatigue. He dropped to the floor and pumped out thirty push-ups and fifty crunches, trying to get his blood flowing. A little out of breath, he stood under a cold spray as long as he could stand it before turning the handle to warm and finishing his shower.

A late breakfast consisted of a stale piece of bread, popped in the toaster and slathered with butter, all washed down by the morning's most important ingredient: coffee. Ethan enjoyed his second cup of brew while contemplating his plans for the day. A knock on the door interrupted his thoughts.

"Surprised to see me?" said Chloe once he opened the door.

"Yes. I thought you'd be packing stuff today." Ethan stepped back so as she entered the apartment.

"Well, my flight has been delayed, so to speak."

"What does that mean?"

"I had a long talk with my father this morning and he agreed to give me a few more days. I told him about the possible lead you discovered and convinced him that we would take all the precautions necessary to stay safe."

"We?"

"Uh, yeah. I told him that I would stay close to you. I hope that's okay."

"Are you sure that's a good idea? Trouble managed to find us in recent days, no matter what we did."

"So you don't want to stick close to me. Is that what you're saying?"

Ethan wasn't sure how to respond. Was she asking on a personal level or only about their current situation?

She noticed his brief hesitation and didn't look pleased.

"You have to think about it. Is that it?" Chloe's voice increased in volume.

"No, Chloe, it's just that you caught me off guard. I didn't expect...."

"You didn't expect what?" she interrupted. "You didn't expect to have to put up with me anymore? You didn't expect to have to keep me out of trouble again? What is it?" Her hands were now on her hips, her eyes fixed on his.

Ethan took a step closer until he was within arm's reach. "I didn't expect to care as much as I do. That's what I was going to say. I don't want anything to happen to you and thought flying home was your best option."

Her features softened as any potential anger drained away.

"If you're sticking around, I'll be glad to stay close," he said.

"Sorry. I know that I've been a little on edge the past few days. I'm usually not quite so emotional."

They stared at each other for a few awkward seconds. A toilet flushed in the back of the apartment, breaking the moment. Dale soon walked out rubbing his eyes. Ethan was glad his roommate at least had pants on.

"What's all the noise out here?" Dale headed straight for the coffee maker. "I thought I heard someone yelling."

"Just having a discussion," Ethan replied. "We're about ready to take off."

Ethan slipped on some shoes and picked up the bag with his computer in it. He used his eyes and a tilt of his head to indicate to Chloe that they should be leaving.

"Nice to see you again, Dale," said Chloe over her shoulder as she went through the door.

"Now where are we going?" she asked Ethan once they were on the sidewalk, outside the apartment.

He looked in both directions, sorting through the options in his mind.

"Let's try the Mercado Centrale. I know there's Wi-Fi available, and we have some time to find a good table before the lunch rush. In another hour, we'll be lost in the crowd."

"Two small fish in a crowded pond. Sounds like a plan."

The Mercado was a short walk from the apartment. They acted like normal tourists as they wandered through the market stalls, checking out the merchandise before finding a table in the corner of the expansive interior. Ethan opened his laptop and navigated to the Laurentian Library site. Chloe sat next to him as the photos of the book of poems by Cem loaded.

"I'm not sure what we'll be able to determine from looking at the pictures," Ethan admitted. "I assume the writing is some type of Turkish script, but it's tough to determine."

He scrolled down the screen, allowing time for them to examine each section of the small book; only twenty pages in all. The lines, curls, and dots of the writing were unrecognizable, looking almost like the script Ethan saw during trips to the Middle East with his Army brigade.

"Open up another window on your computer, so we can do a search," said Chloe.

Ethan minimized the library site and clicked a link for a browser.

"Type in a search for Turkish languages and see what comes up."

He clicked on the first link that appeared in the results and they both read through the page.

"This looks like the same script," Chloe said,

pointing to a section near the bottom of the screen. "It says that Ottoman Turkish writing is a version of an Arabic script, but was replaced as the official Turkish alphabet by a Latin-based version almost a hundred years ago."

"So, if that's the case, the form of writing used for these poems no longer exists," stated Ethan. "How in the world do we translate a language that hasn't been used for at least a century?"

Neither of them had an answer.

Ethan typed another search into the browser. "Maybe we go right to the source," he said.

"What are you searching for?"

"Here is a list of museums in Istanbul," Ethan pointed out. "It's the largest city in Turkey and is a significant historic location. I assume someone there can translate the writing of Cem's poems."

"You're just going to call up somebody at a museum and ask them to translate a book of poems that could be five hundred years old? How are you going to explain that?"

"I'm not sure yet," he responded. "Do you have a better idea?"

Ethan picked out the one museum he had heard of—the Topkapi Palace Museum—and found the phone number on the museum's website. "Here goes nothing," he said as he dialed the long number.

Chloe could follow only one side of the conversation after someone answered the call.

"Hello, do you speak English?"

A pause.

"Great. Can you connect me with someone who can help translate writings in the old Ottoman

Turkish script?

"Thank you." He turned to Chloe and whispered that he was being transferred to a professor who was the Director of Ottoman Research.

"Professor Yildiz, thanks for taking my call. I've come across some writings that I believe are in the old Ottoman Turkish script and would like to get them translated. Can you help me?"

Ethan listened to the response.

"There are about twenty small pages of writing. I believe it is a book of poems."

Another response from the professor.

"I am not in Istanbul at the moment. I'm calling from Italy."

He listened again. Then dug a pen out of his computer bag, along with a scrap of paper. He wrote down an email address while the professor spoke.

"I think I have it. Thank you for your help, professor."

After the call ended, Ethan turned to Chloe. "The professor said he would do the translation. He gave me his email to send pictures of the text in the poems. He admitted it might take two or three days, as he's in the middle of a project at the museum."

Ethan took a few minutes to download the pictures of each page of the poems from the library site. He attached the files to an email and sent them to Professor Yildiz.

"Now, I guess we just wait," Ethan said after sending the email. "Do you want some food? We might as well eat while we're here."

An hour later Ethan finished his fresh baked lasagna, while Chloe took the final bites of her creamy ravioli.

They both flinched when Ethan's phone rang, hoping the Professor moved faster with the translation than anticipated.

Ethan answered and spent most of the call listening, with an affirming "Yes" spoken sporadically. "Thank you. We'll be there."

"What was that all about?"

"That was the officer who took our statement when your computer was first stolen. They think they've found the man who held us up and want us to come down and identify him through pictures."

"Why just pictures? Don't they have him in custody?"

"It seems he was brutally attacked a couple of days ago and is in the hospital with several cracked ribs and two broken legs. They took pictures for us to look at, so we didn't have to go to the hospital."

Ethan and Chloe remained silent for a few minutes, contemplating the news, reminded again about what was at stake if their search crossed paths with the wrong people.

"So how did the police know that this guy might be the one who robbed us?"

"They found a slip of paper in his pocket with our names on it; your whole name and just my first name. It was too big of a coincidence for the police not to connect him to the complaint we filed. We need to be at the police station around four o'clock to meet with the officer and look at the pictures."

Ethan packed up his computer for the short walk back to his apartment. A glorious early summer day greeted them as they exited the Mercado. A few wispy clouds were overhead, and a light breeze provided some relief from the hot sun. The annual summer explosion of tourist activity was in full force, which meant far more pedestrians than vehicles filled the roads in central Florence. They picked their way through the burgeoning crowds and reached the apartment without incident.

The two talked for much of the afternoon, trying to focus on anything but the translation of the poems. It might take days to hear back from Yildiz, though they hoped to get results much sooner. Until then, there were no more leads to follow or clues to research.

When Ethan's watch said it was 3:35, he suggested they leave for the fifteen-minute walk to the police station. Their appointment with the officer went quickly. The pictures he had them look at were graphic—even with just the man's bruised face showing. Despite the bruising, though, the pictures obviously showed the person who had held them at gunpoint. The officer said the young man's name was Adolfo Caputo and he was a small-time thug in the area. So far, Caputo hadn't admitted to anything or given any indication of whom he might be working for. According to the officer, the threat of another beating might be Caputo's motivation to stay quiet.

Ethan and Chloe chose not to talk about the second time the man approached them. If that incident were reported, then they would have to bring the wooden box from the Medici chapel into the conversation. They signed an affidavit confirming their identification of the man and then left the station.

"What now?"

"Maybe we just act like tourists and enjoy some of the sites," suggested Chloe.

"Sounds like a good plan."

They were both familiar with Florence and had spent time in all the primary attractions. Chloe took Ethan to her favorite, the Uffizi Gallery. It was one of the most important Museums in Italy and the home of a massive collection of Renaissance art. The end-of-the-day crowd forced a long wait, but they were able to get in before the doors closed. Chloe served as a personal tour guide, showing off paintings like *The Annunciation* by da Vinci, *The Birth of Venus* by Botticelli, and *Flora* by Titian. The gallery was huge, holding hundreds of paintings and sculptures. Visitors often spent hours looking at the priceless collection. Their visit to the Uffizi ended when the staff informed the patrons that the museum was closing.

Ethan chose to guide Chloe to the nearby Ponte Vecchio, the famous bridge that had spanned the Arno River for centuries. The pedestrian bridge included numerous shops that once were filled with butchers, tanners, and farmers selling their wares. Those stalls were now home to jewelers, art dealers, and souvenir shops. The structure served as the only bridge across the Arno until the early 1200s. It was also the single surviving crossing after the German army retreated at the end of World War II.

"Did you know the Medici added a corridor over the Ponte Vecchio?" Ethan asked Chloe.

"I've heard that before, but don't know the

details," she responded.

"Cosimo I Medici, a distant relative of the Cosimo we've researched, had a special corridor built in the late 1500s. The family was back in charge after their exile and no longer lived in the Medici Palace, but moved to the much larger Palazzo Pitti on the other side of the Arno. They wanted an easy and discreet way to reach the city offices without mixing with the commoners and salespeople on the bridge. The private corridor above the other shops allowed them to go to and from the main government buildings in Florence without being detected. It's called the Vasari Corridor, named after the man who built it for the Medici."

"You're full of all kinds of interesting facts." Chloe slipped her arm into Ethan's, and they mixed with the crowd traversing the bridge. They enjoyed the late afternoon sun reflecting off the gentle ripples of the river.

Chapter 18

One day passed. Then two. Still no reply from their Turkish translator.

Ethan used the time to work on his thesis, despite having a difficult time focusing. Writing about the Medici's impact on the architecture of Florence proved difficult while thinking about the impact that the clues left by the Medici clan could have on the history of Christian scriptures.

Chloe spent most of her time hanging out at Ethan's apartment, not wanting to venture out on her own. She researched more about the island of Rhodes, the Knights of St. John, and the Ottoman dynasty. She even had some extended conversations with Dale, realizing there was a decent, thoughtful man under the somewhat rough exterior.

On day three of their wait to hear from Professor Yildiz, Ethan crossed the street to pick up another pizza from Fuocco Matto and bring it back to the apartment.

During the meal, Chloe updated Ethan on her research.

"So many of the people and situations we've been looking at are connected in some way," she said. "Sultan Mehmed attacked Rhodes in 1480, about fifteen years before his son, Cem, would be exiled there. The Knights of St. John withstood the invasion attempt at that time, but forty years later, Mehmed's great-grandson, Suleiman the Magnificent returned. Suleiman sailed with over four hundred ships to the island and managed to take control after a six-month siege. Cem would have been long gone by that point, but it makes you wonder if Suleiman was still looking for the manuscripts stolen by Cem."

"It also makes you wonder if Suleiman found the manuscripts or destroyed them," said Ethan.

Neither Ethan nor Chloe wanted to consider that option. The odds of finding anything at the start of this search were close to zero, so they were already ahead of the game. They both wanted to keep moving forward until the game was officially over.

Ethan went back to his room to continue working on his thesis, only to hurriedly return carrying his laptop.

"I just got a reply from the Professor." He set the computer on the table, where he and Chloe pulled up chairs so they could see the screen.

Ethan started to read through and summarize the message from Yildiz.

"He was able to translate most of the pages but said a few sections were too faded to read. He confirmed the poems were by Cem, the son of Mehmed, and said some of the poems also appeared in books in Turkish historical libraries. At least two of the poems he translated were unique and to his knowledge did not appear in any other writings."

"I hope one of those unique poems is what we're

looking for," said Chloe.

A quick look at the translations showed ten separate poems. They started reading the first one, some type of lament about being in a dungeon and shedding tears of blood. The second was a love poem, with Cem imploring a woman to make herself beautiful and come to him.

"I don't think those are what we're looking for," commented Ethan.

They began reading the third translated poem and the recognition of potential clues hit Ethan and Chloe at the same time. Words like *sacred texts*, *Saint*, and *treasures* immediately jumped out at them.

I sacrificed, I sacrificed, now with sacred texts I rest.

Though my body is guarded, my mind soars through the gates of my captors.

Priceless writings are hidden in my heart and the stones.

Will a Saint watch over the treasures and offer them to those who search?

Will his sword point the way to discovery?

Or will Allah find the marker, holding it like a seashell in his hand?

I sacrificed, I sacrificed, now my offering I submit.

"This might be it," said Chloe. "I'm not sure what it all means yet, but there's too much here to ignore."

"Is there anything that could relate to the research you've done?"

"Nothing I see right now."

They read the poem several times.

"The word *'Saint'* is capitalized," Ethan pointed out. "Could that mean anything?"

"He could be referring to a particular saint. Since we assume the writings are from Paul, let me do a search of Saint Paul on Rhodes."

Chloe pulled Ethan's computer in front of her and typed the words into a search engine. In seconds, numerous results appeared.

"Look at this," she pointed to the screen. "There's a St. Paul's Gate on the northern end of Rhodes. This says it was constructed in the fifteenth century and was part of the fortification for a nearby harbor." She continued to read.

"This article states that locals believe the gate is on the exact spot where Paul and Luke landed as described in the book of Acts." She became more excited as she read. "It also says that there's an image of Paul carved into a stone on the walls surrounding the gate. His left arm is raised, and his right arm holds a sword."

Chloe found a picture of the carved likeness of Paul. The image on the stone appeared faded after more than 500 years, but they could easily identify the sword pointing straight down.

"Amazing," was all that Ethan managed to say at first. After they basked for a few moments in the satisfaction of another step forward, he added, "It looks like we need to find some tickets to Rhodes."

Within an hour, Ethan had them scheduled for an early-morning train to Rome, then a flight from the Fiumicino Airport to the Diagoras Airport on Rhodes. The entire trip should take almost ten hours, including a layover in Athens. That would put them on the ground in Rhodes at five o'clock the following evening. Ethan also reserved a car, not wanting to rely on public transportation to get around the island.

"Are you sure you want to cover all those costs," asked Chloe.

"It's not a problem," Ethan assured her. "Although the military doesn't pay that well, I've always been frugal with my money and saved a nice amount during my time. The government paid for my college, and I lived with my parents for a couple of years when I first left the Army. I'm certainly not rich, but I have a bit of a nest egg set aside for something special. I think this qualifies."

"Your contributions are appreciated," said Chloe.

She offered to use the available travel points accumulated on her credit card to secure a place to stay on Rhodes. She found two single rooms at the Lydia Hotel, located in the historic Old Town of Rhodes and very near the site they wanted to explore. She booked the rooms for two nights and hoped that would be enough time for them to determine if the poem from Cem provided clues to help find the writings of Paul. Neither Chloe nor Ethan wanted to entertain the possibility that they were following an imaginary roadmap.

They ate dinner with Dale that evening and described in broad strokes what they were planning. He asked a few questions, but let their basic explanations stand. Ethan said that he and Chloe planned to be back in three days. That would leave another week until the lease on the apartment ran out, giving the roommates time to clean the place and get ready to travel back home: Ethan to Indiana and Dale to New York. Chloe, obeying her father's edict, would schedule a flight back to the States as soon as the trip to Rhodes was over, whether the trip was successful or not.

Chloe tapped on the apartment's door at 6:30 a.m. the following morning. She pulled a small rolling suitcase and carried a purse-like satchel over her shoulder. Ethan answered, ready to go with a duffle bag and a backpack for his computer. Both of them packed light. They weren't planning to stay long and with the warm June weather, clothing needed to be lightweight and breathable.

"Is that a purse or another suitcase over your shoulder?" Ethan chided. "You could carry a small person in that."

"Hey. A girl's got to be prepared at all times. You never know when an extra nail file or hair clip will come in handy."

They both laughed as they retraced their steps from a few days earlier to the train station. They were full of expectations, but wary of the unknowns.

— • ● • —

It was day three in Amalfi, and Morelli was already going stir-crazy. He loved the location and even appreciated the extended time with his family. With so many questions hanging over him, though, he couldn't relax and truly enjoy the forced vacation. His wife realized something was wrong—especially when he forbade her to make any outside calls.

Morelli remained quiet on the details, not wanting to sow panic and reap the consequences of any bad decisions she might make.

Morelli kept his outside contacts to a minimum, talking only with those he had absolute confidence would keep his whereabouts secret. The authorities would be watching some of his business associates—and maybe tapping some phones—to track him down. He couldn't let that happen.

Buyers for the Medici manuscripts already in his possession needed to be found. He also would speed up the process to identify buyers for some of the artwork and antiquities he had previously acquired. The usual waiting time to approach buyers was at least a year to let some of the initial heat of investigations cool off. With his cut of those potential sales being in the millions after expenses, he couldn't afford to wait. Those millions may not be the buy-my-own-island type of money, but it would be enough to disappear and continue to live comfortably.

The one opportunity that remained for Morelli to move up from the *live comfortably* level of wealth to the *ridiculously rich* level would come by finding the original works of the Apostle Paul. He needed to complete the search that the Medici family began centuries ago. It might be his last chance for a massive payday, and he was determined to succeed.

Morelli sat on one of two terraces featured in his home, contemplating his next moves. The view of the Amalfi coast—when he took time to appreciate it— was breathtaking: the sun glimmering off the calm waters, sailboats and small yachts gliding toward the harbor. Sophia and the kids were at a nearby private beach, reserved for select homeowners in the area.

He slipped a burner phone out of the pocket of his shorts and dialed The Seeker. He was taking a chance by contacting a man who was surely being sought after as much as himself, but Morelli wasn't satisfied with playing defense. He wanted to play some offense.

"I have another job for you if you're willing." Morelli didn't waste any time with niceties or small talk once The Seeker answered.

"I can't work in the Rome area right now. I need to lay low, at least for a couple of weeks," replied The Seeker.

"Then I have the perfect option for you. I want you to fly to the island of Rhodes."

"What is my objective?"

"The clues we've acquired so far indicate that some very important historical documents are hidden on Rhodes. My people are still working on possible locations, but I want you in place and ready to move as soon as I have more detailed information."

"When do you want me there?"

"Tomorrow," said Morelli. "Get a centrally located hotel and secure transportation on the island. I'll call the second my researchers have a location for the hidden manuscripts."

"I can do that. What about additional men?"

"I'll let you make that call. And one other thing."

"Yes."

"I wouldn't be surprised if the Conrad woman and her helper end up on Rhodes following the same clues."

"I would very much look forward to meeting them once again," said The Seeker.

"If you do, make sure they don't ever leave the island."

Chapter 19

Ethan and Chloe parked their rental car and checked into their hotel on Rhodes as the time neared ten o'clock in the evening. The ten-hour trip from Florence stretched into almost fourteen hours, thanks to a flight delay in Athens. They were both tired, but full of pent-up energy after sitting in trains, planes, and uncomfortable airport chairs for more than half a day. The fact that they might be within reach of their goal also served to provide an energy boost to their systems.

Their long travel day allowed them to read about their destination. The fourth largest of the Greek islands, Rhodes had a population of around 115,000. Only a few miles to the west lay the continent of Asia, almost viewable from the high spots on the island. Rhodes was a melting pot of culture and heritage, mixed over many centuries. There was proof of inhabitants as far back as the Stone Age, followed by a revolving door of cultures trading control of the 1400 square miles of land. The Minoans were first, followed by the Dorians and the Persians, who gave way to Alexander the Great who conquered the island in 322 B.C. The Byzantines were next in line, before turning over the island to the

Knights of St. John in 1309. Once Sulieman defeated the Knights, the Turks remained in control until 1912, when the Italians took over. Rhodes, along with the other Dodecanes islands, was incorporated into Greece after World War II.

"Do you feel like walking and exploring the area for a few minutes?" Chloe asked as they rode the elevator to the third floor.

"I'm up for a walk. Maybe we can scout out the area around St. Paul's Gate," said Ethan. "We might not be able to see it all in the evening, but at least we can get the lay of the land."

They dropped off their bags in their respective rooms and met a few minutes later in the lobby. Ethan picked up an area map at the front desk and the two studied it to get their bearings. Soon they headed east on a street called Martiou, then turned south on Amerikis.

"We should be able to follow this street to an entrance to Old Town Rhodes," said Chloe. "I read that the Old Town is the oldest inhabited medieval city in Europe. We can walk through one side of it and get to St. Paul's Gate."

Ten minutes later, they entered Old Town Rhodes through D'Amboise Gate and almost immediately came upon the Palace of the Grand Master. The Knights of St. John built the massive structure in the fourteenth century. After a gunpowder explosion damaged it in the 1850s, the Palace underwent repairs by the Italians in the early twentieth century.

"This entire area was named a UNESCO World Heritage Site several years ago. That boosted the tourism to the island," said Chloe, as they walked the cobbled streets past the Palace.

They pair soon found themselves on Ippoton—better known as the Street of the Knights—surrounded by buildings made of porous sandstone. Despite the hour, tourists still milled about, heading to and from eateries and other nightspots. Ethan stopped to look at the Inn of Spain, which was a barracks for knights of Spanish heritage before the Ottomans captured the city. Chloe read a placard outside the Holy Trinity Church, a structure built by the knights and dedicated to the Catholic denomination. It later turned into a mosque after Suleiman captured the island in 1522. The base of the minaret added by the Muslims remained.

"If it wasn't for the lights and few modern conveniences, this would truly feel like a medieval town," admitted Chloe. "I keep expecting to see a modern building or lighted billboard, but it's kept the look and heritage of the old city."

Ethan took her hand. "This is all interesting, but I'm ready to get to St. Paul's Gate. I think we turn up here."

He pulled Chloe along as they took a left on Apellou and then crossed through the Liberty Gate. The waters of nearby Kolona Harbor reflected the moonlight and held a row of yachts parked in their slots. Wealthy owners appeared on many of the decks, enjoying the warm summer evening with family and friends.

Just beyond Liberty Gate, Ethan checked the map and found a sidewalk that turned into a rough path.

Straight ahead in the shadows was St. Paul's Gate.

"It doesn't look very impressive," commented Chloe.

They walked over a gravel path, noting the arched entryway of the gate, as well as several circular openings in the surrounding walls. Just inside the stone entrance stood a display board, which noted the completion of the protective gate around 1477. The design included twelve cannon holes and a drawbridge—destroyed long ago—operated by a system of beams and counterweights.

Limited lighting at the site made it difficult to examine the walls for the carved image of St. Paul. Ethan and Chloe walked around the courtyard, using the lights of their cell phones to see as much as possible. Chloe walked to the right of the entrance and cast her light on the outside wall of a semi-cylindrical tower. She could see well enough to know something was carved into the stone about twenty feet above the ground, but couldn't be sure what was there.

"This might be what we're looking for," she said to Ethan.

He walked over and shined his light on the wall, as well. The faded image of St. Paul was barely visible in the stone; just enough for them to match what they saw to the picture Chloe found online a day earlier.

They stood and stared at the image until their necks were tired of looking upward.

Chloe pulled out a sheet of paper from her back pocket, unfolded it, and read the translated poem by

Cem.

"I've read this poem a hundred times in the past day, so should have it memorized," she said. "I believe we've found the *Saint* and the *sword* mentioned in the poem, but I'm not sure where we go from there."

"I wish we could see better," said Ethan. "Since there's no one around, this would be the perfect time to search for some type of hiding place."

They strained their eyes to detect anything on the stones that appeared to be a clue. Nothing was visible in the limited light.

"I guess we need to return in the daylight to examine the walls," suggested Chloe. "If we find something, maybe we can be better prepared tomorrow night."

"That sounds like the best plan. We'll get some sleep and come back in the morning."

— • ● • —

The Seeker, whose given name at birth was Fadi El Din, perfectly used the nighttime landing lights to guide the Cessna 206 aircraft in for a smooth arrival at the Diagoras Airport.

His real name and the ability to pilot small airplanes weren't the only things he kept secret from most people.

The native of Lebanon moved with his family to the outskirts of Rome when he was just a baby. His skin tone and dark hair allowed him to blend into the Italian culture much more easily than his Muslim parents would have liked. Rebellious by nature, he fought against any type of authority, from his parents to the Italian polizia.

His knack for solving problems—regardless of the consequences—caught the eye of a Mafia boss named Bruno Corsini when Fadi was eighteen. Fadi couldn't reveal his true heritage to the hard-core Italian, so he gave himself the name Cercatore—The Seeker. Corsini provided the type of education that doesn't happen in schools. He taught his young protégé the finer points of tracking human beings— using legal and illegal means. Along the way, the Mafia boss paid for The Seeker to get a pilot's license, which provided Corsini the ability to transport products and people quickly and privately.

The Seeker still did a few jobs for his Mafia brethren but was able to break away on his own when a rival Mafia family had Corsini gunned down more than five years ago.

The plane he landed on Rhodes came from an associate who owed The Seeker a favor. Anyone checking the tail numbers on the craft would find it belonged to a rich winemaker in the Tuscan town of Montepulciano. A year earlier, The Seeker tracked down a former business partner of the winemaker; a partner who had disappeared with more than a million euros of the winery's profits. The business now had a single owner, and he was an owner who liked to spend his money on seeking thrills: mountain climbing, bungee jumping, and even skydiving. The winemaker traveled all over Europe to find his next adrenaline rush. The Cessna not only allowed him to travel without the headaches of commercial airlines, but it was also a popular airplane for his occasional skydiving fix. The roomy cabin and big cargo door in the rear made it easy to step right out of the plane.

Besides The Seeker, the six-seater carried three additional people and all the supplies they might need to search the island, whether that search would be for people or hidden artifacts. It was after midnight as he taxied to the private aircraft section of the international airport. The debarking group met a pre-arranged customs agent who happily disappeared after accepting a roll of Euros from The Seeker. A pair of Peugeot Traveller vans were waiting on the tarmac, each with the back seats removed to allow for more storage. The Seeker and his three companions transferred their gear into the vans and drove the two vehicles through an exit gate less than ten minutes after landing.

The warm evening air smelled of the sea as they headed up the coast to the four-bedroom rental home awaiting them in Trianda. The small resort town provided easy access to several main roads and was a short distance from the city of Rhodes, which would allow them to travel to any of the major areas of the island in thirty minutes or less.

The only thing needed was a phone call from Morelli to pinpoint a search location.

Chapter 20

The persistent pulsing of a phone set to the *vibrate* mode eventually caused Morelli to stir. The device shook itself against the wooden nightstand creating just enough noise to wake him after another fitful night of sleep. He was in one of the guest rooms of his vacation home, choosing to sleep alone. He knew his constant tossing and turning—caused by frightening dreams of incarceration—would not endear him to his wife. She slept perfectly well on most nights, unencumbered by outside concerns.

Morelli's eyes focused enough to grab his phone before it vibrated itself off the edge of the nightstand. "What?" he said, in a dry scratchy voice.

A high-pitched, very excited voice responded. "Signore Morelli, we've been up all night and learned more about Cem and his poems. We have found some new clues and think we might know where more manuscripts are hidden and...."

"Slow down. I'm not awake enough to follow your ramblings."

Morelli heard one of his researchers taking a couple of deep breaths, trying to overcome what was likely a caffeine-induced high.

"Sorry. We finally had a breakthrough and then worked all night. We believe we've found some clues, and those clues could lead to the manuscripts hidden by Cem on the island of Rhodes."

"Speak slowly and explain to me what you've found."

The researcher explained how they discovered that Cem wrote a series of poems and wondered if any of them were composed while he was in exile on Rhodes. After confirming that the dates of some of Cem's published poems corresponded to his time on Rhodes, they came across a book of poems in the collection that was sent to the Medici family. They looked at the book on the Laurentian Library site, printed off copies of the pages, and then tracked down a Turkish professor in Rome to translate the Ottoman Turkish language. The professor didn't appreciate being woken well after midnight but agreed to translate the script as quickly as possible for a substantial fee.

"Don't worry about the fee. I'll cover it," said Morelli. "What did he find?"

The researcher continued, recounting the receipt of an email from the professor at four-thirty in the morning with rough translations of each poem in the book. After looking through the translations for nearly an hour, one poem stood out: it talked about sacred texts, hidden priceless writings, and a saint.

"Did you figure out what it means?"

"We can't be sure, but we believe it's saying that the sacred texts are hidden somewhere around a structure called St. Paul's Gate on Rhodes."

Morelli was fully awake now—no caffeine

needed. "Send me all the information you have and your best guess of where the texts are hidden. If you're correct, a bonus will be coming your way."

———•●•———

Ethan pulled back the curtains to enjoy the early-morning sunshine as it sliced through the opening and illuminated his room. The view out the window included the Fortress of St. Nicholas in the distance and a glimpse of the waters of Mandraki Harbor. He slept well after the previous day of travel but felt anxious to get the new day started. He and Chloe hoped to fly back to Italy tomorrow, so there was some self-inflicted pressure to be successful with their search in the next twenty-four hours.

A set of push-ups, sit-ups, squats, and lunges got Ethan's blood flowing. After four more sets of body-weight exercises, the sweat dripped off his chin, and his breathing came in rapid bursts. He filled the small plastic cups offered in the room with water multiple times from the tap, drinking one cupful after the other. He did some easy stretches and let his body cool down. Thirty minutes later he was shaved, showered, and ready for breakfast.

Ethan knocked on Chloe's door, assuming she would be awake, but she didn't answer. He knocked again a little harder, but still no response. He started to get a little worried, wondering if she was okay.

"Are you trying to break down my door?" came a voice from down the hall.

He turned and watched as Chloe approached, wearing shorts and a t-shirt that showed signs of perspiration.

"Where have you been?"

"I woke up early, so went on a little jog before it got too warm," Chloe responded. "I found a path that took me around the tip of the island. The scenery was awesome.

"You look all ready to go," she said.

"I am," said Ethan. "But I'm also ready for some breakfast. There's a complimentary buffet downstairs."

"I smelled it as I came through the lobby. Let me take a quick shower, and I'll join you."

Ethan found his way to the buffet, going back for seconds and thirds before Chloe arrived. She was wearing white shorts and a yellow top with a pair of tennis shoes that looked both fashionable and comfortable. Her hair was still wet, and she didn't appear to have taken the time to put on any makeup.

She still looks good, thought Ethan, unsuccessfully trying to keep his mind focused on their search. A few heads turned as Chloe entered the breakfast area, confirming that others felt the same as Ethan.

Chloe piled a plate with fruit and added some yogurt with honey. She picked up one piece of paximadia—a twice-baked Greek biscuit—and a glass of juice. After sitting down at the table across from Ethan, she bowed her head, moving her lips in a silent prayer.

"This is the day," she said, looking up.

"The day for what?"

"We are going to find the oldest known New Testament writings."

"Is that right? You sound pretty confident. Is that what you're praying for?"

She thought for a moment. "In a broad sense, I guess that is what I'm praying for."

"So, you want to be famous?" asked Ethan.

"No, I don't think it's about me—or you—at all," Chloe replied. "Just think of what it would mean to Christians around the world. Despite ample proof that the writings of the Bible are authentic, there are still so-called experts out there who poke holes in what they see as contradictions or discrepancies in the scriptures. They point out that some of the earliest authenticated manuscripts were produced at least a hundred years after Christ. The same experts use that fact to imply that much of the New Testament is made up or is manipulated to fit into some orally transmitted storylines."

"Do you think producing an original text from the first century will change anyone's mind?"

"There will be some who'll never believe, no matter how much proof is put in front of them. That's a rejection of the overall message of Christianity more than any scientific or historical objection. But, I think an original epistle of Paul that's universally confirmed would get people asking questions and open some minds to what might be true."

"I hope you're right," said Ethan.

The two sat in silence for several minutes as Chloe finished her breakfast.

"So, what do we do after we find the manuscript?" she asked, continuing her positive tone.

Ethan worked through some options in his head

before responding. "I think the first thing I would do is contact Martin Scheidt from Interpol. From what he told me last week, he's worked with numerous investigations into the illegal antiquities market so should have a good idea of how to proceed. I'm sure there are procedures to follow with any new historical find, like working with local authorities and determining who has actual ownership."

"That's not exactly how we handled what we found in Florence."

"Yes, and now someone else has possession of those valuable manuscripts," admitted Ethan. "I hope we've learned from our mistakes."

"Well, keep Scheidt's number on speed dial because I think we're going to need it," Chloe said with a smile.

An hour later, Ethan and Chloe slid into their rental car for the short trip to St. Paul's Gate. The Fiat Doblo—a cross between an SUV and a mini-van—was Ethan's idea. Most rentals on the island were so small he could practically sit in the back seat and drive. It was worth it to spend a few extra dollars and not feel like he had to shrivel up to squeeze into the driver's seat. He started the vehicle and turned right out of the hotel parking lot. A short trip down Martiou and then a quick jog to the left to reach Platia Elifthirias. Another right turn and then it was less than a mile until they reached a small parking lot between the harbor and the entrance to St. Paul's Gate.

The late-morning sun began to increase in intensity as they walked through the gate. Unlike their solo exploration of the previous night, at least a dozen tourists checking out the historical site now surrounded them. Ethan and Chloe went straight to the area below the carving of St. Paul, squinting into the sunlight as they studied the stone walls.

"Last night it was too dark, and now the sun shining off the stones makes it tough to see," said Chloe. "Can you make out anything?"

Ethan continued to look at all the stones around the carving, trying to follow a grid pattern, his eyes moving up and down, back and forth.

"Do you have that copy of the poem with you?" he asked.

Chloe pulled out a sheet of paper from her rear pocket and unfolded it. Both read through the poem again.

"I'm confident we found the *Saint* and can follow the direction the sword is pointing," said Ethan. "But all I see are a bunch of stones that all look the same."

"The next line in the poem must mean something. '*Or will Allah find the marker, holding it like a seashell in his hand,*'" Chloe read aloud.

They continued to stare at the wall as others moved about the area taking pictures of the main gate and zooming in for pictures of the carving of St. Paul.

"Let's walk around for a few minutes and then come back," suggested Chloe. "Maybe something will jump out at us then."

They left through the gate and walked up Platia Neoriou, a small road that was part of the land surrounding Mandraki Harbor. At the end of the road stood the Fortress of St. Nicholas, which Ethan had seen earlier that morning from his hotel window.

They stopped to read a display board with descriptions of the fortress in both Greek and English and learned that the stronghold was one of many construction projects completed by the Knights of St. John.

Even more interesting, the floor of the fortress contained a circle of sandstone blocks which some believe served as the original base of the famed Colossus of Rhodes. When Charles of Lyndus completed the statue of the sun god Helios around 282 B.C., the 105-foot-tall sculpture was considered one of the Seven Wonders of the Ancient World. An earthquake brought down the bronze and iron structure sixty years later, but the broken remains stayed in place for more than eight centuries. Arabian forces raided the island in 654 A.D. and sold off the bronze for scrap. It's rumored that it took more than 900 camel loads to transport the pieces.

Ethan and Chloe walked through the fortress and saw the circle of blocks, trying to imagine a statue erected almost 2500 years earlier that stood two-thirds the height of the Statue of Liberty. Their interest soon waned as thoughts returned to St. Paul's Gate. Without saying a word, they both quickened the pace, retracing their steps.

By the time they were back standing below the carving of St. Paul, the sun had moved just enough across the sky that the stone wall in front of them no longer reflected the light. It would remain bathed in shadows as the day progressed and the sun moved westward.

The two were almost alone inside the gate, with most tourists off in search of a cool place to eat lunch.

Both moved close to the wall and began to examine each brick anywhere in the vicinity of the sword of St. Paul was pointing. The pale sandstone appeared pitted and scratched, showing the wear of five centuries of use and weather.

"What's that?" Ethan pointed to a particular stone just above the reach of his arms and a few feet below the carving of St. Paul.

"What do you see? It all looks the same to me," said Chloe.

Ethan put his hand on a stone at his eye level. "Count five bricks above this one. Do you see something in the center? It looks like a seashell might be embedded in the stone."

Chloe stood on her tiptoes, straining to get a closer look. "It does look like there's something in the stone, but I can't be certain."

"A shell would fit the clue in the poem that talked about Allah holding a marker like a seashell."

The stone Ethan pointed to looked about two feet wide and maybe a foot high. It had a slightly darker color than the stones on either side, but not enough contrast to make it stand out. An indention in the center held a small, perfectly formed seashell; at least that's what Ethan believed.

Still looking up, examining the stone, Chloe asked, "How do we get up there to look at it more closely?"

"I suppose we find a ladder and a flashlight and come back this evening after dark."

"That sounds like a good idea." The statement came from a man behind them who had approached unnoticed.

Ethan spun around, the familiar voice already setting off alarm bells in his head. He caught a glimpse of Chloe as they turned, seeing the jolt of recognition in her eyes.

"It's very interesting who you can run into on a Greek island," said The Seeker, a smile—or maybe a sneer—appearing on his face.

Two other men stood a few paces behind The Seeker, both failing in their attempt to dress like tourists. They boasted thick arms and foreboding stares, not to mention the obvious bulge of handguns under their shirts.

Ethan glanced around the area, seeing the only other visitors scurrying to exit through the main gate, either finished with their exploration of the site or scared off by the menacing new arrivals. Ethan stood tall, trying to look confident. He put his arm around Chloe's waist, but didn't speak, his thoughts vacillating between *How did they find us?* to *What do we do now?*

"My boss called this morning and told me I might run into the two of you here," said The Seeker in his thick accent. "I'm very pleased that he was correct."

The Seeker nodded to his associates, and they moved to stand on each side of Ethan and Chloe. They looked like bookends from the Thug-of-the-Week Club. One wrapped his meaty hands around Chloe's upper arm and pulled her away from Ethan. The other slipped out his gun and pressed it into Ethan's spine. The Seeker turned to walk toward the exit. The two pairs—after some not-so-gentle nudging—followed close behind.

Ethan locked eyes with Chloe as they walked, trying to convey some type of positive assurance. He felt he could take the thug walking behind him, but that still left a two-on-one battle with Chloe in the crosshairs. This situation wasn't like the confrontations in Florence. The extra men changed the odds. Odds that were now significantly in the favor of the three aggressors.

Waiting for a better opportunity was the smart move.

The chances for such an opportunity took a negative turn when the two chaperones split Ethan and Chloe up and placed them into the rear seats of identical vans. A third thug—who could have been the ugly little brother of the other two—was in the driver's seat of the van with Ethan. The Seeker slid into the backseat with Chloe in the other van, her minder taking over driving duties. The matching Peugeots pulled out of the parking lot, spinning their wheels to head away from the area.

Ethan hated to be separated from Chloe. He knew that she would be beyond frightened; reliving bad memories from the first time she was forced into a van with The Seeker. Ethan found a way to get Chloe out of the first situation, so had to stay positive and keep looking for the right opening. A couple of facts kept occurring to him, though, that put a damper on his positivity level. First, they were on an unfamiliar island with no close contacts. Second, the man who was holding them had already lost one battle, but now had reinforcements in an attempt to win the war. The Seeker would not underestimate Ethan again.

With his mind continuing to search for ideas and his fear factor rising, Ethan took a deep breath and let it out slowly. He closed his eyes, and he did the only thing that he could. He prayed.

———·●·———

Chloe tried not to show the dread that was churning inside of her.

Just a week ago, the man called The Seeker took her captive, and she experienced more fear than at any other time in her life. With The Seeker sitting next to her once again, her fear level now spiked to a new high. Being on a Greek island so many miles from the previous encounter in Rome had provided a false sense of security, but now that safety net had suddenly been ripped away. She was struggling to keep her spirits from sliding down a pit of despair; a pit she may never escape.

Memories of her mother's battle with cancer managed to break through and push aside Chloe's negative thoughts. She remembered how her mom's consistent positive attitude allowed her to rise above the constant pain. Then Chloe thought about her mother's faith, and how she didn't show any fear despite facing almost certain death.

Chloe's body began to calm, and her breathing became more controlled.

As the vehicle moved along a coastal road, Chloe began saying a verse over and over in her head: *"He will never leave me or forsake me. He will never leave me or forsake me. He will never leave me or forsake me……"*

Chapter 21

Less than thirty minutes after being forced into the back of a vehicle, Ethan found himself tied to an uncomfortable wooden chair in a room containing limited furniture. The van that transported him around the northern tip of the island and through a seaside community eventually pulled down a short driveway and into a three-car garage. The garage connected to a large Mediterranean-style home, complete with a red tile roof and stucco exterior. The van carrying Chloe pulled into an adjoining space and Ethan caught a glance of her before they were taken to separate rooms.

The curtains hung open in the room where he was being held, his captors not concerned with Ethan seeing out or others seeing in. There was no fence around the property, but a variety of trees blocked the view from any of the surrounding homes. All he saw out the window were the full branches of a Kermes oak tree, a pair of pine trees, and a dense grove of thin, cone-shaped Mediterranean cypress. Besides the bright afternoon sky and a few wispy clouds, there was nothing to provide any hope that someone might see through the window and notice a man tied to a chair.

The shadows lengthened across the ceramic tile floors and up the plain white walls as Ethan waited for his captors to appear. His mouth was dry from thirst and the hunger pangs in his stomach grew more insistent with each passing minute. He tried to remember the training he received in the military concerning the possibility of capture and interrogation: stay mentally alert, not be too passive or too aggressive, and only give up important information in small pieces.

All of those directives are simple in simulated situations. No matter how real the course instructors want it to feel, there is always the realization that the captive will walk away at the end of the day. Being tied to a chair in a foreign country with no guarantee of release and at least four unfriendlies in the vicinity creates a much different set of circumstances. Knowing a woman you care about is in the identical situation in a nearby room, raises the stakes even higher.

The door to the room finally opened and one of the muscled sidekicks entered. He untied Ethan's feet but left his hands secured in front of him with a large zip-tie. A firm grip wrapped around Ethan's arm and helped him stand on legs that suffered from less-than-normal blood flow after a few hours of sitting on a hard chair. His escort took him to an interior restroom with no windows and told him in broken English that he had two minutes.

Ninety seconds later Ethan opened the door to see a gun pointed at his chest. A wave of the gun guided him toward an open-concept living area, nicely appointed with stylish furniture—a significant upgrade from the bare room where he spent the last few hours. Chloe was there, sitting in a modern, black leather chair with swooping chrome legs. She appeared unharmed, but there was a gag in her mouth and her wrists were secured, just like Ethan's. Once their eyes met, Ethan resisted the urge to go to her, not wanting to add additional drama to the room. He settled for a weak smile and a simple nod, hoping to show some confidence and some sense of control.

The Seeker sat in one of two designer white chairs in the room; chairs that featured sharp right angles and square wooden legs. Whoever purchased the furniture must have thought that the stark contrasts between black and white, curved and linear would be appealing. As Ethan followed the pointing gun to the other white chair, the thought crossed his mind that the interior designer might have trouble finding more work.

"The décor is a little artsy for a mafia man from Rome," said Ethan, pretending to pay special attention to the surrounding furniture, as well as the framed canvases on the walls. He also wanted to send a message that he would not be easily intimidated.

The Seeker shrugged. "We could do our business in a barn or a fine home. Only the time needed to clean up afterward changes," he said with a smirk, turning to look at Chloe. "With your cooperation, this doesn't need to get messy."

Ethan glanced at Chloe, recognizing the fear in her eyes. "In a show of cooperation, why don't you tell your goons to remove her gag?"

A chuckle escaped The Seeker's throat. "Very well. Despite your poor choice of words to describe my men, I'll make the first move." The Seeker motioned and one of his helpers used his sausage-thick fingers to untie the gag.

Chloe moved her jaw around and cleared her throat before mouthing a *Thank you* to Ethan.

"Now that we are more comfortable, I expect some cooperation from you," stated The Seeker.

"It's obvious you know enough to be on Rhodes and to be checking out the area around St. Paul's Gate," said Ethan. "I'm not sure what else we can tell you."

"Yes, we have been provided some quality information and were fortunate to cross paths with the two of you again. From what we overheard, you know more about the exact location of the item we both seek."

"I'm not sure what you heard, but we were just discussing some ideas. We haven't found anything."

The Seeker shook his head, looking like a frustrated parent. He motioned to his men. The first two goons stepped in to hold Ethan. They forced him to watch as the third put his large hands around Chloe's neck and began to squeeze. Her tied hands were no match for his strength, her fingers trying in vain to break the grip as she struggled to breathe.

"Okay. Okay," blurted out Ethan, still straining against the strength of his captors. "I'll tell you what we know."

"I thought you would see my way of thinking," said The Seeker as his thug released his grip on Chloe.

She sucked in a breath, trying to fill her lungs. After a cough and another deep breath, she turned her head, speaking in a scratchy voice to the man behind her. "Did you enjoy that? Must be fun choking a woman who can't fight back."

The man's smile showed the gap of a missing tooth and highlighted a scar running along the edge of his jaw.

I would love to knock that smile off his face, thought Ethan.

The Seeker started the conversation again. "Now that we have that unpleasantness out of the way, maybe you'll be more willing to share information with us."

Ethan chose to nod, not trusting himself to refrain from a confrontational reply. Chloe started to say something, but a serious gaze from Ethan and a slight shake of his head convinced her to remain quiet.

"My employer very much wants the manuscripts that he believes to be hidden here on Rhodes and most likely in the area of St. Paul's Gate," said The Seeker. "The two of you have made progress in finding the exact location and now is the time to share that information. If not, the next demonstration of our seriousness will not be so friendly." The Seeker again turned to look at Chloe. "It would be a shame for Signorina Conrad to have an accident while vacationing on this lovely island."

Ethan finally lost the internal battle to keep his façade of calmness. He bolted up out of the chair and extended his bound hands toward The Seeker. He instinctively knew it was a foolish effort, but could no longer remain passive.

After a blur of punches, Ethan soon found

himself seated back in his chair, bloodied and semi-conscious. The Seeker had never even flinched as two of his cohorts intercepted Ethan's futile advance. The pair demonstrated their ability to win a two-on-one battle against a foe with tied hands.

Tears were flowing down Chloe's cheeks as Ethan tried to shake the fog from his head and assessed the damages: a bloody nose, soon-to-be black eyes, and a possible cracked rib. Ethan spit blood out of his mouth and looked up at The Seeker, trying to look defiant despite being in significant pain.

"I admire your courage, but hope you can see that you're only prolonging the inevitable." The Seeker leaned forward in his chair, his dark eyes boring into Ethan. "Now, you need to tell me what you know about the manuscripts. My patience has about reached its end."

Ethan still had some fight left in him, but knew he needed to save some of that energy for a more opportune time. He glanced at Chloe and then began to tell The Seeker what they knew about the poem and its clues to the location of what they believed were original manuscripts by the Apostle Paul. However, Ethan did change the final clue.

"We believe the manuscripts might be hidden behind the stone right below the carving of St. Paul," Ethan lied, knowing the stone with the seashell embedded was several bricks lower. "The sword Paul is holding points downward to that stone. When you found us earlier today, we were discussing ways to get up to the stone and remove it."

The Seeker continued to stare at Ethan,

evaluating what he heard. "Is this true?" he asked, turning to Chloe.

She hesitated but soon responded. "Yes," she said, still wiping away tears. "We were going to find a ladder and some tools and go back at night."

The room remained silent while The Seeker contemplated the news. After some thought, he stood and fired off some orders to his men in swift, terse Italian. Then he turned to Ethan and Chloe. "We are going to explore the information you provided. For your sakes, you better hope we find what we're seeking."

———•●•———

The sky had turned completely dark by the time Ethan was manhandled into the back seat of the same vehicle that transported him to the house. Clouds blocked any chance of seeing the moon or stars and a stiff breeze flowed in from the nearby Aegean Sea. The Seeker slid into the front passenger seat, while one of his men took the driving duties and another sat by Ethan in the back. A gun stabbed into his sore ribs.

The final member of the group—the one with the wicked smile—was left in the house to watch over Chloe. That arrangement worried Ethan more than his own safety.

During the past hour, Ethan and Chloe were allowed to eat a small meal, and Ethan spent some time cleaning up his battered face. Two of the hired hands disappeared for much of the time, but the extension ladder now secured to the top of the van indicated they had been preparing for the evening's activities.

Where do you purchase a ladder after normal business hours on Rhodes? Ethan asked himself. He shook his head at his stupidity, realizing these were the type of men who thought nothing of acquiring what they needed by any means necessary.

As the van traversed the long, crushed stone driveway and then took a right onto the road, the vehicle's headlights illuminated a street sign just enough for Ethan to see the name: Ialisou. He repeated it to himself several times, locking the street name into his memory. He didn't know how, but he would make it back to get Chloe and needed to have some idea of her location. A left turn onto Dimosia Rodou provided another clue. The van remained on the same road into the city of Rhodes, a route that flowed along the seaside and turned into a four-lane highway.

Ethan assured himself that he absorbed enough information to find the house where Chloe was being held. He only needed to get free from the three men surrounding him, make sure they couldn't warn the final goon watching over Chloe, and then secure a vehicle to get back to her. The gravity and difficulty of those tasks threatened to suck the hope and faith out of him, but Ethan fought to remain positive. He mouthed a silent prayer as the van pulled into the parking lot across the street from St. Paul's Gate.

The ambient light from the surrounding city served to offset the darkened skies as they pulled Ethan from the van. One man kept a firm hand on Ethan's arm and a gun stuck into his back. Another unhooked the ladder from the roof, while The Seeker pulled a large canvas bag from the back of the vehicle. Ethan looked around in vain for others in the vicinity but saw no one. The late hour and the threat of rain combined to keep both tourists and locals off the streets.

"The moment of truth has now come," said The Seeker, leading the group of four men through St. Paul's Gate.

Ethan knew the moment was soon approaching where his *truth* would be found to be *a lie*. What he didn't know, was what he would do when that moment arrived. He was confident that nothing would be found behind the stone directly below the carving of St. Paul. What would The Seeker do when he realized that the manuscript wasn't there? Ethan needed to make something happen before the search reached that point. But what?

Two of the goons erected the extension ladder so that it reached the needed height. The Seeker pulled a roll of yellow caution tape out of the canvas bag and strung it across the entrance to St. Paul's Gate, hoping to ward off any late-night visitors. With the ladder in place, the men took a pair of flashlights from the bag and directed their beams toward the stone wall. The gun in Ethan's back nudged him forward.

"You now have the chance to prove your words correct," The Seeker said to Ethan. "Climb up and find the manuscripts that are waiting for us."

One of the men tried to give Ethan a hammer and chisel, as well as another flashlight. Ethan held up his tied hands. "I can't do much with like this," he said.

The bonds were removed and now three guns pointed in Ethan's direction. "Be very careful up there. Accidents can happen quickly," warned The Seeker.

Ethan took the tools, stuffed the chisel in his back pocket, and slid the hammer through a belt loop. He then grabbed the flashlight and began to climb the ladder, hesitating on each rung—not from a fear of heights—but because he continued to think through his options.

The stone below the carving of St. Paul looked like most of the stones in the structure. The large sandstone brick appeared to be around eighteen inches wide and close to twelve inches high. Only a thin layer of lime mortar separated the well-shaped bricks used to build the structure, proving that medieval craftsmen built things to last.

With the appointed stone now in reach, Ethan wasted time, pretending to use the flashlight to study the surface and the mortar joints. He looked down at the three men staring up at him from fifteen feet below. The site of the men gathered in a small cluster at the base of the ladder sparked a crazy idea. His mind flashed through probabilities and consequences. With limited options, Ethan realized that even a low probability of success was better than he could expect if he came down the ladder empty-handed.

"Time to use some muscle and remove that stone," The Seeker said from below. "Your life very much depends on your success."

Ethan managed to hold the flashlight between

his teeth. He then removed the chisel and hammer and held them as if to drive the chisel into the thin mortar around the stone. After one timid tap, a small sliver of the six-hundred-year-old mortar came loose and dropped straight down. Ethan took a deep breath before the hammer came down again. *I must be crazy*, he thought as he let the chisel slip from his fingers. The three men below instinctively followed the descent of the chisel with their eyes. This allowed Ethan to snatch the flashlight from his mouth and drop his two-hundred-pound body off the ladder.

The Seeker and his goons were too surprised to do anything but try to protect themselves as Ethan crashed down. The bulk of Ethan's weight fell onto the biggest man, bashing him out of the picture and providing some cushion for the fall. Ethan made sure to extend his arms as he fell. He used the flashlight and the hammer as weapons, causing each to make contact with one of the other adversaries, knocking them both to the ground alongside their comrade.

Ethan felt a sharp sting in his side as he landed, but pushed the pain away. He rolled off the unconscious man and stood on wobbly legs, still holding his makeshift weapons. The Seeker had been hit in the head with the flashlight but was moving and trying to stand. The other goon suffered a hammer blow to his lower arm, his moans testifying to a probable shattered bone.

The Seeker managed to get to his feet, a large lump already appearing on his forehead. He looked around the area and caught a glimpse of his gun on the ground only feet away. Two unsteady steps took him in that direction, but Ethan beat him to the spot and used his fist wrapped around the handle of the flashlight to land a devastating blow to The Seeker's jaw. Two men were now unconscious.

While Ethan made sure that The Seeker was down for the count, the man with the broken bone found a way to stand, his rage blocking out the pain in the injured arm. His good arm scooped up one of the guns, while a string of unintelligible words spewed from his mouth. Ethan turned to see the gun rising in preparation for a clean shot and did the only thing he could. Though he never played baseball growing up, his pitch of the flashlight was a strike. The third man failed to get off the shot as the blow to his head knocked him out before his finger could squeeze the trigger.

Ethan slumped to his knees, both from thankfulness and from exertion. His brain knew that he needed to move, but his body was screaming for rest. The phrase *mind over matter* resonated somewhere in his head. Moments later Ethan rummaged through the pockets of each of the unconscious men for their phones and the van keys. He pocketed those items along with the guns carried by each man.

The need to make it back to Chloe drove him forward, despite his injuries. Ethan looked around for something to bind the three men but found nothing. He dragged them to a corner, out of the view of anyone who might be making a late-night walk by the site. Even if they regained consciousness, the men lacked communication or transportation. That gap in time should allow Ethan to reach the house and surprise the final member of The Seeker's crew.

———•●•———

Chloe's wrists were raw from the constant rubbing of the plastic zip-ties. She had been bound to a hard chair in the middle of a mostly empty bedroom since Ethan and the other three men left. That was more than an hour ago. Her blood pressure—and fear level—shot up every few minutes when her guard entered the room, making her emotions as raw as her wrists. The guard's face continued to be filled with an evil smile, his eyes leering at her as he pretended to check her bindings. His hands became a little friendlier with each visit.

The phrase *fog of war* circled through Chloe's mind as she attempted to stay alert and look for a way out. Her father talked about the phrase in military terms. He described the state of a commander who, in the heat of battle, becomes uncertain about his capabilities as well as the capabilities of the adversary. That uncertainty could lead to delays in making important decisions.

The uncertainties in her situation were many, but Chloe knew she had to be ready to act when the smallest opportunity appeared.

Chapter 22

Ethan drove as fast as the van could handle while navigating his way back to Chloe. Unfamiliar with driving protocols on Rhodes, he honked the horn at any car that impeded his progress, swerved dangerously around several slow-moving vehicles, and generally ignored most traffic signs. After twenty minutes and only one wrong turn, he recognized the road named Dimosia Rodue and then slowed until he found the next street ingrained in his memory: Ialisou. A right on Ialisou meant he would approach the turnoff for the house in less than a mile.

Things moved so rapidly back at St. Paul's Gate—his crazy plan to fall off a ladder, the brief scuffle, and then his high-speed drive—that Ethan hadn't thought through any realistic plan. Now, as he neared the house, he tried to reign in his emotions enough to formulate some type of coherent strategy. The *unknowns* outweighed the *knowns* of the situation. Ethan hoped the element of surprise would tip the scales in his favor.

He switched off the headlights of the van when he approached the final turn onto the gravel drive, using the ambient light to see the trees on each side.

Ethan pulled in and parked next to a tall Cyprus. He waited several long minutes before starting his approach to make sure there was no movement in the house. He wanted to remain unseen and unheard as long as possible.

He carried one of the guns he took from The Seeker's crew. The firearm was an Italian-made Tanfoglio pistol, which was designed for competition shooting but had turned into a status symbol among Italy's criminals. Ethan hoped not to use the weapon, though he was prepared to do whatever was necessary to free Chloe.

A soft breeze blew, rustling branches over his head while Ethan approached the home with caution, using the various trees as cover. He planned to do a complete circle of the property to check for possible entrance points, hoping to catch a glimpse of Chloe or her captor through a window.

Ethan learned during his time in the Army that information drove strategy. Gathering correct and relevant data almost always took precedence over speed because the side with the best information was able to devise the best strategy. Strategy—not greater numbers or better technology—won battles. Still, time was a factor. The men Ethan left unconscious back at St. Paul's Gate would eventually come around and try to find a way to warn their partner.

Muted light escaped through curtains covering the large windows in the front of the home. Ethan paused to check for any moving shadows but saw none. He stayed low as he skirted from the cover of one tree to the next, progressing until he rounded the back corner of the house. There he was able to see another illuminated room, this one with the curtains standing open. Ethan crawled until his back rested against the rough stucco exterior, his ragged breathing an indicator of nervousness more than physical exertion. After several deep breaths, he moved into a squat position and grabbed the ledge of the window above him. He rose slowly until one eye peaked into the room, where he saw Chloe tied to a chair, relieved that she looked unharmed.

A few seconds later, the sight of her captor entering the room with an evil grin, turned that relief into concern.

———•●•———

Footsteps in the hallway and the turning of the doorknob alerted Chloe to the return of her captor. She tried not to show the fear she was feeling as the man circled the room, a crooked smile locked into place. He looked like a lion closing in for the kill.

"Niccolo is bored and wants to play game," the man said, seeming to struggle for the correct English words.

He moved closer until the barrel of the gun in his hand came to rest behind Chloe's ear. Her battle to remain stoic soon slipped away. She closed her eyes, feeling a tear escape and roll down her cheek. She hated showing this man any fear.

The man named Niccolo used the barrel of the gun to trace a path around her neck, under her chin, and then down one arm. Chloe shuddered, repulsed by the man whose breath smelled of alcohol— probably the fuel that gave him the bravery to go against The Seeker's orders to leave her unharmed.

"Niccolo asks for favor. You give me what I ask, then you win prize," he said, followed by a drunken, maniacal laugh.

"I won't give you anything," Chloe managed to say through her tears.

A swift, but off-target backhand grazed Chloe's forehead, hurting Niccolo's hand as much as it did Chloe. He broke into a rage and spewed indecipherable Italian while shaking his injured hand. He used his other hand to grind the gun barrel into the back of Chloe's head.

Chloe was sure her life was over.

A crashing noise nearby caused Chloe to flinch. Niccolo appeared confused as well. Ending his rant, he moved toward the door, stumbling out of the room in seconds. Alone now, Chloe realized the noise came from the next bedroom down the hall. She heard a door open, followed by a guttural scream and then what felt and sounded like a boulder bashing against the adjoining wall. A gunshot rang out, prompting a shriek from Chloe. After one more massive thud against the wall, there was only silence.

Chloe tried valiantly to escape the bonds that kept her immobile. She figured she had nothing to lose at this point, but her efforts only managed to cut further into her wrists. She shifted her weight back and forth, hoping to break apart the wooden chair. The action caused Chloe to tip sideways, crashing her to the floor where she sobbed in frustration and fear.

Someone entered the room, but she couldn't contort her body enough to see who it was. When a familiar voice softly spoke her name, Chloe cried in relief.

Ethan found a knife and cut away the bonds securing Chloe's wrists and ankles. He helped her stand on wobbly legs. She immediately wrapped her arms around his neck and buried her face in his shoulder, the tears still flowing, which left damp spots on his shirt.

Ethan whispered, "You're safe. You're safe."

A few more sobs escaped before Chloe composed herself. She backed away and used her sleeve to wipe her face. Before she said anything, Ethan clutched her hand and started walking toward the door.

"I'm sure you have questions, but we need to get moving. I'm not sure how much time we have until The Seeker and the rest of his crew manage to get back here."

Chloe pulled up, giving Ethan a quizzical look as all the facts failed to coalesce in her mind. A string of questions almost came spewing from her mouth, but she held them back as Ethan guided her through the house and out the front door. She saw Niccolo as they passed the next bedroom, sprawled in the middle of the floor, chest rising and falling.

Once away from the house, Ethan and Chloe stayed at the edge of the driveway, near a row of trees. As her eyes adjusted to the limited light, she saw the van parked near the tree line and recognized it as one The Seeker and his crew had been driving. She followed Ethan's lead when he jumped in and started the engine. As soon as her door closed, Ethan gripped the steering wheel and hit the gas. The spinning tires threw dirt and leaves as the rubber found its grip. Once backed up onto the road, Ethan shifted into drive and stomped down on the gas again, moving them away from the property.

"Where are we going?" asked Chloe.

Ethan took a few turns before answering. "I'm not sure. I just know that I want to get away from the area and away from Old Town Rhodes."

Ethan headed north toward the sea and then west, winding through several seaside properties. He turned on the small streets of Ferenikis, then Akousilaou, and then Papaflessa before coming to a four-lane road named Leoforos Iraklidon. He turned west again, putting as much distance as possible between themselves and anywhere The Seeker might show up.

Twenty minutes after leaving the house, Ethan calmed enough to answer Chloe's questions. He told her about his choice to fall from the ladder at St. Paul's Gate and leave The Seeker and two of his goons unconscious. He described his speedy navigation back to the house and then circling the house until he saw a light on in a bedroom. Once he saw the man enter the room where Chloe was being held, Ethan knew he had to move fast.

"I didn't know if I would have a good shot at him through the window," said Ethan. "Plus, I didn't want you to be caught in any crossfire, so I decided to create a distraction. I tossed an old potted plant through the window of the bedroom next to you. I lost my gun when I dove through the shattered glass but managed to get to my feet just as the man entered. He seemed a little slow, so I was able to rush him and knock him into the wall, which caused his gun to go off. He hit his head when I body-checked him into the wall again, and he was out."

Chloe sat in silence for several minutes while Ethan kept driving, the road taking them near the airport where they arrived on the island barely twenty-four hours earlier.

"Ethan, I just want this to be over," Chloe said, looking down at her hands and wiping the occasional tear from her face. "There's no artifact or discovery that's worth what we've been through. If we leave the island and go back to our lives, won't the men chasing us just let us go?"

She turned to look at Ethan as he considered her question. Before answering, he pulled over while going through the small town of Soroni. He parked in an empty lot in front of what looked like an elementary school. There was a small supermarket on one side and a drugstore across the road, both closed for the night.

"I don't know if they will leave us alone," he answered. "They know who we are and they know we have a great deal of knowledge about what might be hidden in the area of St. Paul's Gate. Even if they manage to find the manuscript themselves, they won't want someone out there who knows the whole story. They can't take a chance that we could ruin their discovery."

"What can we do?"

"I think we do something they won't expect. They will most likely look for us at the airport or one of the boat docks. I'm sure they expect us to leave the island and get as far away as possible. But, I say we go back to St. Paul's Gate tonight and try to find the hidden manuscript. Making the find before anyone else is the only way we can protect ourselves."

"What if there's nothing to find? What if we've been chasing something that's not real?"

Ethan thought a moment before replying. "We've believed in this search enough to get us to this point. You've believed in it even longer than I have. If there's nothing to find, I guess we'll deal with the consequences."

Chloe's mind raced through the events of the past few weeks: her excitement of finding the initial code in the Medici books, the death of Pietro Vesuchi, the thrill of the discovery in the Magi Chapel, and the stark fear she felt while being held hostage, not once, but twice. Then she again remembered the bravery of her mother while fighting a losing battle against cancer.

She wiped away the last of the tears and turned to look at Ethan, her gaze focused and her jaw firmly set. "Okay. Let's go get what we came here for."

It took most of an hour to wind their way south and then east back toward the city of Rhodes. Much of the interior of the island appeared to be sparsely inhabited and primarily covered by pine and cypress trees. They did pass through some arable strips of land, though, where groves of wine grapes and olive trees were evident. They joined the Rodou Lindou highway, taking them to within a few blocks of their hotel.

Ethan parked the van in a vacant lot between two nondescript buildings. One looked to be near the end of its lifespan with crumbling bricks and a faded wooden sign advertising what must have been a little-used travel agency. The other building was newer with an engraved sign by the door indicating a law firm filled the premises.

"Our hotel is close, so let's go grab our stuff," said Ethan. "We can use a back entrance and should be able to leave without being noticed. I don't believe The Seeker knew where we're staying, but we need to be careful that no one is watching the entrance."

Chloe looked at her watch and saw that it was approaching 2:00 a.m. "At this hour, anyone hanging around the outside of the hotel should be obvious."

They approached the hotel with caution and tried to examine each potential hiding spot for someone who might be watching. Seeing no one, Ethan pulled his key card out of his wallet—something The Seeker didn't take—and scanned it through a reader near the back entrance. Nothing happened with the first scan, but he tried again and heard a soft click. He pulled open the door and looked down the hallway before allowing Chloe to enter. They were able to get to the stairs without passing through the lobby or by the front desk and climbed to the third floor.

Was it only this morning that we were eating breakfast together here? thought Ethan as they walked down the hallway. *It feels like days ago.*

Within minutes, they were exiting the same rear door, pulling suitcases behind them.

Back at the van, they deposited their bags behind the front seats. Ethan then took a few minutes to rummage around the back of the vehicle.

"Look what I found," he said, holding a cell

phone up for Chloe to see. "My phone was in a small duffle bag. They must have thrown it in there after they first took it from me."

"Does it have any battery left?"

"It looks like they turned the power off, so let me check." Ethan pushed the small button on the side of the phone and waited. Within a few seconds, the screen lit up and the familiar tone chimed to indicate the phone was connecting to a local network. "There's about fifty percent power remaining. It should be good for a few hours."

Ethan returned to the back of the van and came out carrying the small duffle bag in one hand and pulling a wheeled shipping case behind him. The case was a little larger than a briefcase, with an extended handle and wheels.

"I found a few tools we might use and put them in the bag," he said. "I assume they brought this case to transport the manuscripts. I looked inside and it's filled with foam padding. I hope we're able to use it."

Ethan slid the case to Chloe and hiked up the strap of the duffle bag higher on his shoulder. Tools clanked as he walked, the sound echoing off the concrete buildings on either side of the parking lot.

"Our rental car was still parked close to St. Paul's Gate. The Seeker took my keys, but they weren't with my phone or anywhere else in the van. I searched his pockets after knocking him out and didn't find them there. One of his other men must have had the keys and I just missed them," said Ethan. "If he figured out the car was parked that close, he might have used it for transportation once he and his men came around. The good news is that they couldn't have taken the ladder or some of the larger equipment in our small car. It would still be there for us to use."

"What if the men are still unconscious?" asked Chloe.

Ethan now looked at his watch. "It's been a few hours, so I assume at least one of them woke up and then would wake the others. If any of them are still unconscious, they were hurt worse than I thought. We'll take our time once we get there and make sure the site is deserted."

———•●•———

Middle-of-the-night phone calls are becoming far too frequent, thought Morelli as he fumbled for his buzzing phone.

"What?"

Morelli listened as The Seeker described the events of the evening. The antiquities dealer's face became redder and his grip on the phone became tighter as the conversation happened.

"I don't care what you have to do, but find them," Morelli screamed in reply. He was no longer concerned if he woke his wife or children. "Don't let them leave the island."

He listened again.

"I don't want your excuses. You're supposed to be the best and the Conrad girl and her boyfriend have beaten you twice."

There was silence on the line until Morelli calmed himself enough to speak, this time with less volume, but just as menacing.

"And get some of your men back to St. Paul's Gate as soon as you can. I don't care how many stones have to be moved. I don't care what you have to destroy. I want those manuscripts."

Morelli ended the call, closed his eyes, and took a deep breath. His life was unraveling while he was stuck in Amalfi hiding from the authorities. Worst of all, he felt helpless to do anything about it.

His thoughts drifted to the hurtful things he would like to do to the two people at the center of his current problems. Soon, his breathing became more rapid, and his hands clinched into fists.

Morelli's wife appeared at the doorway just as a primal yell poured from his mouth. Her face showed fear and confusion when she recognized the fury flowing from her husband. She recoiled as his eyes bulged and spittle dripped from his chin.

Chapter 23

Perspiration appeared on the faces of Ethan and Chloe by the time they covered the distance to St. Paul's Gate. He carried the tool-laden duffle bag, and she pulled the wheeled case. The summer temperatures on Rhodes usually neared ninety degrees during the day and only dropped into the mid-seventies overnight with the humidity often on the high side. Nervousness, weariness, and a general fear of the unknown also played a part in their elevated body temperatures.

Instead of approaching the gate from the inland side of the structure, they followed a path around the back side, which jutted out into the bay. Their path took them by numerous boats moored along the water's edge before they turned the final corner near the gate.

Ethan pointed to a crevice in the foundation large enough to deposit their baggage, then motioned for Chloe to stay put. She shook her head, making it obvious she was not leaving Ethan's side. He didn't waste time—or make noise—arguing, but put his forefinger to his lips. The pair crept along the stonework until Ethan could see through the gate. Chloe moved behind him, her hand on his back and eyes peering over his shoulder.

Ethan turned and whispered into her ear. "I only need to move a little further to tell if there's someone still inside. Please stay here until I know more."

He pulled back to look into her eyes and this time she gave a small nod of agreement. Ethan moved forward as silently as possible, checking each step for loose stones that would give away his approach. There was one small safety light along the path up to St. Paul's Gate. He moved to the far edge to avoid the arc of illumination and create any moving shadows. Still within sight of Chloe, he reached the entrance and peeked around the edge to the spot where he left the unconscious men a few hours earlier. He saw nothing but the cobblestone floor. Then he squinted in the limited light to look around the rest of the area before motioning Chloe to join him.

"It looks like they've all cleared out," Ethan said, still talking in a soft tone. He took her hand, and they walked toward the wall with the carving of St. Paul and, more importantly, the stone with the embedded seashell. The ladder was still in place and a few tools remained strewn on the ground, which indicated that The Seeker and his crew left in a hurry.

Ethan found the flashlight he used as a weapon earlier in the evening and turned it on. The covering over the bulb was cracked, but the light still worked, allowing him to find the hammer he'd wielded, as well as the chisel.

"You go ahead and get started working on the stone with the seashell. I'll go get the bag and the case," said Chloe, turning to retrace their steps.

Ethan climbed the ladder in the same manner as when The Seeker had been watching over him. This time he stopped a few stones lower on the wall and examined the stone that could be protecting the hiding place of an original writing of St. Paul.

The flashlight between his teeth, the hammer in his right hand, and the chisel in his left, Ethan gave a slight tap along the mortar joint around the stone. His action reminded him of the caution he used when trying to chip away the seal around the Medici box they found in the Magi Chapel.

"I think you might have to hit it a little harder." Chloe was back and standing at the bottom of the ladder, the bag and case at her feet. "That mortar has withstood the elements for several hundred years, so doubt that it will break away easily."

Ethan acknowledged her comment, then placed the chisel along the right side of the sandstone brick, in the middle of the half-inch vertical strip of mortar. He gave the chisel one soft tap to create a small groove before swinging the hammer with greater power. A chunk of the mortar flew off, just missing Chloe.

"Stand back."

He worked for the next ten minutes, being as careful as possible while still using the force necessary to break away the mortar. Once the chisel reached about two inches into the mortar, Ethan felt no more resistance, a sign to him that there was something different about this particular stone. In a normal building process, the sealant would have been evident along the entire depth of the stone. A stonemason didn't build walls by putting mortar only on the front half of a brick—in today's world or five hundred years ago.

Ethan stopped momentarily to put the tools in his pocket. He held the flashlight in one hand and used his other hand to pull his shirt up and wipe the sweat from his forehead. He looked down at Chloe, her eyes showing the anticipation that he was feeling.

"Once I chip away the rest of the mortar along the bottom edge, I hope to be able to move the stone," he said. "I don't know how deep it is, but it could be heavy. I'm sure some of the stones in this wall weigh a couple of hundred pounds."

"Is there any way I can help?" asked Chloe.

"I'll let you know once the stone comes free. For now, just stay out of the way in case any part of it falls."

Ethan put the flashlight back in his mouth, noticing the beam was getting dimmer. He needed to hurry or they would have no light to work with.

The mortar along the bottom of the stone broke away grudgingly. It was like the mixture of lime and sand was trying to keep the large brick—and perhaps the secret it kept hidden—locked away as long as possible. The final piece of mortar finally fell away, and Ethan could tell the stone settled slightly. He put the tools back in his pockets and attempted to fit his fingers in the gaps at each end, but couldn't get them in far enough to create any leverage. He thought for a moment and then looked down at Chloe.

"Look in the duffle bag we brought. I think there are a couple of screwdrivers in there."

Chloe rummaged through the bag and came away holding a pair of screwdrivers, one a Phillips head and one a flat head; both about eight inches long. She climbed up a few rungs of the ladder until Ethan reached down and grabbed the tools.

He used one screwdriver like an ice pick, jamming the tip into the same space where he had used his fingers. After several attempts, the tool managed to stick in the sandstone. Ethan repeated the action on the other end with the second screwdriver. Now he had makeshift handles on each end of the brick. Pulling gently at first, making sure the screwdrivers would remain embedded, the stone moved an inch. He began to use a bit more force and shimmied the brick side to side until it slid out three inches from the face of the wall.

Afraid that he would pull the stone out on top of himself, Ethan climbed down and moved the ladder to the side. If the stone came loose, now it would fall straight down without any harm.

Back at the top of the ladder, Ethan used his long reach to grab the far side of the stone. He pulled it out another fraction of an inch. He worked on the side nearer to him and then repeated the actions until the sandstone brick felt like it was ready to fall at any point. He put his hand along the top edge, made sure Chloe was away from the ladder, and pulled forward. The stone seemed to hang on a moment, then tumbled down and broke apart in the courtyard below.

The bulb in the flashlight flickered and went out just as Ethan turned back to look inside the crevice created by the removed stone. Chloe heard his growl of frustration, but struggled to see him, as darkness enveloped the area. She heard him tap the flashlight a few times—to no avail—and then let out a deep sigh.

"You know, you could use your phone," suggested Chloe in a calm voice.

Another sigh. "Good call. I guess I'm a little tired and not thinking clearly."

Ethan pulled the phone from his pocket and found the flashlight app. The bright light initially showed straight into his eyes, causing him to recoil, but he managed to steady himself on the ladder. He turned the phone to shine toward the wall, his head leaning in enough to stick into the gap.

"There's definitely something in there," he said, his voice dripping with anticipation.

The arm holding the phone disappeared into the hole in the wall. Ethan stretched and strained as if he was about to crawl into the opening. Leaning out again, he turned the light to point down at Chloe and saw the expectation on her face.

"It looks like some type of stone box, but I couldn't quite reach it. I'll try again."

The light and Ethan's arm vanished into the opening again, only a halo of illumination escaped around his body. After a long grunt of exertion, words sounding like "I got it," echoed from within the wall.

Ethan leaned out, the flickering light from the phone in his right hand highlighting evidence of rock particles and dust in his hair. In his left hand was a rectangular box, about eighteen inches long, a foot wide, and four inches deep. He couldn't formulate any words. The awe of holding what he hoped was inside the box left him speechless.

Looking down at Chloe, he could tell she was feeling the same emotions, her eyes wide and mouth hanging open.

Once off the ladder, the two of them examined the ancient container without speaking. The undecorated box was made of limestone and heavy enough that it was difficult for Ethan to hold in one hand. The top appeared to be sealed with some type of substance, similar to the decorated box hidden by the Medici. The outer surface was discolored and pitted but remained intact, with no obvious breaks or cracks.

Chloe spoke first. "As much as I want to see what's inside, we should find a better place to open it."

Ethan didn't speak but nodded his head. He stepped to the case lying on the ground a few feet from the ladder, opened it, and gently laid the package inside.

"We need to clean up this area the best we can so it's not so obvious that something has gone on here," he said. "I'll carry pieces of the broken stone up the ladder and try to fit them back in the hole. You pick up all the tools and put them in the duffle bag. Once I'm done, we'll carry the ladder outside the walls and put it somewhere that it won't be seen right away."

Chloe went to work gathering up the hammer, chisel, and screwdrivers. Ethan made four trips up and down the ladder, carrying chunks of the broken stone and maneuvering them around the open space like puzzle pieces. The finished product wouldn't fool anyone for long but would stand up to any casual observers who visited the site.

They only needed enough time to get somewhere safe—preferably off the island where The Seeker and his men were surely looking for them.

The two of them hauled the tall ladder outside the gate and placed it along a wall. Anyone passing it would assume that workers left it while doing repairs.

Ethan carried the duffle bag full of tools. Chloe pulled the case along behind her, gripping the extended handle as if her life depended on the firmness of her grasp. They checked the nearby lot and didn't see their rental car, confirming The Seeker must have used the keys he had taken earlier from Ethan.

Chloe led the way as they began walking back toward the van. The rapid cadence of their strides was fueled by newfound adrenaline, which somehow disguised the fact that they were both near exhaustion.

As the pair moved along empty sidewalks and crossed deserted roads, the shadows formed by a sliver of moon and sporadic streetlights created an eerie atmosphere. Ethan and Chloe spoke little during the walk, both straining to see into every darkened corner where someone could be hiding; someone waiting to take what they worked so hard to find.

The four men in the van looked like they were

coming back from a battlefield. The Seeker's left eye was circled by various colors—ranging from blues to black—and his jaw ached so bad he struggled to open it to speak. The first of his men lay across the back seat, groaning with each breath. Another had a knot on his head and a makeshift splint around his wrist; a piece of a cardboard box wrapped with duct tape. The fourth—Niccolo—didn't show any outward damage, but sat gingerly nursing his ribs. He also suffered from a hangover, giving him a massive headache and a mouth as dry as the Sahara.

Once regaining consciousness an hour earlier and realizing his phone and van keys were gone, The Seeker asked the others if one of them had Ethan's keys. The man with the broken wrist wrangled the keys from deep in his pants pocket. The Seeker assumed the rental car was parked close to St. Paul's Gate and pressed the panic button on the key fob. His reward was a high-pitched horn blasting from the parking lot. The three injured men stumbled to the car and squeezed themselves in before speeding back to the house. They arrived a few minutes after Ethan and Chloe escaped in one of the vans.

Enraged by the turn of events, The Seeker took out his frustration on Niccolo. He kicked the still unconscious man twice in the side, further injuring ribs that might have already been broken. The Seeker searched the house for Niccolo's phone, finding it on the floor in the living room. A call to Morelli had to be made, even though there was nothing the Italian antiquities dealer could do to help the situation. The Seeker reached his employer and explained what happened, then suffered through the expected yelling and obscenities.

Once that task was complete and Niccolo was conscious, The Seeker directed his injured and beaten crew to load their belongings into the second van. The small rental car no longer served a purpose.

They drove first to the airport and were told by a security guard that there were no flights—commercial or private—scheduled to leave until seven in the morning. Confident their two former captives couldn't fly off the island for at least a few hours, the foursome next drove toward the main cruise ship port located back near Old Town Rhodes. Again, finding the security office, a guard told The Seeker that no cruise ships were docked at the port and the next ship wasn't expected for two days. When asked about smaller ships leaving Rhodes for the mainland, the guard just shrugged and said passenger boats regularly left from commercial and private docks all over the island.

His frustration building, The Seeker drove the short distance to St. Paul's Gate. His men found a flashlight in the van and, after entering the gate, watched as The Seeker became incensed. Someone—most likely his two former captives—had been to the site in the last couple of hours. A stone on the wall looked like it had been broken into pieces and then fitted back in place; a different stone than Ethan Montgomery pointed out earlier. The ladder and other tools were also gone.

Did they find the manuscripts?

The foursome walked back to the van, looking tired, beaten, and dejected. The Seeker slid into the driver's seat and sat silently for a few moments.

Without warning, he let out an ear-splitting growl and pounded his fists on the steering wheel. Once calmed, he started to rub his tired eyes but winced at the pain when his knuckles touched his bruised face. No one else in the vehicle said a word, realizing the boss was on the verge of a meltdown. When that happened, someone usually ended up dead.

Now, with his crew waiting for him to explode, The Seeker suddenly sat up straight and reached across the dash to open the glove compartment. His hand rummaged around in the small opening, coming out with a folded sheaf of papers between his thick fingers. Without saying a word, he scanned the top page, then grabbed Niccolo's phone from the console below the dash. He checked the papers before punching in a series of numbers on the phone. He waited for multiple rings for an answer to his call.

"Sorry to bother you at this hour," said The Seeker in a calm voice that contradicted his mood. "I rented two vans from your company and my friends took one of them for a joyride. When they wandered back to our hotel, they were drunk and couldn't remember where they left the van. Is there any chance you have GPS trackers on your vehicles?"

He waited for a response, then read the reservation numbers off the pages in his hand and explained which van was missing.

More waiting.

"I would rather not get the police involved. Once my friends get sober, I'm sure we will return the vans in good shape."

The Seeker listened again before finding a pen on the console and scribbling on the top sheet he was holding.

"Thank you," he responded. "Yes, I will be careful."

Once ending the call The Seeker turned to his crew. The initial upturned edges of a smile appeared on his face for the first time in many hours.

"The van is close. We've got them."

Chapter 24

Martin Scheidt spent the last decade working as a Criminal Intelligence Officer at Interpol. He started in the Human Trafficking Division, a job that opened his eyes to the cruel and despicable lengths some criminals will go to make money. While the successes in his position meant that many people—mostly women—were saved and restored to their families, the mental anguish associated with the job became too much for him. He knew that thousands of the most vulnerable in society were sold into modern-day slavery every year and many were never recovered. That knowledge made it difficult for Scheidt to sleep at night or have a pleasant conversation with his wife. The burden of feeling as if he was the final hope for people facing a life of slavery and abuse turned out to be more than Scheidt could handle.

Three years into his time at Interpol, he asked for a transfer to another division and was offered a role in the division looking into Cultural Heritage Crimes. He would be working to apprehend those who dealt in stolen artwork and historical artifacts.

Scheidt took to the new job quickly. He realized that growing up in Geneva, Switzerland, with parents who both worked in the art world—his mother as a university art history professor and his father as a museum curator—gave him valuable background knowledge. He swiftly advanced within the division, serving in the Director's position for the past four years. He was more satisfied with his work, his home life was much better, and his superiors were thrilled with his success.

Scheidt recently completed a year-long operation resulting in multiple arrests and the recovery of thousands of artifacts. Codenamed *Pandora's Box*, Scheidt and his team worked with representatives from several agencies, including the Spanish Civil Guard and the Italian Carabinieri, to facilitate arrests in more than a dozen countries.

Now, he was two days into a summer holiday with his family, something he had promised for months. His wife, Tessa, along with his moody teenage daughter Lorna and his eight-year-old budding soccer star Roger—named after Scheidt's Swiss sports hero Roger Federer—took the train from the Interpol headquarters city of Lyon, France to Geneva to spend a night with Scheidt's parents. He then rented a vehicle and drove the two hours east, crossing back into France and arriving at Chamonix.

The site of the first Winter Olympic Games in 1924, Chamonix is known for its skiing options in the French Alps, with the 4810-meter-high Mont Blanc overlooking the entire region. There would be no skiing with the kids in the summer, but there were plenty of hiking and biking options. Scheidt also hoped to convince Tessa to let him take the kids paragliding with a local company that offered tandem rides over the Chamonix Valley.

The family settled into their rustic, but modern chalet in the early afternoon and took their first hike together. They scouted out trails they wanted to traverse later in the week. Scheidt splurged for an expensive dinner in downtown Chamonix before returning to the chalet. Roger went directly to grab his iPad and started playing video games, while Lorna disappeared into her room, likely posting an exaggerated account of her daily activities on social media. Simply spending relaxed time with Tessa was a treat for Scheidt.

Lights were out in each bedroom, and all were asleep long before midnight.

The shrill of a phone jolted Scheidt awake. His job often required late-night phone calls, but he was supposed to be off-duty. After fumbling to find his phone on the nightstand, Scheidt looked at the unfamiliar number and almost didn't answer. When Tessa stirred with the sound of another ring, he pressed the connect button.

"Hello. This is Martin Scheidt," he said softly as he made his way out of the bedroom.

"Director Scheidt, this is Ethan Montgomery."

The name took a few seconds to register in Scheidt's mind. So much had happened in the last couple of weeks with the *Pandora's Box* operation, the situation in Italy and the search for a lost epistle had dropped from his focus. Before he replied, Ethan continued.

"Chloe and I are in Rhodes and believe we've found something, but we may need some help."

Ethan recounted for Scheidt the past couple of

days: being captured by The Seeker, the subsequent escape, and the eventual discovery at St. Paul's Gate.

Scheidt explained that there would be some legal issues to work out because of the damage done at St. Paul's Gate, a protected heritage site. For now, though, getting Ethan and Chloe to safety—along with their find—would be the top priority.

Ethan admitted he understood there would be consequences for their actions. "We aren't positive of what we've found yet, but we're confident that something special is inside the box we found."

Scheidt asked several additional questions while scribbling notes on a sheet of paper he found in the chalet's kitchen.

"I will call a contact at Interpol's National Central Bureau in Athens," explained Scheidt. "He will be able to arrange transportation to get you two out of Rhodes. Can you get to the airport?"

"Yes, we still have the van we acquired," replied Ethan.

"Once you get there, call me back. I should have more information by then and hopefully, a plane will be ready. And Ethan, be careful. From what we know of the man they call The Seeker, he is smart and can quickly become violent."

— • ● • —

Chloe listened to one side of the conversation as Ethan spoke with the man from Interpol. Her firm grip around the handle of the protective case remained. Her body was beyond tired, but her mind raced at warp speed knowing what could be in the box, secured within the foam padding of the case. Weeks of research, setbacks, discoveries, and more fear than she had ever experienced all brought her to this point: standing in an empty parking lot in the middle of the night on the island of Rhodes.

Now she was within an arm's reach of perhaps the greatest Biblical discovery of modern times, right up there with the Dead Sea Scrolls. She might have laughed if she wasn't so weary. The convoluted path that led her—and Ethan—to this spot was so unbelievable that the best screenwriter in the movie business would only be able to sell the story as fantasy.

She ran through scenarios and made make-believe plans for how the original Pauline epistle could be revealed to the world. What she would say to the press, and what she would wear to the many receptions honoring the industrious and resourceful pair who made the find of the twenty-first century?

A small laugh did escape her lips when Chloe realized the foolishness of her thoughts. "I must be tired," she whispered to herself.

Not only were the exact contents of the limestone box still unknown, but even if they did turn out to be original writings of Paul, it was unlikely that her and Ethan's names would ever be associated with the discovery. The general public would find it hard to honor two people who stole valuable relics from both Florence and Rhodes and did damage to a historical site. She and Ethan would be fortunate to avoid significant time in jail.

"Are you okay?" Ethan's voice interrupted her thoughts. He ended the call with the Interpol agent without her noticing. "You look like you're in a daze."

"Sorry. Just tired, I guess. And anxious."

"The good news is that Martin Scheidt is going to make a call and help us get off the island. He wants us to drive to the airport and then contact him again. If all goes well, there'll be a plane waiting for us."

Ethan opened the rear door of the van and motioned for Chloe to put the case inside. She pushed in the extended arm on the case and swung the rugged container onto the floor of the van. Her grip remained on the handle for an extra second before she allowed herself to uncurl her fingers.

"We should be at the airport in less than half an hour," said Ethan. "We'll be in the air and headed to the mainland shortly after that. Maybe we can get some rest, and then figure out the best way to examine whatever's in this case."

Chloe hesitated in closing the back door of the van since she didn't want to lose sight of the case for even a few moments. Once she did swing the door shut, she threw her arms around Ethan and pulled him close. He reciprocated the sentiment, wrapping his arms around her entire torso.

"Thanks for saving me again," she said softly.

The two clung to each other, appreciating what they had been through, not wanting the moment to pass.

"Well, look at our loving couple."

The voice startled Chloe and Ethan, causing them to jump away from each other and turn toward the sound. An unwelcome feeling of déjà vu settled over them as they watched The Seeker approach with a smug smile on his bruised face. His three goons followed a step behind.

The Seeker spoke again in his accented English. "We need to stop meeting like this."

————•●•————

Ethan still had a gun stuffed in the back of his pants, his right hand twitching to grab it. He hesitated, not knowing what weapons the four men in front of him might have and not wanting to endanger Chloe.

Before he could make a decision, The Seeker barked orders in Italian—something about securing the two lovers. The man who had taken a hammer to his wrist and a flashlight to his forehead strode toward Ethan. A pistol appeared as his good arm swung upward, the aim leveled at Ethan's chest. The other two sidekicks joined in and soon had Ethan and Chloe's hands secured behind their backs with zip ties. They confiscated the gun at Ethan's back, an identical model to the one still pointed at them.

The Seeker now moved forward with supreme confidence, glaring at Ethan with bloodshot eyes. Without warning, he threw a massive punch to Ethan's midsection, followed by a roundhouse to his jaw.

Ethan somehow managed to remain conscious as he fell to the ground, writhing in pain and gulping for air. He heard Chloe scream and sensed her at his side for a moment before the men pulled her way. Despite his blurry sight, he sensed The Seeker move to stand over him.

"That's just the start of the pain you'll feel tonight," The Seeker spat out through clenched teeth. "I'm tired of being nice. You've caused me enough trouble."

The last thing Ethan remembered was a size twelve boot being directed at his head.

———•●•———

The men dragged Chloe kicking and screaming to the side of the van. The one with a broken wrist raised his good arm and placed a bear-like hand over her face. He spoke a sentence of untranslatable words into her ear, no doubt, some version of *"Shut your mouth!"* She shook her head from side to side until the man removed his hand, but obeyed with his implied direction to remain quiet. They forced her inside the van and secured her to the seat behind the driver. She turned enough to watch as the rear doors of the van opened and heard The Seeker exclaim with excitement in Italian after seeing his missing case. One of the men pulled out the case and flipped the latches open. Silence followed for a few moments before rapid directions began flowing again from The Seeker. The next sound came from Ethan, an involuntary groan as the men tossed him into the back of the van. One side of his face was badly swollen, and blood leaked from his nose and mouth.

"At least he's still alive," thought Chloe. She worried the kick to the head might have killed him.

The man she knew as Niccolo—who appeared to be moving gingerly—slid into the driver's spot holding the keys he'd found in Ethan's pocket.

Broken-wrist-man took the front passenger seat after re-checking Chloe's bonds. Niccolo started the van, backed up into the street, and then waited until the identical van driven by The Seeker passed by. Both vehicles roared through the barren streets, soon leaving Old Town Rhodes behind.

The time between embracing Ethan in relief and once again being a helpless captive was so brief, the change from feeling safe to being in ultimate despair so quick, that Chloe's entire body trembled. She experienced adrenaline spikes before but felt too exhausted and too overwhelmed to have her body summon any reserves of energy. Even her tears had dried up, though she badly needed to cry.

She slumped in the seat once the trembling subsided.

The van rounded the northern-most tip of the island, before following the highway in a southwest direction; the same route they took the first time The Seeker and his men drove her and Ethan away from St. Paul's Gate. Chloe saw the waters of the Aegean Sea off to her right, the small waves glistening in the slice of moonlight. She imagined floating in the water, the warmth of the sun on her face, letting the gentle waves wash away her fears and concerns.

Another groan from Ethan broke up her brief, mental interlude and snapped her back to reality; the reality that the time clock for both of their lives could very well be nearing its end.

Chapter 25

The cool air rushed by him like being in the midst of a wind tunnel. Something wasn't right. His descent should have been slowed by now...

He grasped the emergency pull cord and ripped it away. The auxiliary chute broke free and began to fill with air, rapidly slowing his descent...

The not-so-gentle bouncing in the rear of the van produced another extended groan from Ethan. He trickled back to consciousness over several minutes, the daggers of pain shooting through his body enough to rouse him from one nightmare and straight into another. He attempted to open his eyes, only to be hit by a wave of concussion-caused nausea, a symptom that could put him out of commission more quickly than a bruised rib or swollen face.

Though his thoughts were fuzzy, Ethan remembered being in the parking lot with Chloe and the brief beating by The Seeker. The sound of tires buzzing over concrete—not to mention his uncomfortable position on the floor—indicated to Ethan that he was in a van moving at high speed on a highway. He had no way of knowing how long he'd been out but managed to open one puffy eye enough to realize there wasn't a hint of sunlight coming into the vehicle. That meant it was still very early in the morning.

With turtle-like movements, Ethan stirred his body parts enough to take stock of his injuries. Legs uninjured—a positive. Ribs were very sore, but no sign of a break that might eventually puncture a lung—also a positive. Hands still zip-tied—short-term negative as long as circulation could be restored. Head throbbing, possible broken nose, swollen eyes, and a probable concussion—big negatives. Even if all his limbs were working, he would need clear thinking and quick reaction time to have any chance of getting out of his current circumstances.

And then there was Chloe. *Where was she? What kind of condition was she in?*

The cadence of the tires going over the pavement changed as the van slowed and turned to the right. The motion caused Ethan's body to roll slightly and provided a glimpse of the passenger sitting nearest to him. Though he saw the back of her head for only a second, the fact that Chloe was close and sitting upright was welcome news. He had to swallow the urge to call out, not yet wanting his captors to know he was awake.

Streetlights broke up the darkness as the van took a few gentle curves before coming to a complete stop. Ethan heard two men talking in the front seat but was unable to make out exactly what was said. The men went silent a minute later when a familiar voice began talking loudly and angrily from somewhere outside his vehicle—the voice of The Seeker. Once the shouting ceased, a door slammed and within seconds, Ethan's van began to move.

It was a short trip. They soon pulled into what felt like a dark tunnel from Ethan's viewpoint on the floor of the van. Once the lights came on, he could see they were in a hangar. The two front passengers exited the van and Ethan heard other doors being opened and shut. A group gathered outside the back of Ethan's van, speaking loud enough for him to hear.

"What was the problem at the gate?" asked one man.

"The guard said he was told not to let any private planes get on the runway because an important flight was coming in from Athens. Some type of special government operation." Ethan knew this was The Seeker speaking and knew the government flight was probably coming for him and Chloe.

The Seeker kept talking. "Since it was the same man who let us bypass customs a couple of nights ago, the threat of exposure convinced him to cooperate."

"What now?"

"I'm going to make sure the plane is fueled. Then I'll call Morelli and tell him we'll be landing in Naples in a few hours. That's the closest airport to his home in Amalfi, so he should have plenty of time to drive and meet us there," The Seeker explained. "You three transfer the case and our passengers to the plane."

"We're taking those two with us?" asked one of the men.

"Only for part of the trip," snickered The Seeker. "Since the owner likes to use this plane to go skydiving, I'm going to treat them to an adventure they'll never forget."

Upon hearing the last line, Ethan wished he couldn't understand Italian.

Minutes later, two of the goons roughly pulled him from the van. He gave up trying to fain unconsciousness once he realized the men would simply drag him along the ground. Walking was easier. Chloe, her hands also still bound behind her back, looked relieved to see Ethan and see him upright.

She's lucky she doesn't know what's coming, Ethan thought to himself.

The men led them to a nearby airplane and forced them to slide in on their backsides. Ethan wasn't an expert on private planes, but he knew this aircraft was a Cessna. The section where he and Chloe were sitting appeared to be space for additional seating, probably removed to allow for more storage. There were still four seats, which were being filled by The Seeker and his crew. The fact that The Seeker was qualified to fly an airplane came as a surprise. It also meant the leader of the outlaw foursome would be too occupied navigating the aircraft to provide much aid if Ethan came up with some way to cause a commotion. He figured one-on-three was better than one-on-four.

With his hands still locked together behind him by zip ties—not to mention the tight confines of the small plane—the number of opponents was almost immaterial. Unless Ethan discovered some hidden ninja talents, he was in no position to battle anyone. With what The Seeker had planned, though, he didn't have much to lose.

He talked quietly to Chloe, attempting to be as positive as possible. She asked several times if he was okay, and he repeatedly said he was, even though his body felt like it had been run over by a truck. *I must look really bad if she keeps asking me the same question,* thought Ethan.

The plane taxied a short distance before accelerating down the runway. It took off into the early morning sky, a hint of the coming sunrise appearing on the eastern horizon. The motion of the aircraft made it difficult for Ethan and Chloe to stay in any one position. Their bound hands were useless for balance. Ethan pushed with his legs to steady the rest of his body against the sidewall, grimacing when his hands ran over something sharp. He slid around and saw a bolt and a small bracket protruding above the thinly carpeted floor. Looking at the surrounding area, he found three other similar brackets spaced in a rectangle, likely used for securing the missing row of seats.

The brackets presented an opportunity.

Ethan slid close to Chloe and whispered his thoughts. She nodded that she understood, and they pushed and spun their bodies until each was in a good position, their zip-tied hands over one of the brackets. If they were as sharp as Ethan thought, the brackets might be able to cut through the zip ties. Getting the use of their hands back was something; maybe not a game changer, but at least it would move the dial in their favor.

They found it awkward working behind their backs, suffering multiple gashes to their hands and wrists as they used trial and error to get the zip ties in exactly the right spot over the brackets. Every time Ethan felt like he was making progress, gentle turbulence or a turn of the plane caused his body to move. They were fortunate that the men in front of them seemed unconcerned about their captives, convinced Ethan and Chloe were beaten and out of options.

Before Ethan or Chloe managed to cut through the ties, The Seeker turned and spoke to his men. Again, Ethan's ability to understand Italian provided him with information, but not encouraging information.

"I think it's time for our two guests to be rewarded for all the inconvenience and pain they've caused," said The Seeker. "Open that cargo door and let them spend eternity together in the beautiful Aegean Sea."

The two men seated in front of Ethan and Chloe unbuckled their seatbelts and stood, their over-six-foot frames forcing them to stoop in the small fuselage. The men squeezed through to the back of the cabin and hung on tight as they unlatched the cargo door. The combined sounds of the engine and the wind now rushing by made it impossible to communicate verbally. Ethan looked over at Chloe and could tell by the strained look on her face that she was beginning to understand what was about to happen. She sat closest to the door but pushed with her feet to slide up against Ethan's body, squeezing in tight, as if melding together would make them too heavy to move.

The man that Ethan landed on when dropping off the ladder at St. Paul's Gate looked frightened to be so close to the open door. He grabbed at any handhold he could find to steady himself. One of his hands shot out and wrapped around a small handle against the back wall of the plane. The handle turned and a panel popped open exposing a small storage compartment, the only apparent contents being an overstuffed backpack. The man glanced at the compartment and then adjusted his balance, more concerned about staying inside the plane than anything else.

Seeing the backpack gave Ethan some optimism. He knew it was more than a backpack. It was a parachute assembly and looked to be packed and ready to go. He recalled The Seeker mentioning earlier that the plane's owner liked to use it for skydiving. Ethan doubted The Seeker realized what Ethan used to do in the military.

Perhaps there was hope. But one parachute wouldn't save both him and Chloe.

Or could it?

An idea circled and solidified in his mind. It had to be the most radical idea of his life.

The one major obstacle would be getting his hands free. Without the use of his hands and arms, nothing else would work. Ethan pressed his wrists down as hard as he could, dragging the zip tie over the sharp bracket. Despite the numbness in his hands, he felt blood running down his fingers from the cuts he'd caused.

The second man standing—the one they called

Niccolo—came to pull Chloe away. Her piercing screams found a way to resonate above the roaring of the wind. Niccolo grasped her by one leg and jerked her toward the cargo door. Chloe kicked him repeatedly with her free leg but had little leverage to put force behind the effort. As she was writhing around, her zip tie finally broke loose, and she instinctively reached out to Ethan, but he was feverishly working to cut through his zip tie and couldn't reach back.

Niccolo wrapped both of her legs with one of his powerful arms, using his other arm to maintain balance. Once closer to the opening, the second man joined in and took hold of Chloe's two swinging arms. While she continued to scream and fight back, the two men picked her up off the floor as if she weighed nothing. She turned toward Ethan again with an unfathomable look of terror on her face.

The two goons were rocking Chloe back like a pendulum, gaining momentum to cast her from the plane.

That's when the zip tie on Ethan's wrist finally gave way.

His free hands had enough feeling to push his body up off the floor of the plane, the unexpected action causing the men holding Chloe to hesitate. Ethan moved with near-supernatural speed to grasp the shirtsleeve of Niccolo and pull him off balance. The action sent Niccolo to the floor in the direction of the cockpit.

The other man looked in disbelief at the turn of events. He let go of Chloe to get into a fighting position, something difficult to do in a plane with a door standing open only feet away. Ethan grabbed onto Chloe to keep her from sliding out of the opening, then surprised the man with a kick to the midsection, causing the big guy to double over. Ethan took advantage by grabbing the man's collar and jerking him forward so that he landed on Niccolo, who was just up on one knee.

The two men looked like they were in a slapstick comedy, falling over each other while attempting to get up.

The altercation took all of about five seconds, enough time for The Seeker and broken-arm-man to turn in the pilot and co-pilot seats and draw their weapons. Firing a gun in an airplane is never a smart decision, but Ethan doubted The Seeker was concerned with anything except ending his and Chloe's life. Fortunately, the pair of thugs grappling to stand in the middle of the plane blocked any direct line of sight.

Ethan dove on top of Chloe, stretched out one hand to take hold of the parachute, and shimmied one strap up toward his shoulder. He then wrapped his arms around Chloe, put his mouth close to her ear, and said, "Trust me."

The look of confusion on her face soon turned back into terror when Ethan leaned his body back toward the open cargo door, pulling Chloe with him. His last sight before he and Chloe plummeted out of the plane was The Seeker. The criminal's face appeared contorted into a mask of rage.

The deafening noise of the plane's engine and the rushing wind disappeared; at least for a few seconds until their bodies neared terminal velocity and the force of the air whistling by their faces made it impossible to communicate verbally. Ethan could tell Chloe was near hysteria—as anybody would be that just got pulled out of an airplane without a parachute—but he barely heard her screams. Chloe's frenzied state made it difficult for him to keep a grip on both her and the parachute. He had to get the parachute straps over both shoulders and hooked in tightly before there would be any chance to pull the cord. He also couldn't let go of Chloe. Though they would fall at roughly the same rate, Ethan knew if they became separated, it would be tough to reconnect. The added factor of having unprotected eyes against the rushing wind made it difficult to see what he needed to do.

There was another very important issue: time.

Ethan estimated that the plane had been flying at between eight and ten thousand feet of altitude. It took about ten seconds for a person to freefall the first thousand feet, but just five seconds for every successive thousand feet. His experience in the 173rd Airborne Brigade taught him that pulling a parachute at around three thousand feet is very safe. Getting as low as a thousand feet could be dangerous. A very experienced skydiver might wait until five hundred feet, but that's not something Ethan wanted to try.

Some hurried math in his head told Ethan that he had less than forty-five seconds to get strapped in, wrap his arms and legs around Chloe, and pull the cord.

They both turned and tumbled through the sky, the vertical and rotational forces fighting against any normal human motion. His eyes squinting against the rushing air, Ethan struggled to get the parachute straps completely in place. He switched his hands holding onto Chloe and then slipped his second arm through a flapping strap. As if that wasn't difficult enough, now he had to buckle the straps across his body, something that took two hands.

Six thousand feet.

With no time to spare, he circled his legs around Chloe's twisting torso and let go of his grip on her arm. He managed to get one buckle connected before their somersaulting forces pulled Chloe away. Ethan reached out a hand, succeeding in entwining his fingers with hers. The grip was not strong, but he used every ounce of his remaining strength to pull her closer. She looked into Ethan's eyes with fear, but also an inkling of hope. As he stretched out his other hand, their initial grip broke and Chloe spun away, arms and legs flailing as she fell.

The dream Ethan had so many times now played out in real life. A person in need was in his grasp and he couldn't hold on. *This can't happen. Lord, I need your strength.*

Four thousand feet.

Beyond panicked, Ethan found the focus to buckle the parachute straps before going after Chloe. He hurriedly balanced himself into the neutral freefall body position: belly down, back in a relaxed arch with hips pushed forward into the wind, arms and legs spread out evenly, and chin up. Once his own body was steady, he saw Chloe still spinning erratically to his left and below his current position.

Even though the average freefall speed is around 120 miles per hour, a skydiver can alter that speed by changing body positions. Ethan pointed his head straight down and brought his arms into his side, making himself into a falling torpedo. He used his arms like fins, moving them slightly to modify his direction. Seconds later, he came up on Chloe and crashed into her tumbling body.

Two thousand feet.

He was fortunate to dive right into her back, quickly wrapping his legs around her and slipping his arms under hers. It took a few more seconds for him to wrangle both of their bodies into the correct alignment, so he could open the parachute.

They were close enough to the water below to see the early-morning sun reflecting off the small waves.

One thousand feet.

Ethan brought one hand into his chest and grappled for the ripcord. He pulled the handle, then locked his hands together in front of Chloe as the canopy deployed. The jolt of the parachute catching air attempted to pull Chloe from his grasp, but this time Ethan hung tight. Her body was now empty of energy and sagged like a limp rag doll. The limited distance to descend after deploying the parachute meant it would be a short flight, but they were floating smoothly and would survive the drop from the airplane.

Thank you, Lord.

Only now did Ethan think of the next issue they faced. He and Chloe were about to land in the Aegean Sea, maybe fifty miles from shore with no way to signal for help. Just before they entered the water, the thought crossed Ethan's mind that they pulled off an amazing feat in the air, only to face drowning in the sea.

Chapter 26

Morelli motored along Strada Statale—state highway—163 for twenty kilometers until picking up the A3 Highway near Salerno. Twenty-five kilometers later he sped by the exit for Pompeii. He drove with the top down on his Alpha Romero, enjoying the lack of early-morning traffic and the relatively cool air. By early afternoon, the summer sun would be beating down with a vengeance.

For once, the phone call from The Seeker that woke Morelli from a sound sleep turned out to be good news. What appeared to be the hidden manuscripts from the Apostle Paul had been found. In addition, the two people responsible for Morelli's flight from Rome and potential ruin were hopefully at the bottom of the Aegean Sea by now. The Seeker should land in Naples in less than two hours, giving Morelli ample time to get to the Capodichino Airport.

He would owe The Seeker a substantial finder's fee, but if the package being delivered turned out to be authentic writings of Paul, Morelli wouldn't have to worry about his finances. Along with the Medici documents and the single page of Paul's letter already in hand, the biggest payday of his career was within reach. He had some feelers out to potential buyers and expected several to be interested. Morelli hoped to create a fierce bidding war, driving the price upward to a number that would make him financially set for life. Just as important, the money would allow him to disappear before authorities closed in. He wasn't sure how long he could continue to hide out, so he planned to get the bidding process started within days, if not hours.

Morelli found himself whistling along to some catchy pop tune on the radio as he buzzed along the highway, the stress of the last couple of weeks melting away in the coastal breeze. He viewed the Bay of Naples in the distance off to his left, the rising sun providing a view of the turquoise waters.

A road sign indicated that only twenty kilometers remained until he arrived in Naples, the third largest city in Italy. The airport was located a few kilometers north of the city, meaning Morelli had less than thirty minutes to enjoy his drive. He would meet The Seeker at a private airplane hangar and collect his prize.

Less than an hour until I set eyes on my just reward, he thought.

———•●•———

The Aegean Sea encompasses 214,000 square kilometers or about 83,000 square miles. Even if authorities launch an extensive search, those lost at sea may very well never be found.

The initial plunge into the Aegean ended one

harrowing experience and started another for Ethan and Chloe. The lifesaving parachute quickly became a liability when it tried to drag Ethan under the water. Since he was struggling to help Chloe at the same time, the prospect of them both drowning minutes after landing became a real possibility. Ethan let go of Chloe and pushed her away, hoping she would swim clear of the parachute's canopy. He fought against panic even though his head struggled to stay above water. He took a deep breath, let his body relax, and sank below the surface. Without the arm and leg action required to tread water, he was able to unhook the parachute pack strapped to his back and swim away. He remained underwater until he was out from under the canopy, then surfaced and took a needed gulp of air. Swiveling his head, he saw Chloe bobbing in the gentle waves only yards away. They swam to each other and embraced awkwardly while working to remain afloat.

Then Chloe punched him lightly in the shoulder.

"Don't ever pull me out of an airplane again," she said, showing a strained smile.

Ethan could tell she was still frightened but appreciated her effort at humor despite the circumstances.

"The next time I plan to jump out of an airplane, I promise not to take you with me," he replied.

Chloe's smile grew a bit wider at his response, but she did so with quivering lips and eyes that looked somewhere on the other side of exhaustion. Ethan knew her energy levels had to be low and treading water, especially in a choppy sea, was hard work. Between lack of sleep and enduring traumatic situations—plus a couple of good beatings absorbed by Ethan—neither of them would survive an extended amount of time in their current situation.

"Tuck in your shirt," directed Ethan.

"What?" Chloe still had on the white shorts and yellow top she dressed in the previous day.

"Tuck in your shirt and button it all the way up," Ethan demonstrated with his shirt. "Blow into the opening around the collar, then grip it tight around your neck. The air should rise to your shoulders and help you float."

Chloe followed the directions and an air bubble appeared in the yellow material. She stopped kicking her feet and still kept her head above water. "I think it's working."

"You'll have to keep blowing into the shirt every minute or so, but it'll give you some added buoyancy."

They didn't talk for several minutes, neither wanting to voice their fears or admit the inevitable.

"Do you think it was in there?" Chloe asked after blowing into her collar for at least the fifth time.

Ethan understood her vague question, despite its lack of detail. The same question circled through his mind.

"I have to believe it was. Everything else we found, every clue along the way, turned out to be true. I think that small, stone box held an original writing by the Apostle Paul."

Time passed as they floated, not knowing which direction the tide carried them. Soon the hot sun—as well as thirst and hunger—would add to their growing list of life-threatening issues.

Chloe's voice broke the silence, with words struggling to be audible above the lapping waves. "I pray to have the power to grasp how long and high and deep is the love of Christ," she recited to herself. "I pray to know the love that surpasses knowledge and to be filled to the fullness of God."

"What was that?"

Chloe, surprised that Ethan heard her words, responded. "It's taken from a verse in Ephesians that's always been one of my favorites." She struggled to blow into her shirt again and keep her head above water. Ethan feared she was nearing the end of her strength.

"Paul prayed for the believers in Ephesus that they would know the greatness of Christ," she added. "I need that for myself. I want to go out praising God, just like my mother."

Ethan floated close to her and positioned his face close to hers. "I want you to see that verse written in Paul's original hand once the manuscripts are recovered." Chloe looked away as if she didn't want to hear any kind of pep talk or false confidence.

"Listen to me, Chloe," Ethan said once she turned back to face him. "We've been through too much to give up. We've been held at gunpoint, taken hostage, and just survived falling from over eight thousand feet. I believe the Lord has a plan and it's not for us to die today. You have to believe that and keep the faith. Can you do that?"

Tears mixed with the seawater on Chloe's face. "I want to believe that," she said. "I truly do. But I'm so tired...so tired."

She sank briefly, before kicking with her legs.

Ethan moved to her side and put one arm under her shoulders, hoping to provide a little support. "I will help you, but I need you to do something for me. Something important."

"What?"

"Keep praying," he said. "Pray out loud if you need to, but keep talking to the Lord."

They continued floating, Chloe's lips moving in prayer, Ethan trying to remember anything from his past training that might be useful. He also scanned the horizon for any sign of a miracle.

In the end, the miracle didn't happen because of military training, ingenuity, or amazing physical attributes—although each of those qualities may have played a small part. It came in the form of a malfunctioning warning light on a night ferry traveling from Karpathos to Rhodes. The anomaly took place before Ethan pulled the stone box out of its hiding place at St. Paul's Gate the previous evening. Without the warning light indicating a mechanical issue in the engine room, the 142-meter-long F/B Pharos would have left port on time. It would have already been past the spot where Ethan and Chloe parachuted into the middle of the Aegean.

The once-a-week route normally left the Greek island of Karpathos just before midnight and arrived in Rhodes around 6:00 a.m. Travelers slept in one of the 250 single beds or reclined in airplane-like seats, depending on how much they were able to spend for the six-hour crossing.

It turned out that the warning light was defective and not a problem in the engine room. The time it took the engineers to figure that out meant the ferry was running two hours behind.

Chloe was the first to notice a small shape in the distance, moving in their direction. Other than a few harmless fish swimming around them, it was the first object of any kind they'd seen since landing in the water—a block of time that felt like several hours but had only been forty-five minutes. The small shape grew bigger and became distinguishable as a seagoing vessel. Then it became so large that Ethan and Chloe's excited anticipation of a possible rescue turned into a fear of being pulled beneath the ship's wake.

A crew member was outside the bridge for an early-morning cigarette and detected something floating in the water ahead of the ferry. At first, he thought it was just sea junk—items that inadvertently fall off the many ships crossing these waters—but then sprang to attention when the *sea junk* started waving frantically. The crew member bolted onto the bridge and hit the alarm indicating an emergency, the blaring claxon putting a mildly rehearsed emergency plan into action.

The large vessel—moving at its cruising speed of fifteen knots—made a slight turn and took more than a nautical mile to come to a complete stop, passing Ethan and Chloe's position in the process. By the time the crew began lowering a lifeboat into the water, the decks were ringed with passengers awakened by the commotion and sudden slowing of the ferry. The crew performed admirably, getting the lifeboat filled with rescue personnel and first aid equipment into the water quickly and safely.

A small outboard motor came to life and

propelled the lifeboat back to the two haggard castaways. A dark-haired sailor reached out a strong hand and pulled Chloe into the boat, while a second man wrapped her in a blanket and started asking questions in rapid Greek. When Chloe didn't reply, the man tried a few basic words of English and sensed the exhausted woman understood. Ethan was next, his larger size creating more of a challenge for the smaller Greek seaman. With some help from the second sailor, Ethan was hauled into the boat and was given a blanket. He quickly became the target of their questions.

He appreciated their concern, but despite his weariness, Ethan held up his hands and asked one question in return.

Ten minutes later, Chloe was on her way to be checked out in the ship's infirmary. Ethan walked unsteadily onto the bridge, still wrapped in a blanket. The dark-haired sailor remained by his side and addressed the captain in his native tongue, passing on Ethan's request.

A snow-white beard covered the weathered face of the ship's captain, the title Cpt. Petsalis prominently displayed on the nametag pinned to his starched shirt. A proud native of the Greek island of Corfu, the captain had been at sea for more than twenty-five years. He looked at Ethan with interest, studying the man who had just been plucked from the water at least fifty miles from land. Captain Petsalis knew there must be an amazing story to be told.

But the story could wait.

The captain motioned for Ethan to follow, guiding him to a nearby lounge where various breakfast foods and coffee were available for the crew. Ethan sank into a chair and grabbed some type of sweet roll and bottle of water, consuming both in seconds. The captain picked up the handset of a phone in the corner of the room and handed it to Ethan.

"Phone, uh, is a satellite phone," the Captain said in rough English, pointing one finger toward the sky. "Can call any number."

Ethan accepted the handset with a nod of appreciation. The Captain retreated from the room, leaving Ethan alone.

Ethan dialed a number from memory, praying that he wasn't too late.

———•●•———

For a man on vacation, Martin Scheidt stood in the kitchen of his rented chalet in a rotten mood. Even worse, the rest of his family would be in a similar bad mood once they found out he might need to cut short their week in Chamonix.

Scheidt had been in constant communication throughout most of the night with his contact in Greece. A plane had been sent to Rhodes to pick up Ethan Montgomery and Chloe Conrad, but the adventurous pair had not shown up at the airport. Numerous calls went unanswered and contacts with local authorities proved unfruitful. The only thing Scheidt could confirm was that there indeed had been damage done to the wall at St. Paul's Gate, matching the information Ethan presented in their one, brief phone call.

He lost track of how many cups of coffee he'd gone through in the past six hours, but Scheidt poured another. He heard someone in the chalet's bathroom and knew he would soon have to explain to his wife and kids why their plans for the day would have to wait.

Today was meant to be one of the best days of their vacation. The planned highlight was a ride on a series of cable cars up to the Aiguille du Midi, a station over twelve thousand feet up the side of Mont Blanc, the tallest mountain in the Alps. They would then cross a national border to Ponte Helbronne in Italy and down to the small town of Courmayeur. There would be stunning 360-degree views the entire time. For those who didn't want to physically climb or ski down mountains, the day Scheidt and his family planned was considered one of the best outings in all of Europe.

Now those plans would have to change.

Scheidt's wife entered the front room, noticed his haggard look and unshaven face, and started to speak, but his ringing phone interrupted. He held up a finger, indicating for his wife to wait as he turned to answer.

"Where are you?" Scheidt practically shouted after realizing who was on the call. "People have been looking for you for hours."

He listened for several minutes, alternating between shakes of his head in disbelief and nods of understanding. His wife stared at him, knowing by Scheidt's facial expressions that something unusual must be happening.

Once the call ended, Scheidt turned to his wife

and said only, "This is big." Then he walked away
and punched a number into his phone.

268

Chapter 27

In the two days since being miraculously plucked from the middle of the Aegean Sea, Ethan and Chloe had done little other than rest and recuperate. Ethan came out of the ordeal with a pair of cracked ribs, a broken nose, and more scrapes and bruises than he could count. Chloe escaped most of the physical injuries, but the moments of terror she experienced still weighed on her mind, and probably would for many weeks to come.

Thanks to the influence of Interpol, local authorities made sure the two were safe and comfortable in a beachside home, several miles from Old Town Rhodes. New clothes were supplied, meals were prepared, and a doctor visited regularly. Ethan appreciated the diligence and professionalism of the guards who rotated shifts on the property.

Chloe talked to her father a couple of times each day, fighting an unsuccessful battle to keep him from flying to Europe to take her home. Colonel Kenneth Conrad usually got his way and would be boarding a flight within hours. Ethan also spoke with his parents, updating them on his situation and promising to be heading back to the States within the week.

The pair enjoyed a great Greek lunch of soutzoukakia—spiced meatballs in a cinnamon-rich tomato sauce—prepared by a grey-haired Greek woman who spoke very little English but served Ethan and Chloe wonderful meals.

While they admired the sea view from the home's terrace, a new man walked through the open sliding doors. The man was dressed in black pants, a starched white shirt, and a conservative blue tie, loosened at the collar. He had thinning blond hair with hints of grey over the ears and a face covered by at least a three-day growth of beard. His eyes were noticeably blue, but ringed by dark circles.

"You must be the adventurous pair who caused me to cut my vacation short." The man spoke in adequate English but with a French accent. Upon hearing the words, Ethan recognized the voice and rose to greet Martin Scheidt. The two shook hands, and then Ethan introduced Scheidt to Chloe. She passed on the handshake and moved in for a hug, a surprise to the usually stoic native of Switzerland.

Introductions and pleasantries accomplished, Scheidt pulled up a chair and joined Ethan and Chloe at the round table covered with their lunch.

"I've been working most of the last forty-eight hours, ever since your call from the ferry," Scheidt said. "And there's much to report."

Though they had been well taken care of, Ethan and Chloe heard little from Interpol, Scheidt, or anyone else in authority since being returned to Rhodes aboard the F/B Pharos.

"Your quick thinking to call me from the ferry turned out to be just in time," Scheidt said, looking at Ethan. "The fact that you overheard The Seeker talk about landing in Naples and meeting Giancomo Morelli there was the break we needed."

Scheidt went on to describe how he reached out to some contacts in the Naples police department, and they, in turn, contacted airport security. Within minutes of Ethan's call from the ferry, Scheidt was pacing in his chalet, coordinating the takedown of a fugitive antiquities dealer and the criminal known as The Seeker.

The Cessna was allowed to land and instructed to taxi to an assigned area for private planes. The area was conveniently cleared of other aircraft and located far enough from the main terminal to escape the view of commercial travelers. Authorities remained out of sight until confirmation of Morelli's arrival. Once the antique dealer stepped from his car, a dozen vehicles hustled into the area and screeched to a halt, surrounding the plane and Morelli. The Seeker and his men started to pull their weapons but thought better of instigating a gun battle once they realized the firepower aimed their way. The experienced criminals accepted their fate with little emotion. Rumor had it, though, that Morelli was crying like a baby when the airport police placed him in handcuffs and led him away.

"I wish I could have seen that," said Scheidt. "By the time I was able to get to Naples, Morelli had called in his lawyer and wasn't talking."

"What about the case with the stone box? Was it on the plane?" asked Chloe.

"The authorities found the case holding the box and it's been handed over to the Italian Ministry of

Culture. They've been in touch with their Greek counterparts and the two sides are working out a variety of issues dealing with provenance."

"Do you know if the box has been opened?" Ethan inquired.

"To my knowledge, until the question of ownership gets settled between the Italians and the Greeks, nothing will be opened or examined. That could take some time, as both sides are very protective of any potential historical finds."

The disappointment of Scheidt's reply showed on Ethan and Chloe's faces.

"The good news is that we were able to find and search the home where Morelli had been hiding out," said Scheidt. "The box with manuscripts you uncovered in the Palazzo Medici was in the house, as were a few other stolen antiquities that will only increase Morelli's time in prison. The Italian authorities can lay claim to the Medici items, so they should be examined and authenticated within days."

Chloe asked the next obvious questions. "Are the authorities aware of our involvement in the whole affair?"

Scheidt nodded his head in affirmation. "They know the broad strokes of your involvement. Both the Italians and the Greeks want to question the two of you and get more details."

Ethan stole a look at Chloe, then stated, "I assume we'll face some type of charges. We've talked about it and are willing to tell our entire story, regardless of what happens."

"Well, I don't think you'll be rotting away in a foreign jail if that's what you're worried about. But there will most likely be some consequences," said Scheidt. "I've tried to smooth some of the egos involved on both sides and was very clear that these historical items might never have been found if it wasn't for the two of you.

"The one thing I know you can expect is a fine for the damage at St. Paul's Gate. From what I've been told, it could cost several thousand Euros to repair the wall."

Chloe and Ethan looked at each other again, both shrugging at the news from Scheidt.

"I think we would be thrilled if that's the worst thing that happens to us from all of this," said Chloe. "We just hope that what we found turns out to be worth everything we've been through."

"I've heard from an expert who's already seen the Medici box, and he's excited about the items it contains," said Scheidt. "That find alone could turn out to be priceless, regardless of what's in the other box."

The Interpol agent rose, indicating he would be right back. A minute later Scheidt returned carrying a bulging manila envelope, which he tossed on the table.

"Speaking of finding things, here are your passports and a few other items we found while searching the plane."

Ethan opened the clasp holding the envelope shut and pulled out two passports, his billfold and a small clutch purse. He handed the purse to Chloe before checking out his billfold.

"I can't believe that everything's here, even the cash."

"Same for me," said Chloe, pulling out her driver's license and a credit card. "I guess I can do a little shopping before leaving Europe."

The comment prompted the expected chuckles from the two men.

"I've arranged for you to fly back to Athens in the morning to have a meeting with the Greek Antiquities Council. Then you have a flight to Florence tomorrow evening," Scheidt added. He pulled a set of airline tickets from his back pocket and placed them on the table. "A representative from the Italian Ministry of Culture will speak with you the next morning. The itinerary and contacts are with your tickets. I'm sure you can arrange your flights back to the U.S. later this week."

"We can't thank you enough," said Chloe, rising to give Scheidt another hug. "My father will be flying into Florence tomorrow, as well. I'm sure he would enjoy seeing you."

"I would love to see Colonel Conrad, but I promised my family that I would get back and finish our vacation. I plan to honor that commitment."

Ethan stood and gave Scheidt a firm handshake. "Keep us updated on news about the stone box and what's inside."

"Most definitely," replied Scheidt. "You'll be the first people I contact."

Scheidt turned and walked back through the sliding door, leaving Ethan and Chloe to finish their lunch.

Chapter 28

Three months later

The pair left the jet bridge together and walked side by side along the bustling concourse to collect their luggage. The Florence Airport was small by international standards, but still welcomed over two million passengers each year. Many travelers flew into the larger Pisa Airport located an hour away, or landed in Rome and took other transportation to Florence. The customs process moved efficiently, and the attractive couple exited into the welcoming sun within twenty minutes of landing on Italian soil.

Early September weather was the best that the Tuscan region had to offer: much cooler than the sweltering heat of mid-summer, though still warm enough to be comfortable in short sleeves. Tourists continued to be obvious—looking haggard from overnight flights, talking too loudly in a variety of languages, and trying to follow travel guides holding up brightly colored flags—but the Disneyesque crowdedness of the peak season had passed.

Ethan and Chloe waited only a short time to secure a taxi and were soon leaving the airport for the short trip to downtown Florence.

The past few months had not gone as smoothly as their travel back to Italy.

After departing Rhodes and meeting with both cultural and law enforcement authorities from Greece and Italy, Ethan and Chloe were allowed to fly back to the States. Ethan went to his parent's home in Indiana and Chloe to her father's residence outside of Washington, D.C.

As Ethan's body healed, he poured himself into finishing his master's thesis. He fought daily battles with his concentration, often finding it to be lacking; at least the concentration on his thesis. Thoughts of Chloe constantly challenged for time.

The two talked regularly on the phone. Ethan even managed to open up to Chloe about the death of his friend, Cam, the recurring dream, and the post-traumatic effects. He described how a long-overdue trip to see Cam's family was one of the hardest things he'd ever done but was able to admit the visit turned out to be a cathartic experience. The dream that plagued him for years seemed to have vanished from his subconscious, though the entire episode in Italy and Greece continued to weigh on him and cause some sleepless nights.

Chloe revealed she spent most of her days close to her father, relishing the sense of safety. She applied for a few jobs but lacked the motivation to pursue promising leads. As nightmares about the ordeal began to fade, she admitted to Ethan that she missed the spikes of adrenaline that accompanied her adventures. She even admitted to missing him.

They both spent time complaining they hadn't

heard anything from Martin Scheidt—or anyone else—concerning the contents of the stone box they discovered on Rhodes or any verification of the documents they found in Florence. Scheidt promised to keep them informed, but their messages to the Interpol agent remained unreturned.

The one item they did receive was an itemized bill for the repair of the wall at St. Paul's Gate. Ethan opened the original letter and was quickly on the phone with Chloe. Both were surprised to see the cost of repairs was just short of 50,000 Euros, or around $58,000. They concluded that the amount was much better than facing the possibility of criminal charges. A combination of Ethan's savings and help from Chloe's father allowed them to pay the bill and avoid any further dealings with the authorities on Rhodes.

More than two months after Ethan and Chloe returned to the States, Martin Scheidt finally made contact. He informed them that the Italian and Greek Ministries of Culture would soon be announcing the Medici documents and the contents of the box found on Rhodes.

After much discussion and political wrangling, the two Ministries of Culture agreed that the announcement would happen in Florence. Ethan and Chloe were invited, and Scheidt managed to find the funds to purchase their tickets. According to Scheidt, who claimed to be uninformed about the content of the announcement, the word on the street was that the occasion would be a major event. According to unconfirmed reports, the guest list would include many noted historians, dignitaries, and a few celebrities.

The five-mile ride from the airport to their hotel happened in near silence. The two were excited about the upcoming announcement but exhausted from overnight travel. Ethan flew to meet Chloe at Dulles Airport outside Washington, D.C. The two then boarded their British Airways flight to London and after a three-hour layover, the connecting flight to Florence.

The long flights provided their first face-to-face time since leaving Europe back in June. They passed the time talking about Ethan's graduate work, Chloe's job search, the potential significance of the Medici manuscripts, and their anticipation of the upcoming announcement in Florence; just about anything, except what might be going on between the two of them. The openness of their long-distance phone calls was no longer evident. Despite all they had gone through together, neither was confident enough when face to face to broach the sticky subject of a possible relationship. There were already too many unknowns in their lives.

Approaching a full day without sleep, both were pleased when the taxi turned onto Via dei Cimatori and stopped in front of the Renascentia Hotel. While Scheidt covered the cost of the airline tickets, the hotel was Ethan and Chloe's responsibility. They chose the Renascentia for its location in the heart of Florence and its comfortable, but not extravagant, accommodations. They checked into adjoining rooms in the middle of the afternoon, readily agreeing that naps were in order to fight off the jet lag. They planned to meet in a few hours for dinner and then try to get a good night's sleep.

The big announcement was scheduled for ten a.m. the following morning in the nearby Palazzo Vecchio.

---•●•---

"How did you sleep?" asked Ethan as Chloe stepped out of the elevator and into the hotel's lobby the next morning.

"Not as well as I had hoped, but I managed five or six hours of decent sleep."

"Well, you look very nice."

Chloe wore a business-like outfit: a grey skirt—long enough to be proper, but short enough to show plenty of her toned legs—with a matching jacket over a maroon blouse. A string of pearls around her neck highlighted the look. Her hair was pulled back and held with a fashionable ivory clasp, which allowed her pearl earrings to be seen. She wore just a hint of makeup, something Ethen knew she didn't need to look good.

"Thank you," Chloe replied, trying to deflect the compliment. "I think this is the first time I've seen you in a tie."

Ethan dressed in business-like attire, as well. He wore a blue suit that fit his frame nicely, a white button-down shirt, and a striped tie. His sandy blond hair was longer than his normal military cut, actually touching his ears.

"A couple times a year, whether I need to or not," joked Ethan about the tie. "I thought the fact that we played a part in a historic discovery being announced today was reason enough to get dressed up. I'd rather be in jeans and a T-shirt."

"I hope you're right about the announcement today," said Chloe. "I can't imagine coming all this way and finding out our discoveries were simply old, but insignificant, manuscripts."

"I think Martin Scheidt knew more than he would tell us," said Ethan. "The fact that he came up with the money to buy our plane tickets tells me he knows the announcement will be big."

"Either way, it's good to be back in Florence. It's also good to be hanging out with you again," said Chloe as she grabbed Ethan's hand. "Come on, let's walk for a while."

Ethan looked down at their entwined hands, appreciating that Chloe took the initiative. "Sounds good to me. We don't have to be at the Palazzo Vecchio for almost an hour."

Their hotel was only a block from Piazza della Signoria and Palazzo Vecchio, but they turned the other way and walked down the Via dei Calzaiuoli. The path took them by the famous Duomo—or Florence Cathedral—and the accompanying Baptistery of St. John. They stopped to admire the bronze doors of the baptistery, designed and sculpted by Lorenzo Gihberti and dubbed *The Gates of Heaven* by Michelangelo.

A short walk later, Ethan and Chloe stopped near the entrance to the Palazzo Medici. They stood in silence, still holding hands. They stared at the building and remembered the thrill of discovering the hidden nook inside the Magi Chapel.

"It seems so long ago that we were leaving here with a five-hundred-year-old box in a backpack," said Chloe, breaking the silence. "I still find everything that happened to us hard to believe."

Ethan showed his agreement with a slight squeeze of her hand and then pulled her to the left. They quickly came up to the statue of Giovanni Medici near the entrance to the Laurentian Library, the spot where they first met. "I thought maybe you would like to go in the library and see if Adelina is still working in the manuscripts office."

"That's a great idea," said Chloe. "She was always very nice to me and was distraught the last time we saw her after the death of Pietro Vesuchi. I bet she would be shocked to know the results of all our research."

"It was mostly *your* research," Ethan pointed out. "I was just along for the ride."

"I guess you were a pretty good bodyguard," quipped Chloe.

The Laurentian Library wasn't yet open for tours or visitors, but Ethan managed to convince the guard that they had business in the Manuscripts Office. Adelina was already at her desk and jumped up to greet the pair, embracing Chloe for an extended hug. A long-time secretary in the office, Adelina informed them that she was retiring at the end of the year. She also told them that Mario Ranallo, the young man who fulfilled Chloe's manuscript requests, had quit suddenly and disappeared. The police came to question Adelina, hinting that Mario was wanted for suspicion of aiding and abetting a crime, including a possible role in the murder of Pietro Vesuchi.

Adelina asked Ethan and Chloe why they were

back in Florence and commented on their somewhat formal attire.

"We have an important meeting this morning that might shed some light on the research we were doing," was all that Chloe would say. "Maybe we'll be able to come back and tell you more after the meeting."

More hugs were in order as they were leaving, this time for both Ethan and Chloe. After breaking her embrace with Chloe, Adelina took hold of both their hands and said, "Possa la tua vita essere come il buon vino."

Chloe smiled and nodded in appreciation. Ethan, who understood the phrase, felt his tanned cheeks turn a slight shade of red, but managed to also smile and nod.

Back on the street, Chloe asked Ethan to translate what Adelina said.

After hesitating, he told her. "*May your life be like good wine,* was the phrase she used." There was a distinct pause before he added, "Uh, it's a common saying at Italian weddings."

Now it was Chloe's chance to turn red.

Chapter 29

The Palazzo Vecchio—or *Old Palace*—remains one of the most recognizable structures in Florence, trailing only the Duomo and the Ponte Vecchio in photographic popularity. Construction began in 1299 under the direction of architect Arnolfo di Cambio, heeding the wishes of the people of Florence to build a secure and defendable palace that lived up to the standards of their important city. The cube-shaped design was made of rusticated stonework and included two rows of arched, Gothic windows, capped by a crenelated battlement. The battlement featured small openings to drop rocks or hot liquids on invaders. An off-center tower soared nearly 300 feet into the sky and came complete with a pair of jail cells.

Those cells once imprisoned the worst criminals and political outcasts of Florence—including a brief stay by Cosimo Medici.

Known as the Palazzo della Signoria when first built and still overlooking the piazza of that name, the building received its title of the *Old Palace* from Duke Cosimo I Medici in the mid-1500s. The change came after Medici moved his family, and the seat of his family's power, across the Arno River to the

Palazzo Pitti—or Pitti Palace.

Ethan and Chloe stood under a clear sky as they joined a line of people entering the main doors of the Palazzo Vecchio. Ethan carried the special invitation that would provide them entrance into the event, scheduled to begin in less than thirty minutes. The line moved slowly as security examined each invitation and any bags carried through the doors. During the wait, a pair of sleek, Ferrari limousines pulled across the piazza and dispatched a group of passengers who were quickly ushered through a side door.

"Did you recognize any of those VIPs," asked Ethan.

"No, but the next time we make a historic discovery, I'm going to request skip-the-line tickets," said Chloe. "Maybe a limousine ride, as well."

The line inched forward, placing Ethan and Chloe just short of the main entrance and between two large statues. A replica of Michelangelo's *David* stood guard on their left, the same spot where the original sculpture was erected in 1504 and remained until being moved to the Academia Gallery in 1873. The placement of the replica occurred in 1910.

On their right, of equal height and almost equal artisanship, rose Bendinelli's *Hercules and Cacus*. The Medici family commissioned both pieces of art, with *David* symbolizing the family's spiritual strength and *Hercules and Cacus* their physical strength.

Just as they reached the entrance and Ethan handed the security guard the invitations, there was a rustle of activity and murmuring of voices behind them. They turned to see Martin Scheidt pushing through some of the other guests.

Before the security guards were able to question him, Scheidt produced both his invitation and his Interpol credentials and held them up at eye level. The guards, who had probably never crossed paths with anyone from Interpol, were intimidated enough to waive Scheidt through the front doors.

"That's quite an entrance," said Ethan. "I'm sure you're popular with all those still waiting in line."

"I only have a few perks with my position, but moving to the front of lines is often one of them," Scheidt commented. "I drove to Geneva and flew in early this morning and am flying back later today. I don't want to waste time waiting in lines. Besides, you two are my main reason for being here. Shall we go find a seat?"

Ethan and Chloe had visited the Palazzo Vecchio in the past, but Scheidt knew his way around as well. He led them across the main entryway, which included several columns and a central fountain. They went up a grand staircase that delivered them to the second floor and the impressive Salone dei Cinquecento, or the Hall of the Five Hundred.

A massive space stretching 170 feet long, the Salone was said to be the largest room in all of Florence. Expansive frescos covered the walls, depicting important battles in the history of the Tuscan region. The ceiling consisted of thirty-nine painted panels, most showing memorable episodes from the lives of the Medici family. The original commission to paint many of the frescos went to Michelangelo, but before he began, Pope Julius II called the artist away to Rome to work on the Sistine Chapel.

Several chairs and a lectern stood at the far end of the room, resting on a raised platform that was part of the original design. Chairs laid out in perfect lines filled about two-thirds of the remaining space, confirming that the expected attendance was in the hundreds. Many of the chairs were filled, which forced the trio of Ethan, Chloe, and Scheidt to slip into open seats a few rows from the back.

Portable stage lights focused their beams on the platform and several television cameras were in place to record the event. One camera prominently displayed the logo of Euronews Italy, and another had a small Greek flag sticker and an ERT International emblem.

"This room was used for a press conference with Tom Hanks several years ago," said Chloe. "It was before the release of one of his movies filmed in Florence."

Ethan and Scheidt turned to stare at her with quizzical looks.

"How in the world did you know that," asked Ethan.

"I'm a Tom Hanks fan, and I've spent time in Florence," she replied. "Plus, I tend to retain a lot of interesting, but often useless, facts."

The two men next to her just shook their heads as they continued to look around the room for people they recognized.

Scheidt pointed out officials from both the

Greek and Italian Ministries of Culture just taking their seats on the platform. "I dealt with both of them during this process. They were so excited about your finds that they didn't put pressure on any authorities to press charges. Did you two ever meet them?"

"Yes. They questioned both of us back in June after we left Rhodes," said Ethan. "I guess we'll need to shake their hands and say thank you when this is over."

"You can do that, but you might want to avoid the man next to them." Scheidt pointed out a man in uniform who sat ramrod straight, his head shaved smooth, with an unnaturally black mustache resting on a chiseled face; a face that seemed locked in an eternal scowl. "That's General Dario Marchese. He heads up the Carabinieri Unit for the Protection of Cultural Heritage, sometimes referred to by outsiders as the Art Police. He's recovered millions of dollars in looted artwork in the last few years. Marchese has a reputation for pursuing severe punishment for anyone who dares try to steal or illegally sell Italian artifacts. You're fortunate that some of your little adventures took place in Greece, or Marchese would have made sure you spent time in an Italian jail."

"We'll do our best to avoid him," said Chloe, slinking back in her chair and taking hold of Ethan's hand. The gesture, noticed by Scheidt, produced a slight smile on the Interpol agent's face.

Before the program started, the Interpol agent also identified two representatives from the Italian government and a few celebrities in the crowd. One of those was an actor who played a leading role in a popular television series based on the life of the

Medici family.

With a few invitees still trickling in and pods of conversation going on throughout the large room, a distinguished gentleman with long, silver hair stepped in front of the dais. He was dressed in a sleek, gray Italian suit, black shirt, and shimmery silk tie that matched his hair. Only the man's deeply tanned face broke the monochromatic look.

"Welcome to the Palazzo Vecchio and today's special announcement," the man began in accented, but articulate English. "My name is Roberto Pedrotti, and I am the director of the Medici Archives, based here in Florence." There was a smattering of polite applause before Pedrotti continued. "As we move forward, I've been asked to inform you that this morning's event will be conducted entirely in English. Transcripts of each speaker's words will be made available in Italian and Greek after the conclusion of the program."

Pedrotti gazed out on the room, looking relaxed and comfortable in front of the distinguished gathering. He paused; both for the dramatic effect and to let a smattering of latecomers find standing room in the back of the large space. Once the crowd settled and became as near to silent as several hundred people could be, Pedrotti began speaking without the aid of notes or prompts.

"As you all know, the Medici family were prominent in Florence for over three hundred years. Their influence stretched from the fifteenth until the eighteenth century. In addition to names like Giovanni, Cosimo, and Lorenzo who ruled in Florence, the Medici family tree includes four popes of the Catholic Church and two Queens of France. Often called the Godfathers of the Renaissance, the Medici championed numerous artists and architects, commissioned hundreds of paintings and sculptures, and financed the construction of many iconic buildings still standing today in Florence and throughout Tuscany.

"Another aspect of the Medici was their vast collection of Classical literature and historical books. The Medici family and their emissaries traveled throughout Europe and much of the known world to search for and acquire a wide range of books and manuscripts. The desire to make their collection available to others inspired the construction of several libraries, including the Library of San Marco, considered the first public library in Europe, and the Laurentian Library, designed by Michelangelo. Cosimo Medici, in particular, was an avid collector of books and is considered by some to be the Father of Libraries."

Pedrotti paused and scanned the room, confirming he held the crowd's attention.

"I remind you of these facts to set the stage for what you are about to hear. The Medici—and particularly Cosimo Medici—set in motion a series of events in 1458 that have taken over five and a half centuries to come to fruition. We are fortunate to be able to witness the culmination of those events.

"Later in his life, Cosimo became aware of the existence of a priceless manuscript of untold importance, but his valiant attempts to acquire the manuscript proved unsuccessful. Though he kept it secret from everyone except a lone trusted associate,

Cosimo—who was near death—decided to pass on the true nature of his quest to his grandson, Lorenzo. Motivated to honor his grandfather's wishes, Lorenzo continued the effort to gain possession of the manuscript but ultimately failed. What Cosimo and Lorenzo did accomplish, however, was to provide a path that someday might lead to success. That path remained hidden until earlier this year, but provided clues and some direction to what I think you will agree, is one of the most significant historical finds in our lifetimes."

Pedrotti's obvious exuberance had the crowd on edge, a wave of murmuring voices rolled down the aisle.

Chloe's grip tightened on Ethan's hand, and both felt their hearts' accelerated rhythm reverberating throughout their bodies. A description like, *'most significant historical finds in our lifetimes,'* was both a relief—that their efforts produced results—and a jolt of adrenaline.

The Director of the Medici Archives continued to talk the crowd through the basic events of the discovery. He was careful to avoid most specifics, including the fact that a pair of Americans did most of the *discovering* involved with the process. Pedrotti did mention that the artifacts were recovered from a group of professional criminals and that the ringleader of the group—a well-known antiquities dealer from Rome—was also in custody. Pedrotti thanked Interpol and authorities from both Italy and Greece for their work in the recovery of the priceless historical finds and the apprehension of those involved in their theft.

No mention was made, either specifically or anonymously, of Ethan and Chloe.

Pedrotti succeeded in getting the crowd ready for the big announcement. He reluctantly gave up the spotlight by introducing two of the other dignitaries on the stage.

The ministers of culture—Dario Francetti for the Italian government and Thalia Giannopoulos for the Greeks—looked like a missed-matched pair as they approached the microphone on the dais. The Italian appeared to waddle to his spot, his large girth and lack of height unsuccessfully hidden under an ill-fitting, rumpled suit. In contrast, his Greek counterpart appeared to have walked out of a fashion magazine. She looked at least twenty years younger than the Italian, with long, coal-black hair cascading over the shoulders of a red, designer suit. Her spiked heels allowed Giannopoulos to tower over the rotund Francetti.

Sporting a bad comb-over and noticeable nerves, Francetti pulled a folded set of papers out of his jacket before speaking. He stared down at the prepared words as a large screen unfurled behind the platform. The screen came to life with a picture of the Magi Chapel in the Medici Palace. The large man described in accented English how research conducted on a select group of books owned by the early Medici family uncovered a sequence of clues left by Cosimo and Lorenzo. Those clues led to a hidden compartment in the Magi Chapel, which—in turn—revealed a hand-made, jeweled box containing four distinct manuscripts.

A picture of the jeweled box appeared on the

screen, causing another stir in the crowd as many recognized the Medici crest carved into the box, complete with rubies and sapphire.

"This is surreal," Chloe whispered to Ethan. "It's like he's describing an experience from another lifetime."

"And, it's another lifetime that we've been erased from," noted Ethan. "He skimmed right over the part about the research. Won't someone ask who found the clues?"

The descriptions from Francetti and the accompanying pictures continued. They started with the letter from Sultan Mehmed and moved to the cryptic note from Cosimo, which echoed the clues left in the Laurentian Library books.

By the time he began to describe the letter from Lorenzo, Francetti gained confidence in his presentation and absorbed energy from the growing excitement in the crowd. When he mentioned the single page of scripture found in the box, the noise level in the room rose to the point that Francetti had to ask for quiet.

"Analysis of the letter from Sultan Mehmed and the two documents attributed to the Medicis have concluded that they come from the appropriate period in the fifteenth century," explained Francetti. "Not only do the paper and ink used correspond to the period, but other confirmed writing samples of Mehmed, Cosimo, and Lorenzo Medici are exact matches for the newly discovered documents.

"The final manuscript is honestly something that I never believed that I would see," continued Francetti. "It's not possible to know whose hand wrote the text, as comparable samples do not exist. However, Carbon-14 dating, a paleographic analysis, and extensive research have convinced our experts that the writing could be an original copy of the early verses of the Biblical book of Ephesians."

Francetti waited for the crowd to quiet down again as a picture of the manuscript appeared on the screen.

"Ladies and gentlemen, it is believed that the text you can see now on the screen, which remained hidden in this beloved city of Florence for over five hundred years, is the oldest piece of New Testament scripture ever discovered. Experts are currently assigning its age as sometime in the late first century, which corresponds with the timelines of Biblical scholars who estimate Paul wrote his letter to the people of Ephesus around sixty-two A.D."

The throng of people in attendance broke out in raucous applause as Ethan looked over at Chloe and saw tears streaming down her face. He reached his arm around her shoulders and felt her body trembling.

"As you can see, the document is in good condition considering it may very well be more than two thousand years old," continued Francetti. "But it remains extremely fragile. Great care is being used in the testing and the plans for preservation.

"There is one surprising aspect of this manuscript and other manuscripts that my colleague here will tell you about shortly," said Francetti, acknowledging his Greek counterpart. "It appears the parchment was rubbed with a chemical or substance that may have helped with its preservation. Testing of this substance shows similarities to a chemical compound found on many of the Dead Sea Scrolls, which are believed to have been written between two-fifty and fifty B.C."

The audience of dignitaries, historians, celebrities, and media had calmed, but many—most likely from the realm of the media—had heads down, frantically sending messages on their devices. A few stood to leave the room with cellphones to their ears, not realizing that another major announcement was yet to come.

Francetti shuffled aside but remained near the podium as Thalia Giannopoulos stepped forward in front of the microphone. The confident and attractive Greek introduced herself, displaying a knack for the English language, with just a hint of her Mediterranean heritage.

Giannopoulos picked up the story from where Francetti concluded, briefly talking about the conflict between Sultan Mehmed's sons and Cem's exile on Rhodes. She referenced the book of poetry Cem authored, and the copy sent to the Medicis in the late 1400s. A picture of a poem in its original Ottoman Turkish script appeared on the screen as Giannopoulos explained its significance. She walked the audience through the clues and explained how they pointed to a unique spot on Rhodes.

"As mentioned previously, an artifacts dealer and his criminal associates were monitoring the search process. They managed, for a short time, to take possession of the artifacts that Mr. Francetti announced, as well as another historical find on Rhodes," explained Giannopoulos. "I want to emphasize our great appreciation for the work of authorities from Italy, Greece, and Interpol in recovering the artifacts. There was also some heroic assistance from a pair of civilians."

Scheidt looked down the row and gave a thumbs-up to Ethan and Chloe. "At least someone recognized your contributions," he whispered.

The Greek woman took a long pause as if she were savoring the moment. During the pause, the picture on the screen changed to a scratched and pitted stone box; the box that had rested undisturbed for more than half a millennium until Ethan and Chloe pulled it out of its hiding place at St. Paul's Gate.

"What you see on the screen is a sixteenth-century limestone box discovered on the island of Rhodes," explained Giannopoulos. "Protected in that box for centuries was the true find; possibly the find of the century."

She paused again, perhaps waiting for a drum roll before the big reveal.

The screen changed again. This time the picture showed two stacks of battered and flaking parchments. Fragments, both big and small, had fallen away or disintegrated, leaving fissures and gaps in the documents. Each set of parchments looked like a puzzle with several pieces missing.

"Ladies and gentlemen, you are looking at nearly complete first-century manuscripts of the Biblical books of Ephesians and Colossians." Giannopoulos waited for the applause to die down. "The single page of Ephesians that Mr. Francetti described is believed to have been the first page from the manuscript you see on the left. Though these texts are fragile and small portions have been lost, they remain in amazing condition. As mentioned previously, our experts believe the treatment with a special substance helped the parchments survive.

"The Ministries of Culture from both Greece and Italy, along with the specialists who have tested the texts, are united in our belief that these manuscripts will alter the course of Biblical research. While many experts believe that much of the New Testament was written in the mid-to-late first century, there has never been verifiable evidence. This lack of evidence served to fuel doubters who dismiss the Bible as second- and third-hand accounts of unprovable events; or worse, made up stories written at least a century after the fact, simply to fit an agenda."

Emotions were evident as Giannopoulos neared the conclusion of her talk. Her lips quivered when emphasizing the overall significance of the discovery to Christians worldwide, and the effect it was having on her faith. Twice she dabbed around her eyes, attempting to brush away tears.

Roberto Pedrotti returned to the podium as Giannopoulos and Francetti took their seats next to the other dignitaries on the platform.

"We hope that each of the items revealed today will be displayed for the public very soon, perhaps early next year," said Pedrotti. "However, there is still much study to be completed on each letter and manuscript before that happens. No specific dates or locations for such a display have been determined at this time. I'm sure the public will be given ample advanced notice when those decisions are made.

"I want to thank…."

A middle-aged man holding a notepad stood up from his seat near the front of the room and interrupted Pedrotti. "Who made these discoveries? Who followed all the clues we were told about?"

Several in the crowd shook their heads in agreement and a smattering of applause followed the bold question.

Annoyance showed on Pedrotti's face, but he quickly recovered his composure. "Press packets with information on the artifacts are available as you leave. Thank you for joining us this morning."

A few reporters tried to yell out more questions, but all those on the platform quickly stepped down and exited a nearby door.

"I guess I'm glad we're anonymous," Chloe said to Ethan, leaning in so others around them couldn't hear. "I'm not sure I'd want to re-live our experience in front of the media."

"I couldn't agree more," he replied.

Scheidt led the way to the exit. He didn't worry about the rude looks he received as he shouldered through the media, dignitaries, and others who thought themselves to be important. The trio exited from the Palazzo Vecchio into the bright sunshine and began to say their goodbyes near the *David* replica. Scheidt was headed back to the Interpol headquarters in Lyon, France, while Ethan and Chloe would spend another couple of days in Florence before flying back to the States.

As more people emerged, the piazza took on a festive feel, with the sound of lively conversations filling the air. Those who attended the announcement seemed animated in proclaiming their thoughts. Meanwhile, tourists and locals looked on with interest, wondering what had caused all the commotion.

Ethan shook Scheidt's hand and thanked him again for all of his help. Chloe began to lean in for a polite hug, but the Interpol agent—eyes looking over her shoulder—suddenly pushed her away, lurching forward as if he were a sprinter exploding from starting blocks. Ethan turned as Scheidt bolted past him, catching sight of Scheidt's target, a large man walking toward them with a gun raised and pointing in their direction.

A thought raced through Ethan's mind in that split second; a thought that the man holding the gun looked familiar. Unfortunately, a split second wasn't enough time for Ethan to react.

A pair of rapid shots rang out, sending the festive crowd into a panic.

Epilogue

Ethan took the elevators up from the Federal Center Metro stop and exited onto street level. A walk of only a half block put him in front of his place of work. Although he had the option of an employee's entrance on the other side of the building, he enjoyed going by the massive bronze doors engraved with verses from Genesis. After crossing the threshold of the entrance, his eyes lifted each day to admire the constantly changing images on the 140-foot-long digital ceiling that lined the lobby. Arriving at work before the building opened to the public was one of the favorite parts of Ethan's day. He often wandered through the multiple floors of the building and spent time in front of the many displays and exhibits before settling into his office on the lower level.

It had been nearly ten months since Ethan met Chloe outside the Basilica of San Lorenzo in Florence and more than six months since a pair of gunshots in the Tuscan capital altered their lives even further. The drama the pair experienced produced fear, redemption, and heartache. The events had dominated Ethan's life for much of the past year and shifted both short and long-term plans. His goals and dreams were transformed—some willingly and some after much wrangling with God.

Normally a regimented and disciplined former soldier, the quick-developing life changes forced Ethan to realize that he couldn't always be in charge. The Yiddish proverb "Man plans, God laughs" came to mind often in the twelve short months since his intentions were set on finishing graduate school and finding a teaching job in the Midwest. Today he entered his office in the Manuscripts Acquisition Department at the Museum of the Bible in Washington, D.C. His work goals now included finding, researching, and negotiating the purchase of rare Biblical manuscripts, with an emphasis on documents from the Renaissance era.

Surprisingly, Thalia Giannopoulos from the Greek Ministry of Culture pointed Ethan towards the position at the Museum of the Bible. After the shooting in front of the Palazzo Vecchio, she visited Ethan in the hospital while he recovered from a bullet wound in his shoulder.

The shooter turned out to be the younger brother of The Seeker or Fadi El Din, as Ethan learned after the episode on Rhodes. The brother—Kashir El Din—arrived in Florence hoping to make Ethan and Chloe pay for their part in the arrest of his older sibling.

The little brother added to the family's criminal accomplishments and, thanks to the quick actions of Agent Scheidt, would join The Seeker in a long period of incarceration.

Giannopoulos arrived at the hospital the day after the shooting and gained permission from

Scheidt to speak to Ethan. After expressing her condolences for all that transpired, Giannopoulos revealed her main reason for the visit.

"I know we were not allowed to mention your name yesterday at the press conference, but General Marchese from the Italian Carabinieri was adamant that you should receive no recognition. I think he still considers you a criminal," she added, noting the irony of the General's views considering what took place after the announcement. "I wanted to take this opportunity to thank you again for what you did. Your research and ingenuity, along with your bravery, produced a truly astonishing find."

Looking at Ethan in the hospital bed and knowing the outcome of the shooting, she admitted to Ethan that he continued to pay a high price.

Ethan was too tired and sore to appreciate her words fully but managed to acknowledge her compliment.

"I know you have other things on your mind right now, but I have a connection at the Museum of the Bible in Washington, D.C. We've worked together on a couple of acquisitions that the Museum made of early Greek biblical manuscripts," said Giannopoulos. "Once you're recovered and back home, I think you would be perfect for a position that they have open."

She continued to explain the position, but Ethan failed to pay much attention at the time. After he returned home and continued to recover—physically and emotionally—he decided to follow through with the lead. He was offered the job and started at the beginning of the new year.

No one at the museum, other than his boss, was aware of his connection to the recently unearthed New Testament manuscripts.

Those manuscripts were now taking the world of Biblical antiquities by storm.

Three months later, he was settled into the position and the daily ritual of living in D.C., a far cry from the pace of life in the Midwest. Ethan had already made two trips to Italy and was close to securing a rare fifteenth-century illuminated manuscript of the New Testament from a private collector near the historic town of Assisi.

Now in his office for a few hours of work, he had emails to return and a video call scheduled with a rare books dealer in Geneva, Switzerland. There was a working lunch at noon for the museum's research and acquisition staff to discuss plans for a special exhibit coming later in the year; an exhibit secured—in part—due to Ethan's contacts.

After the meeting, Ethan planned to take the afternoon off. He had an important date in a cemetery.

Marbury, Maryland, was located about thirty-five miles south of downtown D.C., but it could take an hour to navigate the traffic. Ethan had arranged to leave work early, so took the metro to his small condo, hopped in his car, and started the short trip to Maryland before rush hour clogged the roads. Once out of D.C. and moving along the Maryland 210 highway, traffic thinned out and allowed him to get up to speed. He turned off on Hawthorne Road, followed a mile later by a right onto MD-224 and then a quick left into the parking lot of the Marbury

Community Church.

Ethan was familiar with the church from a previous visit. The 150-year-old main building had been tastefully updated over the decades as it passed from Baptist to Presbyterian, and now to a non-denominational protestant congregation. A newer addition stood to the north side of the property, complete with a fenced-in playground filled with colorful swings and slides.

There were no other cars in the lot, so Ethan assumed the arrangements he made were already complete. He took a moment to gather his thoughts and calm his nerves for what was to come. He knew his plan was unorthodox, but felt it would be appropriately meaningful.

He walked around the older portion of the church to the small cemetery laid out on the back of the property. Small glimpses of nearby Mattawoman Creek—an offshoot of the Potomac River—were noticeable through the trees as he strolled through the grave markers, some from as far back as the late nineteenth century. Ethan walked until reaching a section of newer burial plots at the rear of the cemetery.

Finding the proper gravestone, he took a few minutes to pray and to contemplate the series of events that led to this point: his time in the Army, his education, meeting Chloe, somehow surviving their pursuers in Rhodes, and the shooting back in Florence. Someone had once said, "Life is tough and then you die," but Ethan knew that tough things in life were a chance to learn and grow, even if he didn't always understand the *whys* and *hows* of the process.

Learning to trust God to reveal those *whys* and *hows* in God's own time was Ethan's constant struggle.

He stood in silence, enjoying the early spring sunshine, the calming rustle of the trees, and the soft chirping of birds. The shuffle of approaching footsteps soon interrupted Ethan's quiet reverie, a familiar voice prompting him to turn around.

"My mom would be honored that you came to see her," said Chloe as she came up to stand beside Ethan and look down at her mother's gravesite.

Ethan put his arm around her and held her close, enjoying the moment.

The attack in Florence turned out to be much worse for Chloe. After the first shot winged Ethan in the shoulder, Kashir El Din managed to get off a second shot just before Scheidt tackled him to the ground. The bullet caught Chloe in the thigh, nicking her femoral artery and shattering her femur. The fact that a British surgeon on vacation with his wife happened to be approaching the Palazzo Vecchio that day, probably saved her life. He was able to staunch the bleeding before Chloe lost too much blood. She spent several days in a Florence hospital and then needed weeks of physical therapy once the femur began to heal. Her slight limp was still noticeable.

Ethan accompanied Chloe to the cemetery once before, soon after she was able to get around on her own. She and her family attended the small church when Chloe was in early elementary school and her father was stationed near D.C. before getting his first overseas assignment. Chloe's mother always talked glowingly about Marbury Community Church and the love and support the congregants gave willingly, even though they knew the Conrad family—like many others in the military—would soon be moving on. Once her cancer reached an advanced stage, Chloe's mother asked to be buried in the Marbury cemetery. Colonel Conrad followed through on his wife's wishes.

"I appreciate you driving down here, but why did you want to meet here?" asked Chloe.

"Two reasons, actually," Ethan said as he took her hand. "First, I have some big news from the museum."

Chloe stared at Ethan, waiting for him to continue. "Well?"

"It's not been announced to the public yet, but we received confirmation that the museum will be one of the sites for a traveling exhibit of the Biblical texts found last year in Italy and Greece."

Chloe screamed with joy and threw her arms around him. "That's amazing. I don't suppose you had anything to do with that?"

"I might have had a connection or two," Ethan said with a smile.

"Tell me more. When will the exhibits be here?"

"The page from Ephesians we uncovered in Florence will be on exhibit later this year, probably in the early fall. The other texts we found on Rhodes won't be here for at least another year, but just being chosen as part of the worldwide exhibit is huge."

"Does anybody at your work know about our little adventures last year?"

"My boss knows a few of the details, but I've not told anyone else."

"Do you ever wish that our names were

mentioned in connection with the discovery?" asked Chloe. "We would be famous and in demand for interviews by the media in every city that hosts the exhibits."

"I'm fine with being part of the unknown pair of civilians that played a part in the find. I just pray the epistles open some eyes around the world and draw people to the truth of the Bible.

"What about you? Do you have any regrets that we haven't been in the public eye?" asked Ethan, turning the question on Chloe.

"No regrets at all," she answered, taking his hand again. "Hey, you said there were two reasons you asked me here. What's the other reason?"

"Come with me."

Ethan walked with her to the front of the church and opened the main door, which he had arranged to be unlocked. He guided Chloe into the sanctuary but pulled up when the view ahead caused a small gasp to escape from her lips

Pink rose petals were scattered down the aisle, leading the way to three large arrangements of roses and cherry blossoms near the altar.

Chloe began to tremble as Ethan continued to grasp her hand and lead her forward. Once reaching the front of the sanctuary, Ethan turned to face Chloe and took both of her hands in his.

"Chloe Conrad, we've been through so much together that I can't believe we've known each other for less than a year." Ethan's lips quivered as he continued, not from nervousness, but from excitement. He was confident that he was making the right decision, a decision that gave him such a sense of divine peace.

"Before we returned to Florence last fall, I knew that I had feelings for you. After almost losing you and seeing your strength as you battled back to health, those feelings only intensified and matured."

Tears were now streaming down Chloe's cheeks, her eyes wide with anticipation.

"Once we got back to the States and settled into a somewhat normal routine, I came to realize our relationship was much more than just the adrenaline and adventure we shared last year. We have a bond based on a faith that is greater than anything we could develop ourselves."

Ethan reached into his pocket and continued.

"I believe your mom would approve and I have permission from your father to ask you something."

Ethan got down on one knee and looked up at Chloe.

He was confident that God sent this woman to both save him from his dreams and fulfill his dreams.

Their next big adventure was about to begin.

———•●•———

Afterword

Separating Truth from Fiction

The vast majority of historical characters mentioned in *The Medici Quest* are real.

As described in Chapter 29 by the fictional Director of the Medici Archives, The House of Medici had significant influence in the city of Florence, the region of Tuscany, and beyond for three centuries. Not only did the Medici rule in Florence for all but a few years from 1434 to 1737, but the family line produced four popes of the Roman Catholic Church and numerous other dignitaries, including two queens of France.

Starting in the mid-1400s, the Medici's support for art, science, and the humanities played a major role in the rise of the Renaissance period. Many artists of the time received backing from the Medici, which allowed those like Michelangelo, Leonardo da Vinci, Raphael, and Filippo Brunelleschi to create art and architecture that is among the most revered in history.

Cosimo Medici sparked a family interest in books and amassed an impressive collection for the time. His chief book scout, Poggio Bracciolini, traveled throughout Europe—as well as Syria,

Egypt, and Greece—looking for special volumes for the collection. Cosimo funded the start of at least three libraries, while other family members later commissioned the building of the Laurentian Library in 1571.

To my knowledge, Cosimo Medici never received a message or partial manuscript from Sultan Mehmed.

The Sultan—known as Mehmed the Conqueror—captured Constantinople in 1453 and expanded the Ottoman Empire in ways that concerned Pope Pius II. Mehmed acquired a large collection of Western art, including many produced by Renaissance artists. He also built a massive library that contained more than 8,000 manuscripts. Upon his death, sons Bayezid and Cem fought for the throne, with Bayezid winning and Cem going into exile.

Cem spent several years in exile on the island of Rhodes, both a guest and a prisoner of the Knights of St John. Cem did produce a book of poetry, although there is no evidence that he ever sent his poetry to the Medici family or hid any items inside the structure of St. Paul's Gate.

In addition to the historical characters mentioned in *The Medici Quest*, most of the locations in Florence, Rome, and Rhodes—and facts about those locations—are described as accurately as possible, with only a few exceptions to fit the story. These include the Medici Palace and its Magi Chapel, the Laurentian Library and the Palazzo Vecchio in Florence; the Galleria Corsini, the Biblioteca Angelica and the Pantheon in Rome; and

St. Paul's Gate on Rhodes.

Tom Hanks did hold a press conference in the Palazzo Vecchio before the release of his movie, *Inferno*.

I don't believe there have ever been secret hiding places discovered in the seats below the fresco painting in the Magi Chapel in Florence or below the sculpture of St. Paul on his namesake gate on Rhodes.

The Museum of the Bible opened in Washington, D.C. in 2017. It operates with this mission statement: *The Museum of the Bible is a global, innovative, educational institution whose purpose is to invite all people to engage with the transformative power of the Bible.* Additional information is available at ***www.museumofthebible.org***.

Could a first-century manuscript of a New Testament book be out there somewhere, waiting to be discovered? The second-century message from Tertullian quoted at the opening of the book encourages believers to *run over to the apostolic churches... where their own authentic writings are read.* Most experts believe it is unlikely that Tertullian's exhortation described the literal *authentic* writings or that any original copies of New Testament books could exist in any form. However, many skeptics were previously proved wrong when the much older Dead Sea Scrolls were unearthed in the 1940's.

A unique combination of elements used on the parchment surface is credited with adding to the longevity and durability of the Dead Sea Scrolls; a fact I transferred to the manuscripts discovered in *The Medici Quest*.

The earliest piece of New Testament manuscript uncovered is currently the Ryland Papyrus P52. The small section of papyrus includes a few verses from the Gospel of John and is dated sometime between A.D. 100-150, or 40-100 years after it is believed to be written. Another papyrus collection, called P46, includes most of the Pauline Epistles and is dated around 200 A.D. The earliest complete collection of the books of the New Testament is the fourth-century Codex Vaticanus.

While the gap between the original writing of the New Testament books and the earliest known copies may seem to be wide, the gap is much less than many other non-biblical writings. For example, Julius Caesar wrote about his conquest of Gaul in the first century B.C., but the earliest manuscript in existence is dated to the 8th century A.D.; a gap of 900 years. Similar, or even longer gaps, exist for writings from Plato, Aristotle, and Homer.

It is an undisputed fact that there are thousands more examples of early New Testament manuscripts than any other ancient writing.

Maybe an original is out there waiting to be found.

To learn more about the author, visit
www.jeffraymondfiction.com

9 781962 168571